Jubilant Soul
BOOK TWO

WORTH A THOUSAND WORDS

A Novel

Stacy Hawkins Adams

Revell

a division of Baker Publishing Group
Grand Rapids, Michigan

Published by Revell
a division of Baker Publishing Group
P.O. Box 6287, Grand Rapids, MI 49516-6287
www.revellbooks.com

Printed in the United States of America

Library of Congress Cataloging-in-Publication Data
Adams, Stacy Hawkins, 1971–
    Worth a thousand words : a novel / Stacy Hawkins Adams.
       p.   cm. — (Jubilant soul ; bk. 2)
    ISBN 978-0-8007-3267-7 (pbk.)
    1. African American women—Fiction. 2. Conduct of life—Fiction. 3. Texas—Fiction. I. Title.
PS3601.D396W67 2009
813'.6—dc22   2009011554

To Syd and Jay and all of my other children of the heart,
may you always search for God's light for your path
and his truths for your life.

So Jacob was left alone, and a man wrestled with him till daybreak. When the man saw that he could not overpower him, he touched the socket of Jacob's hip so that his hip was wrenched as he wrestled with the man. Then the man said, "Let me go, for it is daybreak."

But Jacob replied, "I will not let you go unless you bless me."

The man asked him, "What is your name?"

"Jacob," he answered.

Then the man said, "Your name will no longer be Jacob, but Israel, because you have struggled with God and with men and have overcome."

Genesis 32:24–28

1

*I*ndigo Burns peered over the balcony at the crowd that had gathered in the courtyard below to celebrate her achievement and her brief homecoming. "Brief," if that's what one could call the next four months. In a town the size of Jubilant, seventeen weeks could feel like sixty, especially after being away for four years, pursuing your dreams.

"This day is perfect," she said, surveying the colorful variety of flowers that bathed the grounds of Jubilant Botanical Garden. "I feel like God is giving me a thumbs-up and sealing it with a kiss."

Brian tweaked her nose with his thumb and forefinger. "Then I guess you don't need mine, huh?"

She chuckled and raised her head so his lips could easily reach hers. Brian delivered the smooch with a smile and she returned the gesture. She laid her head on his chest and closed her eyes. This man was another special gift.

Without consulting one another, each had come to the party wearing tan linen outfits and brown leather sandals, although his shoes were flat and hers bore two-inch heels.

"How does it feel to be a college graduate?" he asked. "A summa cum laude one, at that?"

Indigo squeezed his waist. "Feels good, babe. I'm excited about the next chapter."

He wrapped his deep brown arms around her, and they both turned their attention back to her friends and family milling about below. The intimate group laughed and chatted as they enjoyed seafood and barbecue and browsed through scrapbooks filled with photos from her childhood. Along with snatches of conversation, the scent of fried catfish and basting ribs wafted upward, and Indigo felt herself growing hungry again.

Young and old guests were dancing to some of her favorite old-school R&B and hip-hop grooves. At one end of the patio, Brian's parents swayed in sync, tucking their round bodies into each other's like matching puzzle pieces. They had surprised Indigo by driving the two hours from Austin to attend the party.

A few feet away, her mom and dad sashayed to the riffs of Chaka Khan, a half second offbeat as always. And holding center court were Indigo's cousins Rachelle and Gabe. Indigo smiled as she watched the tall, lean couple move in close and pull away at the beckoning of the beat. Their eyes remained locked, and at one point, Gabe lowered his head and savored a kiss from his wife.

Indigo blushed and instinctively framed the picture in her mind. If she weren't locked in Brian's embrace right now, she'd grab one of her cameras to capture this miracle. Those two clearly didn't need words to let the family know their marriage was back on track.

The song ended, and before the DJ could start another, one of Indigo's aunts climbed the steps to a small stage adjacent the patio. Indigo's best friend followed on Aunt Melba's heels. A bed of multicolored tulips and roses served as their backdrop.

Each of the women grabbed a microphone from its stand, and

Aunt Melba shushed the crowd by tapping hers. She pointed in Indigo's direction.

"That's where they're hiding," she said into the mic. Everyone looked toward the balcony and laughed. "Brian, will you please escort the guest of honor to the stage?"

In jest, Brian saluted Aunt Melba. He held out his arm so Indigo could tuck hers inside, and they descended the curved stone stairwell. A minute later, Indigo was facing her guests.

Wearing a smile that showcased her perfect teeth, she slid between Aunt Melba and Shelby and waved at her cheering loved ones.

We're in perfect position for a photo shoot. She chuckled inwardly.

One of the companies she had interned with a few years ago was always looking for catalog models of different shades and sizes. Today, the three of them would have been hired at their asking prices—Indigo with toffee skin and a thin bone structure that gave her jaw and cheekbones prominent angles; Aunt Melba with her bronze complexion, full red lips, and thick hips; and Shelby, a dark chocolate Hershey's kiss, whose smooth skin and curves made her eligible for Barbie-doll status.

"Aw, y'all really love me!" Indigo said in response to the lingering applause. Her eyes moistened as she scanned their faces. There was her great aunt Margaret, now ninety and wheelchair bound; her childhood babysitter, Sheila; the leader of her Girl Scout troop, Mrs. Jones; and her favorite instructor ever, eleventh grade humanities teacher Mrs. Hutton.

Thank you, God, for this day.

Shelby opened her palm and revealed the tissue she had tucked inside. She passed it to Indigo.

"Any of us who know this girl well knew this would happen,"

Shelby teased. "We haven't said a word about her yet, and she's acting like the Grammy is hers."

Indigo swatted Shelby's arm.

"Seriously though," Shelby said, "it's an honor to be here to celebrate Indigo Irene Burns. For those of you who don't know, I'm Shelby Arrington, Indigo's friend and sister in spirit. We met at Tuskegee University our sophomore year and graduated together yesterday."

Aunt Melba waved. "If any of you don't know me, you better ask somebody!"

The guests roared.

Indigo shook her head. Aunt Melba was always trying to be hip.

"I am Indigo's favorite aunt and one of her biggest fans," Melba said. "Indigo graduated with honors yesterday, with a 3.9 GPA. She has received a partial scholarship to a prestigious school in New York City, and she'll move there in August to get her master's in digital photography.

"She's going to tell us what her summer plans are in a few moments, but her long-term goal is to become as good as, if not better than, some of America's most famous photographers."

Shelby continued the introduction. "She wants to shoot fine art images for magazines and museums and maybe even still-life for movies. The awesome thing about Indigo is that, not only does she *want* to do these things, being the person she is, she'll get them done."

She turned toward Indigo. "Indie, we wish you much success and Godspeed on your journey. And when you hit it big, I'll be your 'Gail.' If Oprah can have a 'ride or die' girlfriend, you can too!"

Indigo hugged Aunt Melba and Shelby and took Shelby's

microphone. The women stepped aside to give Indigo center stage. She thanked everyone for coming and for supporting her over the years.

"Now, to my parents," Indigo said and shook her head. "I can't say enough. They gave me a camera that used 35 mm film when I was ten. Remember those? I took so many pictures that at some point they began upgrading me to a better model every Christmas.

"They've always believed in me and supported me, even when it meant they had to sacrifice something else. They have taught me, and shown me, that with God and personal grit, there's nothing I can't accomplish. Anything that I've achieved so far, or will achieve—I share those accolades with you, Mama and Daddy. I love you."

Indigo dabbed her eyes with the tissue again and searched the crowd.

"Where are Rachelle and Gabe?" she asked.

The couple waved from their seats, in the last row of black folding chairs positioned near the stage. Their teenage son and daughter sat next to them.

"Rachelle, you're a cousin who's more like a big sister, and I appreciate you for that," Indigo said. "Thanks to both of you for giving me this party at this beautiful place. Our usual backyard barbecue was all I had in mind. You're so good to me!"

Gabe stood up and blew her a kiss. "Remember this day when you're rich and famous and I need a loan!"

Indigo raised an eyebrow and laughed. "Okay, *Doctor* Covington," she said. Just about everyone there knew Gabe was one of the top heart surgeons in the nation and wouldn't need her financial help anytime soon.

"Tell them what you'll be doing this summer," Aunt Melba reminded her.

"I will be interning at the *Jubilant Herald* for ten weeks," Indigo said. "My long-term interest isn't photojournalism, but I'll get to add a range of shots to my portfolio before I head to grad school. Plus, it will be great to spend the summer at home."

Brian approached Indigo and put an arm around her waist.

"No men on the stage!" Shelby teased.

Brian winked at her.

"Hey, everybody," he said in his husky, laid-back drawl, skipping the self-introduction. "I just want to say that I'm very proud of Indigo. We met at Tuskegee when she was a sophomore and I was a senior."

Brian looked in Shelby's direction. "Our friend over there introduced us, and within half an hour of talking to Miss Indigo, I knew she was special," Brian said. "She hasn't proved me wrong. She has big plans for the future, and I'm praying that I'll be part of them."

Indigo felt tears surfacing again. Brian had never been much of a romantic; this overt show of affection surprised her.

Then he knelt on one knee. She stopped breathing.

"Indigo, if you'll take this ring, and agree to become Mrs. Harper, you'll make me the happiest man in the world. Will you marry me?"

Indigo stared at Brian and tried to process what she'd heard.

Did he just propose? In front of everyone she knew? Had this man forgotten that he'd be leaving in a few weeks for the Navy's Officer Candidate School, with plans to become a pilot?

Countless emotions engulfed Indigo, from love and gratitude to a tidal wave of fear. Suddenly she felt her stomach churning.

Please, God, no. Not now. Not here.

As much as she loved Brian, becoming his wife wasn't in her immediate plans. Neither was giving up her first choice grad school.

"I love you too, Brian," she said weakly, hoping her grin effectively masked her mental wrestling match. How could she say no to this fine, smart brother, who had a bright future ahead of him and happened to be crazy about her?

She couldn't. Not in front of all these people.

God forgive me.

"Yes—I'll marry you!" she told Brian.

She flung her arms around his neck and let the tears fall. She did love him, and she did want to be his wife. Just not now—before she, and her dreams, had a chance to blossom.

2

*G*etting her to say yes had been the easy part. Now Brian had to convince Indigo to pick a date.

If he had his way, they would have a small, simple ceremony in late August, and Indigo would accompany him to the Navy's flight training school in Florida instead of heading to New York. He had to graduate from Officer Candidate School in Rhode Island first and would be leaving in two weeks. That would give her all summer to plan.

With her dream of shooting fine art images for magazines and private corporate customers, it wasn't going to be a quick sell. He had seen what he thought was a flicker of doubt in her eyes when he slid the two-carat platinum marquise on her finger earlier today.

Had he imagined it because he had been nervous?

"You've got to help me out, Shelby," Brian said softly as he drove eastward, back to Austin, about two hours east of Jubilant.

His parents had fallen asleep in the backseat, and Shelby, his front seat passenger, didn't seem far behind. She gazed out of the window as they whizzed past desolate small towns that appeared to be abandoned under the dark Texas sky. Her eyes fluttered every few minutes and he knew she was fading fast.

"What did you say?" Shelby asked and turned toward him.

"Did Indigo mention before we left her house when she wants to get married?"

Shelby looked at Brian, but he couldn't read her expression.

"What?" he asked.

"You didn't tell me you were going to propose to her," Shelby said. "We drove all the way from Austin and you didn't say a word. Did your parents know?"

Brian nodded but realized she probably couldn't see him. The veil of nightfall had finally blanketed the car.

"Of course," he said. "I got their blessing, and Indigo's parents', before I decided to surprise her. You haven't answered my question. What's Indigo thinking?"

Shelby still didn't respond, and he gripped the steering wheel tighter. If anyone knew Indigo better than he did, it was her best friend. Fortunately for him, Shelby was his buddy too.

"Shel, we go too far back for you not to be honest with me," Brian said. "We're going to Officer Candidate School together. See how I take care of you?"

Shelby laughed and lightly shoved his shoulder. "We might have grown up in the same church, attended the same high school, and even chosen the same career, but how is it that I now owe you something?"

Brian chuckled. "When you told me you wanted to be a pilot and an astronaut, I taught you everything I knew, remember? Your parents wouldn't have brought you for a tour of Tuskegee if I hadn't already been studying there. They felt safe sending you to Alabama because they knew I'd look out for you."

Shelby sighed. "I wish you could see me rolling my eyes. Yeah, you might have been a few years older and you might have made your career decisions first, but I wasn't following blindly in your

15

footsteps. That full academic scholarship Tuskegee offered me made my choice pretty easy."

Brian twisted the radio dial to raise the volume and let his thoughts wander to Shelby's early days on campus. He dated her briefly during her first semester at Tuskegee, but after a few months, they mutually agreed to end the romance. Two strong-willed pilots, both gunning for military flight school and professional pilot status, wouldn't make it as couple—at least they decided they couldn't.

They managed to remain friends, and that relationship had served both of them better. Brian helped Shelby weed out the players she sometimes wound up dating, and Shelby introduced him to Indigo. She was firm, however, about not crossing boundaries with either friend. When Indigo shared a confidence, she didn't betray it, and vice versa.

Tonight, though, that rule was infuriating Brian. He wanted to know where he stood with his fiancée. Keyshia Cole's "Heaven Sent" wafted through the speakers: *I wanna be the one who you believe, in your heart, is sent from heaven.*

"Give me something, Shelby," he said. "Anything."

Shelby sighed and reached to turn off the music. "Brian, you're getting ready to go to Officer Candidate School. We both are. We'll be on lockdown for twelve weeks, and you want Indigo to spend her summer planning a wedding, all by herself? And what about her grad school plans? It's a prestigious program and it's only for two years. What's the rush?"

Brian loosened his grip on the steering wheel and spoke softly, in case his parents were listening. He answered as if he were addressing a child. "I want to marry the girl I've been dating for the past three years and that's a problem? Maybe I just want to do the right thing, Shelby."

"What's that supposed to mean?" she asked.

Brian paused. "Nothing," he said. "Just know that I want what's best for Indigo too. Let's change the subject. Who are you dating these days?"

Shelby replied by turning toward the window and laying her head against the seat. She drifted to sleep and left Brian fretting over what she knew but didn't care to share.

Indigo loved him; he wasn't worried about that. Now it was time for her to prove how much.

3

*G*etting a shampoo from Aunt Melba was almost as good as a visit to the spa.

Carmen, the salon assistant, usually washed Indigo's hair when she visited during college breaks, but Carmen had requested the day off and Aunt Melba was multitasking.

Indigo rested her neck in the curve of the shampoo bowl and tried not to doze off. Aunt Melba gently scratched, then deeply massaged Indigo's scalp and, in the process, sloughed away the tension filling her neck and shoulders.

"You just graduated from college. What's got you so uptight?"

Indigo laughed nervously. "I'm starting my newspaper internship in a few days. Gotta get ready for grad school soon. And now I've got to think about a fiancé."

Aunt Melba paused and looked at her. "Everything okay?"

Indigo shrugged. No need to raise concern about things she was still sorting out. "Life's just busy, that's all."

Aunt Melba helped Indigo sit upright and quickly toweled most of the moisture out of her hair.

When Indigo was seated under a dryer, Aunt Melba turned and surveyed the rest of the crew. Rachelle had brought them

18

all—herself and her daughter, Taryn; Indigo; and Indigo's younger sister, Yasmin.

"Who's next?"

The two teens, Yasmin and Taryn, looked at each other, but didn't reply.

"Come on, Rachelle," Aunt Melba said and waved her over. "Those divas-in-training are still trying to get it together." She looked at Rachelle's head and chuckled. "It won't take me long to wash what's left anyway."

Rachelle laughed too. "*You* did it. And I still love it."

"Me too!" Indigo piped up from under her dryer. The subtle hum of the low setting allowed her to hear their conversation with ease.

The super-short, layered 'do was a first for Rachelle, and Indigo was still getting used to the fact that Rachelle's soft black hair no longer flowed past her shoulders. The dangling copper earrings that grazed her shoulders complemented her fresh style.

Rachelle had always looked youthful, but this blunt cut made her look a decade younger than her forty-three years. People often did double takes when they saw her with Tate and Taryn, now seventeen and fifteen, and learned that she was their mother rather than an older sister or an aunt.

"You've been a walking advertisement," Melba told Rachelle as she washed her hair. "I'm getting calls every week from ladies who want 'that style you gave Rachelle Covington.' Kelly, my receptionist, has decided to stay home with her new baby. I need to find her replacement soon, just to handle calls from all of these Rachelle wannabes!"

Rachelle chuckled. "It's a great conversation starter with my new clients. I'm trying to do their eye exams and they're trying to figure out how I came to town and within a month found someone to keep my hair looking fabulous. I tell them that before I moved to Jubilant I drove down from Houston on more than one occasion when I needed your special touch."

Melba put Rachelle under the dryer next to Indigo and pulled up a chair to talk with them.

"You aren't going to do the girls' hair?" Rachelle asked her.

"In a minute." Aunt Melba sighed. "All this extra work has me tired. I know I still look good, but I'm getting old! I've interviewed two young ladies who want to rent space and see their own clients here. They'll start next week, and if they're good, I may let them take on some of my new clients."

Aunt Melba looked at Indigo. "While I take a breather, let's get back to you."

Indigo frowned. "What's up?"

Melba and Rachelle exchanged glances.

"What?" Indigo said. She lifted her head from beneath the dryer and leaned toward Aunt Melba.

"We saw you calculating what to say when Brian proposed to you last week." Rachelle had lowered her voice so Taryn and Yasmin couldn't hear. They sat nearby, in Melba's cozy waiting area, flipping through magazines.

Indigo's eyes widened. These ladies knew her too well.

"Well, yes, but . . ."

Aunt Melba put a hand on her thigh and pursed her lips. "Anytime there's a 'but,' you need to tread carefully, Indigo. Do you want to marry Brian or not?"

"I do!" Indigo said. "I love him. He's a wonderful guy. It's just that he's ready now and I'd like to wait until I finish grad school. He's joining the military and all and wants his wife to travel the world with him."

Rachelle sat back under her dryer and folded her arms. "You

know my story. Don't rush into something you'll regret later, no matter how wonderful he is."

"I'm trying not to," Indigo said, "but I don't want to lose him, either."

Aunt Melba nodded at Indigo. "You're right—you don't want to lose a good man, and Brian is that for sure. Here's what I think—"

Before she could finish the thought, Aunt Melba gasped and grabbed her head with both hands.

"Aunt Melba?!" Indigo's breath flew from her body.

Rachelle caught Aunt Melba before she toppled out of the chair. She slumped in Rachelle's arms and her eyes rolled backward. Indigo reached for her purse to grab her cell phone, but when she couldn't find it in the floppy leather bag, she yelled for Taryn and Yasmin.

"Call 911! Aunt Melba has collapsed!"

Yasmin, who seemed frozen with fear, snapped back to the present. She ran to the phone located on the wall next to Aunt Melba's hair station.

Indigo watched her younger sister dial and knelt on the floor next to Rachelle and Aunt Melba. She took Aunt Melba's hand in hers, and rubbed the back of it. A movie scene seemed to be unfolding in slow motion before her eyes.

"She's still breathing," Rachelle said after checking Melba's pulse and placing her ear near her aunt's slightly open mouth. She tilted Melba's head back at what looked like an awkward angle. "This will keep her airway open until help arrives."

Within seconds, Indigo heard the siren as an ambulance approached.

Thank God. She couldn't lose her favorite aunt.

4

The news was good: Aunt Melba was still alive. But Indigo could tell by the doctor's pensive eyes that the Burns family shouldn't be celebrating just yet.

"Ms. Mitchell is stable, but she is a very sick woman."

The emergency room physician, Ray Patterson, stood in the center of the ICU waiting room, surrounded by the entire family, including Rachelle's dad, and Melba's brother, Herbert. He had arrived at the hospital just an hour ago. Soon after Rachelle's call, he boarded a flight from Philadelphia and had flown in a puddle jumper for the last leg of the trip from Houston's international airport to Jubilant's regional one.

A frown creased his otherwise smooth brown face, and he clutched the hand of his other sister, Indigo's mother, Irene.

Dr. Patterson elevated his voice so everyone could hear, but he specifically addressed Irene, who was Melba's designated decision maker.

"She suffered a major stroke in the left frontal lobe of the brain, which means she is paralyzed on the right side of her body, and her speech may be impaired."

Mama and Uncle Herbert looked at each other.

"It's too early to give an accurate prognosis, but she is stable."

Gabe spoke up. "You're not giving us much of anything, Doc."

Dr. Patterson shrugged. "I'm trying to be realistic, Dr. Covington. I don't want to give you false hope. She's not out of the woods. We're doing everything we can to keep her stable and to possibly turn things around. Right now she is awake, but she can't talk or move. We're trying to keep her as comfortable as possible and get her ready for follow-up tests in the morning. We'll know more then."

Indigo wanted to tell the doctor that, while Aunt Melba was a practical businesswoman, her faith would trump all doubt, even in a situation as dire as this. Instead, she zeroed in on how her mother was holding up and prayed that this crisis wouldn't overwhelm her.

"Thanks for all you're doing, Doctor," Mama told Dr. Patterson.

Uncle Herbert shook his hand. "Can we see her?"

Dr. Patterson surveyed the group. "Some of you, but not all of you. I know you want to make sure she's okay, but it would be best if not everyone tried to go in tonight."

Mama looked at Daddy. "You coming with me?"

He squeezed her hand and they followed Dr. Patterson down the hall.

Indigo watched her parents leave, thankful that they had each other.

"Want to go next?" Brian asked her. He hugged her gently, and she realized she was thankful for him too. When she had called him in tears just before noon, Brian jumped in the car and drove down from Austin. He had already resigned from his job in Dallas and was spending the next few weeks with his parents, before leaving for OCS.

"I'll go in after Uncle Herbert, and Rachelle and Gabe," Indigo said.

She would likely be the last visitor of the day since Dr. Patterson wanted Aunt Melba to rest, but she needed to check on Aunt Melba. She couldn't get the image of Melba slumped on the salon floor out of her mind, and she wouldn't be able to sleep tonight if she didn't see for herself how her aunt was faring.

Indigo sat on the edge of her seat, anxious for her parents to return. The ten minutes seemed more like thirty.

Mama's eyes were red and her face was drawn when she entered the waiting area. Rachelle stood and embraced her.

After a few seconds, Mama pulled away and took a deep breath. She mustered a smile. "It's alright. This is all very scary, but I know that God is here with my sister, and with us. We can listen to the doctors, but we really need to just trust God."

Uncle Herbert patted Mama's shoulder on his way out of the waiting room. Rachelle kissed Mama's cheek, then she and Gabe followed Uncle Herbert.

When it was Indigo's turn, she felt like she and Brian had stepped inside an episode of *Grey's Anatomy*. Tubes canvassed Aunt Melba's arms and chest. Her hands were strapped to her sides, and consistently timed beeps and pings from the various machines keeping her alive punctured the silence in this somber, sterile environment.

The right side of Aunt Melba's face appeared slack, and she looked as if she had aged fifteen years in a matter of hours. Where was the vibrant aunt Indigo knew and loved? This couldn't be happening.

Indigo approached Aunt Melba and leaned in close to her ear. She caressed Melba's forehead.

"Auntie, I need you to get better, okay?" she said softly. "You know I love you. Don't let this get the best of you. We need you. And besides, you left me hanging just as you were about to give me some great advice."

Indigo tried to chuckle, but the laugh got caught behind the lump that had formed in her throat. She stood there, taking in this broken image of her beautiful aunt, who had always encouraged her and told her she could do and be anything. Aunt Melba backed up those words with action. Her graduation gift to Indigo was a savings account with a healthy balance that would help pay for grad school.

Based on her aunt's current condition and Dr. Patterson's cautious diagnosis, it would be awhile before Melba would be ready to welcome clients into her seat at Hair Pizzazz. Aunt Melba needed her encouragement now. Indigo was ready to give her whatever support was needed.

Indigo kissed her aunt's forehead. Aunt Melba's eyes fluttered and she tried to talk.

"I can't understand what you're saying," Indigo told her. "What is it, Aunt Melba? It's okay; calm down."

Aunt Melba continued to fidget, and Indigo knew she wouldn't relax until she conveyed what was troubling her. Because the nurses had her hands strapped down, she could only move so much. When she tried to speak, she didn't realize that just half of her mouth was moving. The right side remained slack.

"Har . . . har. . . my har . . ."

Indigo leaned in and grasped Melba's hand.

"Are you trying to say 'hair salon,' Aunt Melba?"

Melba sighed and nodded once. She closed her eyes and sank into her pillow.

"Don't worry about that right now. It will be okay," Indigo said.

Melba grew agitated again and shook her head.

A male nurse entered the room and added more medicine to her IV. Within seconds, she grew calm and dozed off.

"We don't want her moving or trying to talk," he said. "We want her to rest."

But Indigo took Aunt Melba's agitation as a good sign. She was in the fight, and Indigo had to believe she was going to win.

25

5

*I*ndigo knew better. She had learned the skills she should be applying right now in a freshman-level photography course: focus on your subject, put her at ease, and concentrate on making the poses as natural and as unscripted as possible.

Unfortunately for her and for this kind older woman, she could care less about all of that. At least, not today.

Instead of enjoying the photo shoot in this lush backyard, she just wanted it to end. Aunt Melba was coming home from the rehab facility today. She wanted to help her get settled.

Besides, she felt a headache coming on. Those annoying halo-like shapes that sometimes clouded her vision when she spent too much time in the sun had returned. She couldn't tell Ms. Harrow that, though; she had to keep trudging.

"Don't look at the camera, Ms. Harrow," Indigo said. "Keep your eyes on the flowers. Smell them like you normally do and forget that I'm here."

The *Jubilant Herald*'s two photographers despised assignments like this, where they were required to shoot what they considered fluff photos for the paper's Home and Garden section. It thrilled them when a freelancer got the assignment or, as was the case with Indigo, a current or recent college student joined

26

the staff for the summer. The extra help allowed them to skip the lightweight stuff and capture photos for the front page or the local news section.

Indigo didn't care to compete for those assignments anyway. She hadn't wavered from her plans to photograph still life, nature, and other fine art images as a career. This kind of newspaper work was giving her practical experience that would make a difference long term.

Today, however, Ms. Harrow was working her nerves. She bit her lip to keep from saying something she'd later regret. Mama had raised her better than that; respecting her elders was a given, not an option.

Lord, if I can't move her along, will you?

Aunt Melba would be arriving at Indigo's parents' house in half an hour. Indigo had agreed to give up her bedroom so Melba would have easy access to the primary rooms in the house while she recovered from the stroke.

Indigo's bedroom had a small private bathroom and was the closest of the four bedrooms to the kitchen and family room. Melba wouldn't have to navigate too far down the hall in her wheelchair and, eventually, with her walker. To make her aunt feel more welcome, Indigo had removed pictures of herself and Brian from the bedroom walls and had replaced them with images of Aunt Melba in better times. She couldn't wait to see her aunt's face when she was wheeled into the room.

Finally, Ms. Harrow gave Indigo a pose she could live with. The thin, auburn-haired woman cut a long-stemmed rose and held it to her nose. She closed her green eyes and inhaled its fragrance. The sun set on the horizon, behind her, just as Indigo snapped the picture.

Ms. Harrow pushed herself up from the ground with one

fist and wiped grass clippings from the knees of her royal blue capris.

"Did you get what you needed, dear?"

Terms of endearment from strangers or new acquaintances usually annoyed her, but in her second week at the newspaper, Indigo had decided she'd better get used to them. She was interacting with people from all walks of life, trying to make them feel comfortable being photographed for a publication that thousands would see. If they wanted to call her affectionate pet names because she looked eighteen instead of her actual twenty-two years, so be it.

"Yes, ma'am, I think we're good to go," she said and quickly removed her zoom lens. She tucked it and the camera into a black shoulder bag and approached Ms. Harrow.

"I'm sorry to rush off, but I have another commitment," Indigo said. She extended her hand to Ms. Harrow and they shook. "It was a pleasure to meet you, though. I'm going to review the photos when I'm in the office tomorrow, and one of them will be in the *Herald* next weekend, as the cover art for the section."

Ms. Harrow clasped her hands together. "How exciting!"

She walked Indigo from her backyard to the driveway and rattled off everyone she'd be buying a copy of the newspaper for that day. Then she stunned Indigo.

"I've heard that you're related to Melba Mitchell. She's a wonderful person. How is her recovery coming along?"

Indigo's eyes widened. Jubilant was a fairly small city, but everyone didn't necessarily move in the same circles. How did this woman know her aunt?

Ms. Harrow patted Indigo's arm. "Let's just say you can't judge a hair salon by its name," she said and smiled. "I moved to Jubilant about ten years ago and didn't know a soul in town. I woke up one morning feeling sad and started having a pity party about everything that wasn't going right in my life. I decided to get a new look to make myself feel better, but I had no idea where to go. I looked up salons in the phone book and drove around the city to check them out. I stopped by the first shop that appeared to have some class. When I strolled my l'il Caucasian self into Hair Pizzazz to ask for a perm, your aunt Melba and I both were speechless."

Ms. Harrow grabbed her sides and guffawed. Indigo couldn't help but join her.

"Of course she didn't have the appropriate chemicals for my hair texture, so I couldn't get my Shirley Temple curls that day, but Melba graciously shampooed and styled my hair while her other clients watched in amazement. We became friends after that," Ms. Harrow said.

"The fresh flowers that sometimes grace her reception desk come from that very garden you just photographed." Ms. Harrow motioned with her head toward the backyard. "God can bind anyone in sisterhood, you know. Sometimes Melba joins me back there in prayer."

A lump filled Indigo's throat. She'd been so focused on her own agenda during the photo shoot that she hadn't taken time to appreciate the floral sanctuary she'd just left. To know that Aunt Melba sometimes communed there made her want to take another look.

"She comes here?" Indigo asked.

Ms. Harrow nodded. "Usually twice a year. We get together at the beginning and halfway points of each year to agree with one another in prayer about the blessings and miracles we're asking God for. I visited her once, before she left the hospital, but I haven't made it to the rehab center to see her. Can you let her know that I've been in our special place, thanking God for her full recovery?"

Tears blurred Indigo's vision. "A full recovery seemed so un-likely two weeks ago, because the stroke left her unable to talk or walk. Her speech is still slurred, but it's possible to understand her now, when she talks slowly. Her doctors say she'll be able to walk again as long as she continues the physical therapy; and thankfully, her mind is as sharp as ever."

Indigo knew that witnessing her aunt's fight to recover was changing her in ways she couldn't yet articulate.

Now, to hear that feisty Aunt Melba, who rarely attended church or mentioned God, had a personal prayer partner who was a well-to-do white grandmother from the other side of town stunned her.

"I've never been able to pigeonhole my aunt Melba," Indigo finally said. "To hear that you two are friends surprises me, but then again, it doesn't. Thank you so much for praying for her."

"You don't have to thank me, young lady," Ms. Harrow said. "Now that you and I have a connection beyond your job, you feel free to stop by anytime you need my backyard for prayer too, okay? I've groomed that garden as a special place for everyone, not just myself. It's my gift to God for blessing me in so many ways."

The two women hugged. Indigo slid into her Honda CRX, eager to get home and share with Aunt Melba details about how she wound up meeting her friend.

She waved to Ms. Harrow and pulled out of the driveway. Before she could turn the corner and enter the busy intersection, her cell phone rang. It was Brian. Indigo didn't have her Bluetooth in her ear, so she pressed the speakerphone setting.

"Yeah, babe, where are you?"

"I'm pulling into your parents' driveway," he said. "You almost home?"

Hearing his voice always lifted her spirits. It was sweet of him to have driven from Austin for her aunt's homecoming too.

His last day with Hillman Aeronautics had been a month ago. He had submitted his resignation early so he could make more frequent trips before reporting to Officer Candidate School in ten days. Indigo was grateful.

"You know that everything in Jubilant is fifteen minutes from everything else," she told him. "I'll be there in no time. Wait 'til I tell you about the woman whose picture I just shot for the paper."

"Wait 'til I tell you about my day," he countered.

Indigo frowned and lowered her speed slightly.

What was he up to now? Today was about Aunt Melba. She hoped he wasn't planning something foolish, like starting a discussion about wedding dates with her family. The two of them hadn't talked about the logistics of his proposal since Aunt Melba's stroke. With Aunt Melba's life hanging in the balance, little else had mattered. Now she wasn't sure what to expect.

She ended the call with Brian and tapped the code for Rachelle's number. Taryn answered for her mother on the first ring.

"Hey, cuz," the fifteen-year-old said. "You need Mom?"

"You know it," Indigo said. She might be all grown up, but she wasn't going to lose her street cred with this kid. She wanted Taryn and Yasmin to keep looking up to her so she could be the mentor for these two honeys that Rachelle had been for her.

Her older cousin's voice filled the phone. "We're heading to your parents' house now," Rachelle said. "Are you there yet?"

"Not yet," Indigo said, "but Brian is there, and I'm afraid that tonight I might have to tell him the truth."

6

rian Harper had never been arrogant, but he knew his worth.

Indigo shouldn't be taking him for granted, given the women he regularly held at bay. She was so trusting that he could have stepped out on her a time or two; but the thing was, he loved this girl. He was trying to do right by her.

He sat in his car with the engine running and cool air swirling while he waited for Indigo's parents to arrive with Aunt Melba. Melba wouldn't want to be welcomed by a bunch of acquaintances, but she was such a people person that he knew she'd be happy to have the support of close friends.

He and Indigo valued her wisdom, and Brian wished she were well enough to advise him about his efforts to marry Indigo sooner rather than later. He wanted the date set and planning underway before he left for Rhode Island, and he knew it would happen if Aunt Melba were on his side.

Brian flipped open his cell phone and called Shelby for the second time today.

"What do you want now?" she asked.

"Are you in the middle of something?"

"I'm trying to declutter my room and figure out what I'm taking to OCS next week," she said. "I know we're not supposed to bring much, but I don't want to leave anything important behind. Have you talked to Indigo yet? I guess not, or she would be calling me instead of you."

Brian sighed. How had Shelby and Indigo wound up being best friends? They were opposite in personality and ambitions, yet the two of them couldn't be any closer than a pair of fraternal twins.

"You know, Brian, if you have to use coercion, that's a sign that you need to wait, friend," Shelby said. "Indigo loves you, but just like you and I have dreams that we're pursuing, she does too. Why are you trying so hard to convince her to forsake what she wants to make you happy? That's pretty selfish."

Brian bristled. That mouth was one of the reasons they had never gotten along when they were a couple.

"Indigo is pulling up, now," he told Shelby. "One of us will call you later."

He slid the cell phone into the holster attached to his belt loop and stepped out of the car so he could wait for Indigo near the front door.

God, you know my heart. Let her agree that our relationship is worth some compromise.

Brian watched Indigo parallel park and then approach the person in the SUV who had pulled up behind her. He recognized Cynthia Bridgeforth, Melba's best friend, behind the wheel. Cynthia lowered her window and chatted with Indigo for a few minutes before climbing out of the Volvo and accompanying Indigo up the driveway.

Indigo hugged him before she unlocked the door and led him and Cynthia inside.

He inhaled the True Star perfume that cloaked her and tugged her long, thick ponytail. He loved it when her hair flowed free and framed her gaunt face; but when she was working, she kept it pulled back to keep wisps of it from blocking her view in the camera lens.

Either way, she was stunning, and she really didn't realize it. He liked it that way.

Brian, Indigo, and Cynthia were sitting in the breakfast nook, sipping sodas, when Rachelle and Gabe knocked on the side door off the kitchen. Rachelle peered through the multipaned glass and waved.

Brian opened the door and hugged her when she crossed the threshold. Her kids strolled in behind her and waved on their way to the family room, where the Wii was stationed.

Gabe closed the door behind him and slapped palms with Brian. "What's up, man?"

"Not much, Doc," Brian said. "How about with you? You settled into your new digs at Jubilant Memorial?"

Gabe followed Brian and Rachelle to the table. Indigo and Cynthia stood and hugged him.

"I don't know yet, Brian," he said as he pulled out a chair. "It's very different from being the head of cardiology at one of the largest hospitals in Houston, but I'm adjusting."

Cynthia nodded. "Our small-town medicine can't compete with the technology and resources a large facility provides, but we're happy to have you here, Gabe," she said. "You and Rachelle. Who would have thought that the brief time she spent volunteering at my pediatric clinic all those years ago would lead her to eventually open her own optometry practice, and in Jubilant, of all places."

Gabe smiled at Rachelle. "I know," he said. "But change is good. More than good."

Brian knew that Gabe had been "The Man" in Houston medical

circles. Living and working in Jubilant had to be very different, and probably confining.

"Sometimes God leads us to a foreign land so we can take our eyes off of ourselves and our drama, and focus on him," Rachelle said.

Gabe chuckled. "Don't I know that."

"I wasn't talking about your first mission trip to Uganda." Rachelle winked at him. "Just our move here."

Brian's eyes widened. "Mission trip to Uganda?"

"When I was helping with eye exams in Cynthia's office, Gabe was in Uganda, transforming other people's lives with medical care," Rachelle told him. "Little did he know that God was also performing surgery on him."

Gabe nodded. "Well said, babe."

Indigo rose from the table and motioned for them to follow her. "Let me show you what I've done for Aunt Melba," she said. "As independent as she is, you know she hates not being able to go to her own house; but maybe this will make her feel at home while she's recuperating."

They gathered in the doorway of Indigo's bedroom. When she flipped the light switch, there was a collective gasp.

"Oh my goodness," Cynthia said.

"Girl, you are gifted," Gabe whispered.

Brian's heart swelled with love and pride. He couldn't summon the words to match his feelings, so he remained silent.

Indigo had turned the walls of the room into a miniature gallery. The soft lavender paint from her high school days still graced the walls, but each surface was now covered with photos of various sizes, from 4 x 6s to matted 11 x 17s that she had collected of Melba at various stages of life: in her salon; at her fiftieth birthday party; on a cruise with her sister, Irene; singing in the church choir;

35

reading to kids in Cynthia's pediatric clinic; on a mission trip to Kenya with Gabe and his former medical partner, Lyle Stevens.

The black-and-white images were encased in black frames, and some were matted or suspended in glass.

"This is beautiful." Rachelle's voice was trembling. She walked to the wall across from the bed and pointed to a picture of Aunt Melba laughing, with her head thrown back, eyes closed and hands clasped together as if she were in prayer.

"That's my favorite," Indigo said shyly. "I took that picture about three years ago, right after I helped her get dressed for a formal event. It captures Aunt Melba's heart and soul. I hung it there to remind her of who she is, so that when she gets discouraged, she'll remember that the chance to resume her full life is worth the struggle to get better."

Brian stepped toward her and hugged her. When she became Mrs. Harper and he was a top Navy pilot, he'd see to it that she got plum assignments to showcase her talents wherever they were stationed. They were going to be a good team.

7

I can't believe I agreed to this. I didn't sleep all night."

Indigo sat on the edge of her bed, gripping her cell phone so tightly that her hand was beginning to ache. Shelby would tell her what to do.

But her friend remained silent.

"Are you there?"

"I'm here, Indie," she said. "What do you want me to say?"

"I don't know. Something. Anything. What would you do?"

"That's a loaded question and you know it," Shelby said.

Indigo rolled her eyes. So what if Shelby and Brian had dated freshman year? Shelby had been up front with her about that years ago, and Brian assured her that their brief romance had led nowhere.

Indigo trusted him. She trusted Shelby too. Her sister-friend wouldn't betray her.

"I'm not asking what you'd do if Brian wanted to marry you— I'd kill you before that happened," Indigo said and giggled. "I'm asking what you'd do if you were me."

She heard Shelby plop on a bed or sofa.

"That's still a loaded question! I can't tell you to choose grad school over your man or vice versa. You have to do what's right for you, Indie."

Indigo sighed. "Why do I have to choose? Why can't I marry him and then go off to grad school and join him when I'm done? Or better yet, we could just have a long engagement and get married after I get my MFA."

Shelby should have been a psychiatrist. The long silences she could maintain always left room for Indigo to come up with her own solutions.

"Yes, that's what I'll do. See if he'll let me backtrack on what I agreed to last night and instead have a long engagement. Thanks for listening, Shel."

"Always, girl. I'm here for you. Now let me go have breakfast with my family. Mom is already getting emotional about her baby leaving for Rhode Island. It's not like I'm going away to college for the first time. Rhode Island is just a plane ride away. But you know how parents are."

Indigo laughed. "Go give your folks some love. And be prepared to keep an eye on Brian for me when you guys get to Officer Candidate School. I know those little honeys are going to be after my man."

"Hmmm," Shelby said. "Sounds like you do want to keep him. I was beginning to wonder."

They laughed.

"I do love him, Shelby," Indigo said. "I just don't want to make the mistake of throwing away my dreams for someone else's. It happens all the time. I think that's one of the reasons Mama lost herself in alcohol all those years ago. And Rachelle reminds me every chance she gets about the long, rocky road she has traveled to finally practice optometry. I think I can pursue what I'm called to do and still be there for Brian."

Just as quickly as she uttered that reassurance—more for herself than for Shelby—Indigo remembered the cloud that had settled over Rachelle's face the night before, when Brian gathered everyone in the living room, including Aunt Melba, and asked the family to help Indigo prepare for a late summer wedding. She had agreed to a date only moments before.

"Indigo and I have decided that we'd like to get married sooner rather than later," Brian had announced. They stood in the center of the room, holding hands, and Indigo kept her eyes glued to his face while he spoke. "I will graduate from Officer Candidate School on August 19, and I'll have a few weeks of leave before I have to report to flight training school, possibly in Corpus Christi, but most likely in Pensacola, Florida."

Indigo's mother beamed. "I'll do whatever I can to help my baby get ready. That's not a lot of time, though. We have a lot to do between now and August, Indigo."

Aunt Melba, whose face was still slightly twisted from the stroke, had remained expressionless.

Gabe and Rachelle exchanged glances, but didn't speak.

Despite her reservations about his urgency, Indigo knew she was lucky. She had captured the heart of a man who loved God, had a bright future, and adored her. She would be throwing away a blessing to dismiss him.

Yet, she had tossed and turned all night. And it troubled her that Rachelle had gone home without telling her goodbye or wishing her well.

She deserved an explanation. Indigo flipped open her phone again and dialed Rachelle's number. It was Saturday morning and just seven a.m., but she knew Rachelle was already well into her day.

"Hey, cuz, where are you?"

"At Melba's salon, making sure everything's ready for the ten a.m. opening," Rachelle said. "The two girls who've been renting booth space from her agreed to split her clientele today. Carmen will serve as their shampoo girl, like she's always done for Aunt Melba. I'm going to field calls and answer questions about how Melba's doing. Your mom said we might want to set up a schedule to rotate these duties until Aunt Melba's back up to speed. I could tell last night that she's worried about her business falling apart."

"I picked up on that too," Indigo said. "She kept pointing to the picture on the bedroom wall that shows her standing in front of the salon. I told her we're going to take care of everything, but she was really agitated. After I stop by the newspaper, I'll come down to see how everything's flowing so I can reassure her."

"Great," Rachelle said. "But I know that's not why you called."

Indigo took a deep breath. "I noticed your silence last night."

Rachelle didn't respond.

"You still there?" Indigo asked.

"I'm here, Indigo. We should talk in person, okay? Brian's a good guy, but I want what's best for you. That's all. You know I've traveled a similar path."

Indigo felt her defenses rise. "Yes, you have, Rachelle. But I'm not you. This is a different time and a different set of circumstances."

Rachelle fell silent again.

"Let me go," Indigo said. "I've got to get to work. I'll see you later."

She hung up before Rachelle could say goodbye. Minutes before the call, she had been wavering herself, but confronting Rachelle's unspoken judgment of her decision ticked her off.

She didn't need or want to be preached to; she'd lived long

enough and had seen enough to know not to rush into anything. She wasn't going to let Rachelle's misgivings influence her decision. Just because Rachelle's chance at a fairy-tale romance had been pockmarked by poor choices didn't mean she would face the same problems.

Indigo was thankful that Rachelle and Gabe were happy now. They both had put the past, and the relationships they had experienced then, behind them.

Rachelle's college sweetheart, Troy, and his new wife had left Jubilant for Chicago with their blended family two years ago, just as Gabe and Rachelle had begun praying about relocating here. The timing couldn't have been better. Indigo was convinced that God had orchestrated the shuffling game to snuff out any sparks that routine encounters with an old flame might ignite. She had watched God knit Rachelle and Gabe closer together than ever, and she was trusting that he'd do the same for her. In the meantime, she wanted to feel good about her looming wedding.

She jumped off the bed that had once belonged to her older brother, Reuben, before he left for college and moved to Seattle to work for Amazon.com. The twin mattress was firmer than the queen-sized one on her bed; still, she knew that hadn't been the cause of her sleepless night.

She dismissed the worry, attempting to cloak her fears, and strolled across the hall to the full-sized bathroom. When she leaned toward the mirror, a fuzzy spot filled her view in one eye. Indigo yanked a sheet from the paper towel holder on the countertop of the sink and wiped the glass, but the blurriness remained.

She closed her eyes, tilted her head sideways, then opened them to look at the mirror from another angle. Before she could react to the fact that the cloudy spot still remained, she saw her giggling sister behind her.

41

"Why are you making faces in the mirror? Brian's not trying to marry a lunatic," Yasmin said and smirked. "He really should just wait until I'm older."

Indigo rolled her eyes and stepped away from the mirror. "You need to be thinking about college choices right about now, young lady," she said and raised her arm to pat her sister's head. At five eight, Yasmin could already look her in the eyes. "College and career choices. I'm heading off to the newspaper, but I'll be back in a few hours to get you so we can go over to the salon."

She returned to her room to pick out something to wear and tried not to fret about the fuzziness that was now blocking her side vision. She didn't feel a foreign object in her eye, but the cloudy spot was annoying. It had come and gone before, but this morning, it seemed persistent. She wondered for the first time whether she might need glasses.

Maybe she'd ask Rachelle about it when she saw her, if they were speaking to each other by then.

8

*I*ndigo stepped outside the front door and paused to pick up the newspaper. Before she could bend over, she was grabbed by the waist. The scream that filled her throat couldn't break free.

"Good morning, Mrs. Harper. How does that sound to you?"

Brian eased her fright before she could execute the karate move that had earned her a black belt in eighth grade.

"Boy! Where did you come from? Why are you lurking outside my parents' house?"

He laughed, pulled her closer, and planted a kiss on her lips. "You made me a very happy man last night, baby, that's all. I'm just jazzed."

Indigo peered into his eyes. "Have you been drinking?"

He laughed again. "Maybe. I should have brought over the champagne so we could celebrate together. One glass wouldn't hurt you."

Indigo's heart constricted. "You know how I feel about that, Brian," she said. "Mama's drinking still haunts me."

Her mother had been sober for seven years, but she wasn't going to let anything, including a celebratory drink, send her down a path that could alter the course of her life.

She changed the subject. "I'm going over to the newspaper to process the photos I shot yesterday. Want to have breakfast with me first?"

Brian took her to Shoney's, one of the few morning meal options in Jubilant. They chatted about nothing in particular over eggs, bacon, and pancakes.

But his joy was contagious. As Brian rambled on about how their life together would unfold, Indigo pictured herself in a wedding gown, being introduced to their friends and family as Indigo Irene Harper. She saw herself standing next to him as he was commissioned as a naval officer. She visualized him wearing a Navy pilot uniform and climbing into the plane he'd fly on a regular basis, before eventually returning to Houston to don an astronaut uniform. The vision he laid out for both of them seemed wonderful and right.

She held his hands and admired the way her engagement ring sparkled on her ring finger while he mused out loud.

"I'll be at the top of my game, but so will you," he said. "I see you at the commissioning ceremony with your camera, taking photos of all of the officers and being paid by the Navy for your work. You're with me in Houston as one of the official NASA photographers, recording images for the history books and media. We can achieve our goals and still be together."

Indigo's smile weakened. The only problem with this picture was that her dream was being reshaped to fit into his.

Was this the sacrifice required for love? Was this why Rachelle had sounded so cautious when they talked earlier this morning?

If she was going to float the idea of waiting, now was probably the best time.

"Brian, I've been thinking about the decision we made last

night, and I'm having second thoughts about rushing our wedding and giving up grad school. Maybe we could hold off on the wedding? Or if we do get married now, why couldn't we be apart until I finish my master's? This is a great program, and it's hard to think about giving it up completely."

He sat back in the chair and stared at her. "I thought we agreed, Indigo. Now what's the problem?"

Without giving her a chance to reply, he motioned for the waitress to refill his coffee.

"Let's see where they send me after OCS, okay?" Brian asked. "Maybe you can enroll in an art institute near where we'll be based. Besides, you already have your bachelor's degree. It's not like you can't do well without the master's."

She wanted to ask him to slow down, to give her time to process it all and make sure she was comfortable moving forward. At the moment, however, that annoying blurriness had returned to her left eye, and she was concerned that it might blossom into a headache.

Indigo leaned forward and motioned for Brian to do the same, so she could kiss him across the table. The taste of his coffee lingered on her lips.

"I love you, baby," she said softly. "Let's just enjoy today, okay?"

9

The expansive parking lot adjacent to Hair Pizzazz's squat red building was filled with cars and SUVs when Indigo and Yasmin arrived in the late afternoon. Indigo lucked out on a spot near the door, not far from Rachelle's black Beamer.

They walked toward the salon entrance and paused before going inside.

"It feels weird to be here when she's not," Yasmin said.

"Yeah, it does," Indigo said. "Hopefully it won't be for long."

Aunt Melba was at their parents' home, napping and watching TV, instead of delivering the wit and wisdom her customers craved, along with the hairstyles she customized for them. Tears had filled her eyes when they told her they were leaving to check on things at her place.

"Thank . . . you." The effort it took for Melba to utter two words left her spent and tugged at Indigo's heart.

"For what, Auntie? We're family. What you love, we love," Indigo said. "Hair Pizzazz is going to keep thriving until you're ready to take over again. You just focus on getting well."

The two sisters stood here now, but neither made a move to enter.

Indigo took the initiative. "Come on. Rachelle's inside. It will be okay."

She pulled open the mahogany door and stepped back so Yasmin could enter first. The fourteen-year-old gingerly walked in and waited for Indigo to follow.

"What are you afraid of, sis?" Indigo asked. "It's the same place."

"I'm thinking about what happened the last time we were here," Yasmin whispered. "I keep thinking about Aunt Melba lying on the floor."

Indigo squeezed her hand. "Think about the fact that God saved her."

They entered the foyer and found Rachelle sitting at the reception desk, handling a call. "Yes, you can come in today and see Eboni or Carlotta. Both of them are filling in for Melba until she returns, and both of them do great work. I've let them take care of my hair over the past few weeks and I've been pleased."

She jotted a note on her pad and typed something in the file she had open on the salon's desktop computer. "Okay—I've put you down to see Eboni at the same time Melba had you on the books. I'll be here and will look forward to seeing you then."

Rachelle hung up and smiled at her cousins.

"Hey, ladies," she said. "It has been busy this morning! That was the mayor's wife. She's used to only Melba touching her hair, but she's willing to give Eboni a try, if Eboni will take her in the private room in the back to wash and style her. I tell you, I didn't realize how much coddling and ego massaging this business requires!"

The three of them laughed.

Indigo raised an eyebrow. "You mean to tell me you don't get these kinds of requests at your optometry office? It's all customer service, you know."

47

Rachelle raised her palms upward and widened her eyes. "You are absolutely right, and I guess since I don't do the scheduling in my office, I've had no clue about what all is involved. Looks like I need to give my receptionist, Melinda, a raise in another six months."

Rachelle laughed again and rose from the seat behind the reception desk. She came around and hugged Yasmin. "You aren't hanging out with Taryn today?"

"Yes, ma'am, we're getting together," she said. "Cousin Gabe said he'll take us to the mall later, so we can meet some friends at the movies. But Mama made me come here with Indigo first, so I could help clean up or do whatever needs to be done."

Rachelle smiled at Yasmin, who was a thinner, fairer-complexioned version of Indigo.

"Fortunately for you, Aunt Melba uses a cleaning service, so this place is spic and span. What I do need help with is rescheduling the clients who decided not to come in today but want to make appointments with Eboni or Carlotta over the next two weeks.

"I have a list of women who need to be called back. I'm also trying to get a handle on what bills need to be taken care of. I have the key to the business files, and I want to make sure everything has been paid, including Carmen's wages, and that I collect the two stylists' rental fees on time."

Rachelle lowered her voice and leaned toward her cousins. "They missed paying the first month they were here because Melba had the stroke, but I need to collect that fee and this month's as well, without ruffling their feathers, especially since they're taking on Melba's clients. Any advice?"

Indigo shrugged. "I don't know about that one. Ask Mama and Daddy and see what they say. Aunt Melba might have some thoughts about it too."

"I don't want to upset her by telling her that we let a month lapse," Rachelle said. "This place is her baby. She doesn't need to start fretting that we aren't doing things right."

Indigo smirked. "Believe me, she already is. If she could have climbed into my car, she'd be here now, telling you what to do. She's trying not to worry, but I can tell that she wants to be in the loop. And truth be told, she should be. I can't wait until she's a little stronger."

Indigo walked around the desk and plopped in the cushioned chair Rachelle had vacated. The phone rang and she answered on the second ring.

"Hair Pizzazz, how may I help you? Just a moment."

She put the caller on hold and looked toward Rachelle.

"Aunt Melba never did braids. This person wants to know if someone can braid her hair into a single ponytail."

Rachelle shrugged. "I'll run back there and check with Eboni and Carlotta. She just wants a single braid?"

Indigo nodded.

Yasmin walked over. "I can do that and earn some money for the mall. When does she want to come in?"

"This is a reputable place of business, Yas," Indigo said.

Yasmin put a hand on her bony hip and struck a pose with her lanky frame. "Like I said, I can help if she wants to come in. I can braid and do a few other things. Aunt Melba knows I'm into fashion, so she taught me how to create several hairstyles to complement whatever look I'm aiming to achieve. Plus, I braid the neighborhood kids' hair all the time. You know that."

Indigo paused before returning to the caller.

"Ma'am, we don't regularly offer braiding, but we have a teenager here this afternoon who's skilled at it, and she'd be willing to assist you. If you'd prefer a professional, we fully understand.

49

If you still want to come in, Yasmin will be here for a couple of hours."

Indigo grabbed a pen and scribbled some information on a notepad. "Okay, we'll see you in fifteen minutes."

When a striking café au lait young woman strolled into the foyer a short while later, Indigo, Rachelle, and Yasmin fell silent. Her thin black hair fell in ringlets past her shoulders and clearly didn't require the perms that were typically applied in African American salons.

"Hi. May we help you?" Indigo asked, remembering that people occasionally walked in without appointments to inquire about the salon's services.

Her thoughts turned to the conversation with Ms. Harrow, about how she had once stumbled into Hair Pizzazz by mistake, thinking it serviced people with her hair type. She wondered how this woman, who was clearly of mixed heritage, would respond.

"I called earlier and made an appointment with Yasmin to get my hair braided," she said.

Indigo tried to mask her surprise. "You're Nizhoni?"

The woman smiled and nodded. "Yep, that's me. And yep, I want to get this long, beautiful hair washed, brushed, and pulled into one braid. Can the young lady you mentioned do it?"

Yasmin had made herself comfortable on the red sofa in the center of the lobby. She walked over to her potential customer and smiled.

"Hi, I'm Yasmin." She studied Nizhoni's hair. "Mind if I touch it to see how thick it is?"

Nizhoni nodded. "Go ahead. I'm part Navajo and part African American, but it's more curly than thick."

Indigo contained her smile as she watched Yasmin run her fingers through Nizhoni's ringlets. She saw glimpses of Aunt Melba

50

in how her baby sister connected with this young woman and in how seriously she was taking this assignment.

Yasmin stepped back and spoke formally to Nizhoni. "Your hair texture is very soft, but if you don't mind me weighting it down with hair lotion, to help the braid stay firm, I think I can pull it off. It will be long though, all the way down your back."

"I know," Nizhoni said. "When I sit down, I'll have to flip it over my shoulder. But that's okay. I just need it braided."

Indigo quoted her a price and looked to Yasmin. "Do you want to wash her hair or get Carmen to do that?"

Yasmin shrugged. "I've been a shampoo girl, you know. Aunt Melba called me sometimes when she was shorthanded. I'll do it all. It won't take me long."

She led Nizhoni to the back and left Indigo and Rachelle alone.

"That was interesting," Rachelle said. "Wonder why she wants to braid her hair, and in one braid at that?"

"I don't know," Indigo said. "But it's great to see Yasmin stepping up and helping out. The way that girl keeps her room at home, Mama would be shocked. All she does there is watch those TV shows about models, read fashion magazines, and watch her weight, even though she's barely ninety-nine pounds soaking wet.

"She's been asking me to take her pictures so she can visit me in New York and stop by some of the top modeling agencies to drop off her portfolio."

Indigo and Rachelle laughed.

"You never know, though, Indigo." Rachelle, who had settled on the red sofa in place of Yasmin, shrugged. "Yasmin is a beautiful girl, and she does have the bone structure to be a model. She just needs to stay focused—like I'm always urging Taryn and Tate, and even you, to do."

Indigo shook her head. "You're twenty-one years older than me, so I guess you're old enough to be my mother, but I don't like lectures from you, you know. I just want you to be my favorite cousin."

Rachelle walked over to the reception desk. She sat on the edge of it and looked Indigo in the eyes.

"I *love* being your favorite cousin. Sorry if I'm beginning to sound preachy. It's just that I want you to be your best."

"And you don't think that includes Brian?" Indigo was almost afraid to hear her answer.

Rachelle shook her head. "I'm not saying that it doesn't, Indigo. Brian is a nice young man with a good heart and a great future. But sometimes rushing things can alter plans and hinder goals and get everybody involved off track. I hope that you and Brian do make it, and that you'll have a wonderful life together. I just want to make sure that before you settle into being someone's wife, you know who you are and exactly what you want to accomplish as an individual first.

"I was wrong for not congratulating you after Brian's announcement last night." Rachelle leaned toward Indigo and covered Indigo's hand with her own. "But last night took both Gabe and me back to the days when we made choices so we could fit in with our social circle or meet our families' expectations, rather than because they made us whole individually and as a couple.

"We talked about that with Tate and Taryn on the way home. Not because we wanted to put them in the middle of their parents' relationship drama, but because we want them to understand how complicated life can get. The key is to keep prayer at the forefront of every decision. If God gives you a peace about the choices you're making, then it really doesn't matter what anyone else thinks, especially me."

Indigo sat back in the chair and folded her arms. "I guess I do need to pray about this. That's the one thing I haven't done."

Rachelle frowned. "You know better than to skip that," she gently scolded. "Let me tell you this—don't pray for God to make your marriage work or to change Brian's heart about getting married right away or any of the things I already know you're wrestling with. Pray that he sends you the husband he wants you to have, in the season you're supposed to marry him, and that he gives you clarity about when to say 'I do.' Pray that he'll give you peace when you're making right choices and make you very uncomfortable inside when you're headed down a dangerous path. If you ask him to do that, he will.

"Sometimes the feelings will be subtle, but if you're tuned in enough to God, you'll know it's him speaking through your circumstances."

Indigo frowned and held up her ring finger. "See this beautiful diamond? My heart leapt when Brian slid it on a few weeks ago. I felt excited and terrified. I felt special, but also . . . obligated? Do you know what I mean?"

Rachelle nodded. She appeared lost in thought before she replied. "I know you're tired of hearing my story, but I've been there," she said. "Listen to your feelings. Honor how God is trying to speak to you."

Indigo sat back in the chair and closed her eyes.

She retreated in her mind to the night before and how she felt when Brian persuaded her to set a date for their wedding in August. First the dread, then the need to please by appearing exuberant, then the fear of saying "not right now."

His angular, deep brown face and megawatt smiled filled her mental picture box. She dwelled on how safe and happy she felt whenever she was wrapped in his arms, and suddenly, the mild tension that threatened to overtake her dissipated.

What would she lose by becoming his wife now, when he was clearly ready to jump the broom? A chance to shoot photos for some of the nation's top magazines and for galleries that bought fine art images? It was more, she realized. She'd be giving up, or at least altering, a longtime dream of doing things that had become as important to her as breathing.

What would she lose by insisting on a long engagement? The adoration of a good man who wanted to celebrate and support her? There was no guarantee that he would wait, or that she'd find this kind of love in another relationship.

Indigo opened her eyes and stared into Rachelle's. She hadn't budged from the edge of the desk, and she was still eyeing Indigo.

"I know," Rachelle said. "I don't have any answers, but I'm praying for God to give you clarity, sooner rather than later."

10

*B*rian made a controlled, swift swing and hit the tiny white ball at just the right angle. He held his breath and watched the arc of its travel.

Yes!

Another eagle.

He looked at his father, sitting in the golf cart, and grinned.

"Ready for another round or do you need a break, old man?"

Otis Harper grinned and rested a hand on his protruding belly.

"Fishing is my thing. I'll never beat you in golf, Son," he said. "I just enjoy watching you show off. Now that you've done that a few times today, let's go and get something to eat."

Brian laughed. "I'll gather my equipment so we can get outta here."

Twenty minutes later, father and son were sharing a platter of ribs and coleslaw at the legendary Stubb's Restaurant, in Austin's Red River district. Since it was summer, few college students bustled about, but there were enough locals and tourists to keep the area thriving. Because it was a prestigious college town, the city was quite cosmopolitan, especially compared to Jubilant.

Though Jubilant was a student hub too, the small, private

Everson College boasted an enrollment of just four thousand. The demographics of Everson's student body and faculty were similar to Tuskegee's, and Brian had often teased Indigo about leaving her hometown to spend four years in its twin environment.

Today, Brian was appreciating his Texas roots and the accompanying Southern hospitality. The leggy waitress set another platter of coleslaw in the center of the table and refilled both men's glasses with sweet tea.

She straightened her skirt, patted her cornrows, and smiled at Brian.

"Remember, if you need anything else, my name is Anita."

She waited for a response.

Brian's dad cleared his throat. "Thank you, Anita," he said, his gravelly bass echoing in their corner of the restaurant. "This is fine for now."

When she disappeared around a corner, he sat back in his chair and stared at Brian, who continued to wolf down his food.

"I used to pull 'em like that too," he said.

Brian tried to laugh and choked mid-bite. He took a swig of tea to quell his coughing, then finished chewing.

"Alright, Daddy," Brian said. "There you go as usual, telling me too much of your business. I don't want to get you in trouble with Mom."

His father laughed. "She knows how I got her—it wouldn't be a surprise. She wasn't an easy catch."

Brian raised his eyes. He thought about the ambivalence Indigo had been trying to hide since the day he proposed. "Really? How did you two work it out?"

His dad leaned forward and popped a piece of corn muffin in his mouth. "I ain't gone tell you all my secrets, but I'll tell you this—one fine, loyal woman who has a good head on her shoulders and a good heart is worth her weight in gold, compared to hundreds of gorgeous women looking for a man to take care of all their needs. I realized that your mama was going to be my partner as well as my lover and my friend, and when we got involved in church, I saw that she was going to serve God with me too. I couldn't beat that with a stick. She held out for a while to make sure I was her best catch, but I made sure she knew I was."

Brian took it all in and gazed out of the restaurant's palladium windows. Hadn't he done all of that with Indigo? He looked at his father.

"Indigo has passed all of those tests, but I think she's trying to go to grad school before we get married. I'm not so sure about waiting."

His dad grabbed a toothpick from the holder in the center of the table and began working it through his teeth. "Can't she go to school or find work wherever you're stationed? They need good photographers everywhere.

"A man of your stature, doing the great things you're going to be doing as a commissioned officer and Navy pilot, needs to be in a stable relationship so you don't get off track. Plus, it will look good to your commanding officers if you're settled. You'll be one of the first men they turn to for the plum assignments because they'll know you're dependable."

He hadn't been a fighter pilot, but Otis Harper had served in the Navy for twenty years before retiring to Austin with his family to open a carpet supply business. He had ranked high during his years of service and was discharged with honors.

"When are you thinking you'll tie the knot? After your twelve weeks of training?"

"We talked about that when I visited a few days ago, and she

57

agreed," Brian said. "Now she's changed her mind and has started asking about a long-distance marriage or engagement."

Brian shrugged. If he had his way, they would elope tomorrow, so they'd have a few days together before he left for Rhode Island. He pulled himself out of his reverie and looked at his dad.

"She's in the middle of her photography internship at the newspaper right now, and when that's finished, she'll be heading to New York for grad school. I don't know when I'll be able to pin her down."

"She's a great girl, but you sure she's the one? You and Shelby seem to talk quite often. Sure there's nothing there anymore?"

Brian sat back in his seat and ran his hand over his low-cut hair. "Come on, Dad. You know Indigo and Shelby are best friends. What would that look like?"

His dad shrugged. "I'm just checking. You two basically grew up together at Grace Temple. She's going to Officer Candidate School with you. Could be that you and she have feelings for each other, despite her friendship with Indigo. Happens all the time."

Brian was used to his dad nudging and trying to direct his path, but today Dad was getting the best of him. He tried to keep his cool.

"Naw, Dad, it's not like that," Brian said. "I'm not messing around on Indigo with her best friend. If anything, I'm trying to get Shelby to talk Indigo into a wedding sooner rather than later. If Indie has her way, we're looking at a two-year engagement. I'm not feeling that."

But sometimes Shelby understood him better than Indigo, or better than he understood himself. She was just a friend, yet today, she must have telepathy.

His cell phone rang and her number appeared on the caller ID screen. Brian warily eyed his father.

"I was just thinking about you," he told Shelby when he answered.

"You and every other man I know," she quipped. "Just checking in to see what time you're planning to arrive in Rhode Island. I'll get there with my folks on Saturday evening. I thought we might be able to have dinner with each other and with our parents, before the four of them leave."

Brian felt his father watching him and lowered his head and his voice. "I don't know about that." After the comment Dad had just made, he didn't want to stir the pot.

"Your folks are there with you now and you can't talk, right?"

Shelby was good. "Call me later," he said.

"You and Indigo settled on a date yet?" she asked.

Now he was annoyed. She was posing another question she already could answer.

"Only if you've urged her to. Help a brother out, okay?"

Shelby's minute-long pause seemed like an eternity. "You just do the right thing, Brian—by you and her."

He shifted in his seat. "Gotta go. I'll call you later."

Otis Harper eyed his son and picked up another toothpick. "I'm not telling you whom to marry, Son, I'm just saying follow your heart."

11

*I*ndigo stood in the foyer of St. Peter's Baptist Church, waiting for devotions to end so she and Brian could enter. She reached for his hand and tucked her palm in his.

She loved this man, and she was going to miss him. They had dated for three years in college and had seen each other just about every day until last year, when the company he worked for had relocated his job from Tuskegee to Dallas.

Tonight he and his parents would fly to Rhode Island, and tomorrow he'd officially begin Officer Candidate School, or OCS as he always called it. She was excited for him, but she was also nervous about what this meant for their future.

She wore his ring and knew she had his heart, but she also knew he was human, and if she weren't there every day, things could change. Was he afraid of the same thing? Was that why he was clamoring to get married right away?

As things stood today, they were planning to tie the knot in this sanctuary on August 25. That date gave her some bargaining room to win him over. If Brian relented and agreed, she could still become his wife and show up for grad school a week later.

The ushers opened the doors of the church just as the choir launched into the beginning strains of her mother's favorite song these days. Deacon Kevin Bonner lifted the microphone from a stand near the edge of the choir loft and cradled it close to his lips.

"Never would have made it, never could have made it, without you . . ."

Indigo spotted Yasmin sitting on the last pew with several of her friends. Years ago, when Mama's struggle with alcohol made headlines in the *Herald*, some of those same girls and their parents had shunned her baby sister. The fact that Yasmin had moved on, and that she herself still considered this church a haven, was a testament to God's ability to heal and her parents' humble example of how to forgive.

An usher led her and Brian toward the front of the sanctuary to two seats next to Mama and Daddy.

Indigo's parents smiled when she and Brian paused at their row and slid into the pew. Indigo saw tears in Mama's eyes and squeezed her hand. This song made Mama weep every time she heard it. Marvin Sapp's lyrics were a perfect testimony for her. Since joining Alcoholics Anonymous seven years ago and admitting her dependence on vodka, she had reclaimed her life. She received help for the hip injury she had once coped with by drinking and now shared her story with others as often as possible, to free them from whatever problem served as their prison. She *was* stronger. She *was* wiser. She was a better wife, mother, and person than she'd ever been.

Indigo decided in this moment that if her mother could make it through those difficult days, she too could do anything. She could use this gift of photography in fulfilling ways, and she could be a good wife.

She reached for Brian's hand again. "We're going to make it, okay?" she whispered in his ear.

He grinned at her and nodded. She wanted to stroke his goatee or hug his shoulders but instead turned her attention where it belonged, focused on God and this worship service.

It was great to be here this morning with both of her parents, who had been taking turns coming so someone would always be home with Aunt Melba. Rachelle and Gabe had come by the house this morning to keep Melba company so Irene and Charles could attend service together.

The choir rendered another selection, this time an Israel and New Breed praise and worship song, and Indigo stood to her feet to give thanks for the path her life was taking, as well as Brian's.

Then Pastor Taylor approached the podium and opened his Bible to Matthew 11:30. He read the Scripture before walking away from the lectern to stroll back and forth across the raised landing, clutching a wireless mic.

"I can almost guarantee that every single person in this place woke up this morning and asked God to do something for you today. Maybe it was something simple, like help with finding a good spot in the church parking lot this morning. Or maybe you asked him for something big, like to heal your body from cancer or some other chronic disease. Or maybe your request was somewhere in between the minor and the life-changing. Whatever it was, I can also guarantee you that God heard it."

He paused for effect and surveyed the crowd. "Yep, he heard it. The question is, were you asking from a place of integrity, a place of peace, a place of trust? Did you really give it over to God so he could take care of your request, or did you ask for his help while continuing to brainstorm your own solutions?"

Silence enveloped a sanctuary that moments before had been filled with boisterous musical praise.

"You see, most of us want it both ways," Pastor Taylor said.

He spoke slowly and thoughtfully, as if addressing a roomful of timid kindergartners. "We want God to fix things or grant our desires, but we want him to do it in the way that *we* think is best. We want the answer now, in the fashion that *we've* decided would be perfect. Am I telling the truth up in here?"

He seemed oblivious to the chorus of amens and mopped his face with a handkerchief. "God wants you to ask and then release it. Ask him, then trust him. When you step out of the way, he will fix whatever is troubling your soul."

Indigo glanced at Brian. His eyes were glued to Pastor Taylor, but it was clear that he hadn't heard a word. He sat as if transfixed, wringing his hands.

She touched his arm and leaned toward his ear. "Wake up, babe."

Brian squirmed and gave her an awkward smile before turning his attention to the pastor. Why did he seem uncomfortable? Was he upset that she had been stalling on a wedding date? Was he nervous about leaving for Navy training? Indigo couldn't recall having ever seen him in this kind of mood before.

Indigo returned her focus to Pastor Taylor. She didn't hear the rest of the sermon, though. Instead, she talked to the Lord herself.

God, please let me hear from you about what to do. If you want me to marry Brian now instead of going to graduate school, let me know. You know I want to be a professional photographer. You know I want to work for magazines and in other mediums. Am I wrong to pursue these dreams when the man I love has other ideas? Please tell me what to do. Or better yet, God, can you just fix it? Pastor Taylor says you can. Make this work out so Brian and I both can be happy, okay? Amen.

In the movies, the answer would be revealed right about now.

Indigo's heart sank when she realized God wasn't going to tell her what to do before church service ended. The one thing she did know was that she couldn't hang up her camera to please her fiancé.

She was going to have to wait, and like Rachelle had already told her, listen like never before.

12

*I*ndigo had been an intern at the newspaper just four weeks, but even she knew it meant trouble when Claude Ingram approached you first thing in the morning without a smile. She looked into the photo editor's eyes and didn't see one there, either.

"Can I talk to you in my office, Indigo?"

It was Monday, and one of the *Herald*'s two staff photographers worked silently at a twenty-five-inch computer screen, downloading work he had shot over the weekend. He paused and watched as Indigo rose from her swivel chair and followed Claude down a short hallway.

When they reached his cluttered office, Claude grabbed a disheveled heap of papers off the seat across from his desk and motioned for her to fill it. He slid into his chair, placed his elbows on his desk, and rested his chin on his two fists.

"How have you enjoyed working here this summer?"

Indigo peered into his milky gray eyes, and hesitated, unsure whether to treat this as a trick question or as an icebreaker.

"It's been great," she responded. "I've enjoyed getting to meet people across the city and shoot everything from car accidents and house fires to profile photos and community fairs. As you know, my previous internships were with museums and magazines, and I pulled a brief stint at a catalog recruiting company my sophomore year, where I took photos of aspiring models. This is a great opportunity to try a new form of photography, and I especially appreciate being able to work in my hometown."

Claude nodded and continued to stare at her.

"Have you been pleased with my work?" Indigo finally asked.

He sat back in his chair. "That's why I wanted to meet with you this morning. I've heard great things about you from the staff. They think you're wonderful to work with—professional and enthusiastic. And they've heard the same from some of the folks that you've photographed. But I have to admit that the body of work you've produced has been inconsistent."

Indigo's heart lurched. She sat forward in her seat and prayed that her facial expressions didn't mirror the panic coursing through her veins.

"What do you mean?"

Claude turned toward the computer, which sat on a desktop to his left, and tapped the mouse. He opened a digital file that contained at least a dozen photos Indigo had taken over the past few weeks.

Many of them had appeared in the newspaper, but there were multiples of the same subject, and some of them were off center or out of focus.

Indigo held her breath. She remembered taking some of those shots when that annoying blurriness filled her vision in one eye or the other. She would shoot extra frames on those days, in hopes that she'd hit the mark with at least a few of them, despite her inability to properly hone in. Or she'd switch eyes and close the one that happened to be bothering her. She thought she'd pulled it off. Despite the extra shots, she had submitted some really good images, and a few had been featured on the newspaper's front page.

"You do good work," Claude said. "But it appears that you're straining to hit the mark sometimes. It takes extra time to get additional shots or poses from a subject, in hopes of landing one or two usable ones. Why are you having to do that?"

He turned to look at her.

Should she tell him that sometimes her vision got blurry while she was working, or that sometimes, out of the blue, she'd see halos, or occasionally couldn't see out of the side of one eye? That wouldn't be in her best interest.

Then again, Claude already knew something was up, or he wouldn't have pulled her aside this morning.

"Have you been getting complaints?" she asked.

"A few, from the other photographers who have been asked by an editor to work on one of your pictures because something was not quite in focus," Claude said. "They've had to go back through the digital images to find a more suitable one, and on one or two occasions, we've needed an image so badly that we've photoshopped something you've shot to make it work. That's a no-no in journalism. When we go that route with a photo, we have to indicate on the image that it is a photo illustration because we've manipulated it in some way, and we really shy away from that."

Indigo remained silent. She knew all of that, and she had even noticed that label on a couple of her favorite pictures when they had appeared in the *Herald*.

God, please don't let me get fired.

"Are you having problems with your eyesight, Indigo?" Claude leaned toward her, to read her expression. "If you are, it's okay. Photographers can wear glasses or contacts. You know that. Is it your eyes, or is something else going on?"

She took a deep breath before she answered. "First of all, I'm sorry to hear that my work hasn't been up to par," she said. "I'm mortified about that. Really. I thought everything was going okay. I wish someone had mentioned it to me. I would have been happy to come back in after hours and correct whatever needed to be altered.

"But I do have to be honest and say that I'm having some occasional blurriness in my eyes every now and then. Not all the time, so I didn't think it was a big deal."

Claude nodded. "As a professional photographer, Indigo, a little blurriness is a big deal. You can't just live with that and do your job well."

Neither of them raced to fill the long silence.

"Tell you what," he said and sat back in his chair. "Why don't you take the rest of the day off and go get an eye exam. It's still early enough that you should be able to land an appointment today. Get your eyes checked and see what they say.

"If you need glasses, as soon as they can set you up with a pair, then we'll send you back out on assignments. If it's something that's going to require a longer fix, we'll talk and go from there. Maybe we'll let you do some in-house work for a while if we need to."

Claude gave her a reassuring smile and ran his fingers through his dull brown hair. "We just need to get to the bottom of this. It's not benefiting the *Herald*, or you, if you can't do your best work because you're having issues with your vision. Just get it checked and let's go from there, okay? Don't sweat it at all. Take today off, and tomorrow, if you need it."

He pushed himself up from his seat with his thick forearms and walked her to the door. He patted her shoulder. "You'll be fine. You're young. Maybe you'll wind up with a pair of nice frames."

Indigo gave him a weak smile and trudged down the hallway to the photo lab. The staff photographer, James, didn't look her way when she entered and walked to the corner armoire to retrieve her purse.

"See you tomorrow," she said with the ounce of lightheartedness she could muster.

What she really wanted to do, though, was call Brian or Shelby, and have a good cry. But neither of them was available right now. They had been at OCS for a week and wouldn't be able to communicate with anyone off base for at least ten more days. How had she wound up with a fiancé and best friend both interested in becoming commissioned Naval officers and fighter pilots?

She buckled herself into her seat and sped out of the newspaper's parking lot. A few minutes later, she pulled onto Warner Street and parked in the far corner of the library parking lot. The library didn't open until ten a.m., so the lot was empty. She sat there and wept until the sobs left her hiccupping.

Then she picked up the phone and tried to compose her voice.

"Hello, Melinda? This is Indigo Burns, Dr. Covington's cousin," she said thickly. "I need to come in immediately for an eye exam. Can you fit me in this morning?"

13

achelle took one look at Indigo and turned to her exam assistant. "I'll call you if I need your help, but I think I can manage this patient on my own."

Sabrina gave Rachelle the chart she would need to note her findings during Indigo's exam and closed the door when she left the room.

Rachelle approached Indigo, who sat slouched in the high-backed, leather chair.

Indigo was trembling and trying to hold back tears. She was afraid to talk, because she knew if she did, she'd lose her composure again. She kept her head bowed and wiped her eyes with a crumpled tissue.

Rachelle touched her arm. "Calm down. Whatever's going on, we'll work through it. First, you have to tell me why you're here and why you're so upset. Did you injure your eye or is something else bothering you?"

Indigo shook her head. Rachelle turned away and pulled a stool toward her so she could take a seat.

"I need an eye exam," Indigo finally said, and sure enough, the waterfall resurfaced. "I messed up some pictures at work."

"Did the newspaper fire you?"

Indigo shook her head again and dabbed at her eyes.

Rachelle sighed. "Then why are you this upset? We all make mistakes. Maybe you need glasses—so what? You need to calm down so I can take a look."

Rachelle rose and briefly left the office. When she returned, she offered her cousin a damp handkerchief and a Styrofoam cup filled with water.

"Pull yourself together and we'll get this all figured out."

Indigo took the cloth from Rachelle and mopped her face. The cool wetness felt good against her clammy skin, and she took a deep breath. Rachelle stood there until Indigo was ready to take the cup.

Indigo cradled it in her hands, then sipped every drop. She inhaled and finally felt the tears abating.

"Feel better?" Rachelle asked and returned to the stool.

"Yeah, thanks," Indigo said. "I'm upset, but I don't know why I'm so emotional. I guess it's a combination of missing Brian and being reprimanded at work this morning. The photo editor essentially told me not to come back until I'm sure my vision is okay."

Rachelle's surprise didn't escape Indigo, though it was replaced with a professional mask of nonchalance within seconds.

"That sounds fair to me," Rachelle said. "So you're here for an eye exam. We'll make sure everything looks okay. Now the tears about Brian—I know you miss him. I'm sorry I can't help you with that, but it will get easier. He's going to be in the Navy, so you'll have to get used to him flying off on missions, you know?"

Indigo tried to smile. "You're right, this is just the beginning."

"Let me look at your eyes," Rachelle said. She moved closer and used a remote control device to dim the lights in the room.

Rachelle took Indigo through a series of tests and asked about her symptoms.

"How long have you had the blurred vision?"

Indigo was slow to answer. "I'm not sure. It's not always there, you know?"

Rachelle sat back and looked at her. "I need some idea, Indigo."

"I think I've been having episodes of blurriness off and on for almost a year. It will bother me for a day or two and then it will go away and I forget about it."

"That never prompted you to get your eyes checked, or at least ask me about it?"

Indigo shrugged. "I'd think about what I needed to do, then exams would come up, or I needed to complete some paperwork for grad school, or I had to shoot some photos for a project. Senior year was just crazy."

Rachelle nodded. "Not to mention that you were pledging, hanging out with Miss Shelby, and spending time with your honey, whenever he made it back to Tuskegee."

She raised her palms. "I'm not fussing, though. I see plenty of people, some of them much older than you, who know better, and they still think if they avoid a potential problem, it will go away on its own.

"You said the photo editor wasn't pleased with some of your work. Did you find the blurriness to be a problem when you were taking pictures?"

Indigo nodded. "Yeah, I did sometimes. I just tried to work around it."

Rachelle jotted a few notes on the paper attached to the clipboard and pulled a piece of equipment attached to the ceiling close to her.

"Lean forward so I can look into your eyes," she told Indigo.

She shone light in Indigo's eyes, conducted a few air puff tests, and dilated her pupils so more tests could be conducted.

At some point, Indigo realized that the questions and the chit-chat had stopped.

"What's the diagnosis, Doc? Do I need bifocals?"

Rachelle tried to smile, but didn't quite pull it off.

"I'm not sure yet, Indigo. I'd like to have a friend who's an ophthalmologist take a look. I'll call her now and see if she can fit you in."

Indigo felt the fear rising again. "What do you think it is?"

Rachelle sounded calm, but if all were well, Indigo knew that she'd be in the adjacent room by now, picking out a pair of frames. She recognized evasion when she heard it.

"It could be a number of things," Rachelle said. "You have some interesting symptoms, and Yolanda's specialized training will help us make a quicker diagnosis. Sit tight for a minute. Let me see if she's in the office today and I'll ride over with you."

Rachelle left the exam room door ajar. Indigo heard her talking softly to her receptionist.

"Call Yolanda Woodman over at Jubilant Memorial and see if she can see Indigo this afternoon. How many more patients do I have scheduled for today?"

Indigo could hear Melinda's fingers flying over the keyboard, but not her response.

"Good," Rachelle said. "Will you call the three of them and ask if they can come later this afternoon, say after four p.m., or if they would mind terribly if we reschedule for tomorrow? Tell them I have a family emergency."

73

14

*L*ife was about to be miserable, at least for the foreseeable future.

Brian learned in his first few hours at Naval Station Newport that he'd best not refer to Officer Candidate School as OCS when speaking to his leaders; he'd best forget about his personal thoughts and feelings, because only what mattered to the team was important; and he'd best quickly realize that his time was no longer his own. Every waking hour would be filled with academic preparation, physical training, and gouging—memorizing everything from the proper way to address his drill instructor and his candidate officer to all of the material he needed to know to pass each test and move forward with his class.

"If you've seen the movie *An Officer and a Gentleman*, forget about it!" Class Drill Instructor, Gunnery Sergeant Cade McArthur barked his first order as he stalked past each man and woman who stood erect in a ruler-straight line on the lawn. Brian was eighth in the formation and Shelby was three men to his right.

"Of the fifty-four men and women standing here today, I can guarantee you that at least ten of you won't be commissioned with this class. Some of you are going to realize before Indoctrination Week is over that you aren't officer material. Some of you will fail a few tests along the way and be forced to roll back to another class—that is, if you don't give up.

"All of you will leave here, in whatever fashion, with the under- standing that no one is given a commissioned officer's uniform just because he or she looks good in it."

McArthur stopped in front of Brian and glared at him. Brian maintained his one-thousand-yard stare, fixing his eyes on an object in the distance, and tried not to breathe.

"You're going to have to earn it," McArthur spat, before moving on to the next person in the line. "You got here on paper. Now you've got to prove you belong. Welcome to Officer Candidate School, Indoctrination Candidates."

Brian held his pose and waited for orders. If this was what it took, so be it. He had read enough and talked to enough people who had gone through the training to know it wouldn't be a cakewalk. A retired Navy pilot he met last summer during an internship at the Federal Aviation Administration had encouraged him to face the fear and the stress that he would confront with self-confidence, despite his leaders' efforts to see if they could break him.

Achieving that for Brian meant reciting over and over the Scripture his mom had taught him as a child: *I can do all things through Christ who strengthens me.*

He wished he could look to his right to see how Shelby was holding up. She wanted this as much as he did.

God, give her the strength to persevere too.

McArthur made sure everyone had received a manual and ordered them to read the document—all three hundred pages— tonight.

"You will be expected to know everything in this guide. Espe- cially how to appropriately address and respond to me, to your candidate officer, and to a commissioned officer," McArthur said.

"For the next twelve weeks, you will identify yourself as an Indoctrination Candidate and refer to the numbers of your graduating class. This group will be the tenth class graduating in fiscal zero-eight. Read the manual! You will be expected to know what to do—no exceptions, no excuses."

Later that night, Brian lay in his bunk and mentally kicked himself for not bringing along a blanket. If he had, he would have slept on top of the covers and kept his bed in perfect condition for morning inspection. Other guys obviously had been taught that trick, and pulled out covers from home when the drill instructor had completed his nighttime walk-through.

As tired as he was from the day's activities, Brian couldn't sleep. Neither could his two roommates.

"You think we gone make it, man?" Todd Wayland was from Mississippi and spoke with a southern drawl so thick and slow that Brian equated listening to him to waiting for the last drop of molasses to be forced from a plastic bottle.

The room was pitch-black, and Todd spoke just above a whisper.

The other bunkmate snorted before Brian could respond.

"Sounds like you're scared, Wayland," Greg Kemper, a proud recent graduate of Harvard, taunted. "Ready to go home to your mama?"

"Not if yours'll take me first," Todd countered. "Wanna wager on who'll last?"

"None of us will if we don't work together as a team," Brian reminded them. "Have you guys read the manual? Instead of slamming each other, how about you figure out how to get along so all of our lives will be easier? If we pass inspection and all do well on the tests—as a team—we can earn an Honor Class designation. Think about what's important, okay?"

"The resident Goody Two-Shoes has made himself known," Greg said.

Brian ignored him. He closed his eyes and pictured Indigo's smiling face. He couldn't have contact with her for the next three weeks, and he already missed her voice and her kisses. The thought of eventually being able to earn weekends off and see her once or twice before he received his commission would have to be enough to keep him focused.

Nothing was going to stop him from making his parents, or the future Mrs. Harper, proud.

15

*I*ndigo watched Yasmin wolf down a third helping of pancakes and shook her head in disbelief. She and her sister were both naturally thin, but this was ridiculous.

She took a sip of coffee and noted the time on the microwave's digital clock. 9:42 a.m.

Claude usually arrived at the newspaper at 9:50 a.m. sharp, just in time to gather what he needed for the 10:15 morning staff meeting. If Indigo timed it just right, she could reach the photo editor at his desk in about ten minutes and give him an update before he got preoccupied.

While Yasmin ate for three this morning, Indigo didn't have an appetite. Her life was imploding. If she couldn't see, how could she pursue her dream?

Mama returned to the kitchen and approached her. She hugged Indigo's neck and planted a kiss on the top of her head.

"You're going to be alright," Mama said. "This is not the end of the world. It's not a life-threatening condition and you're nowhere near blind. Rachelle told you that over and over yesterday. So did Dr. Woodman."

Daddy, who sat at the table next to Indigo, looked up from the newspaper.

"That was nice of that doctor to stop by the house with Rachelle to talk to all of us," he said. "It was the first of many blessings that I believe will come out of this situation, Indigo. So don't get yourself all worked up. God has the final say."

Indigo looked from one of her parents to the other and tried to contain her exasperation. "I am twenty-two years old and I have glaucoma. There's a blessing in that?"

She rose from the table so she could retreat to her brother's bedroom to sulk.

Aunt Melba had joined the family at the table for breakfast and was finishing a second cup of hot tea. She called out to Indigo, causing Indigo to stop in her tracks.

"Wait."

Aunt Melba had progressed from using a wheelchair to a walker, and her mind was as sharp as ever. Her challenge these days was that her speech didn't always keep up with her thoughts.

Indigo turned to look at her aunt and pursed her lips.

"One . . . day . . . at . . . a . . . time . . . God . . . will . . . bless," Aunt Melba said.

Indigo stared at Aunt Melba and allowed angry questions to race through her mind without uttering them. What about the School of the Visual Arts? What about her summer internship hanging in the balance? What about Brian? He had plenty of options and had no reason to settle for a wife with a chronic illness.

Before some of that turmoil bubbled over, Yasmin pointed to the digital clock.

"It's 9:51," she said and took another bite of food. "Thought you were going to check in with The Man."

Indigo held up the cordless phone. "I'm going to the bedroom to give Claude a call. He'll be all over the place after the morning meeting and hard to catch."

79

When she had settled on Reuben's bed, Indigo sat there in the dark for a moment, wondering what to do and say.

Mama would tell her to pray before she dialed his number. Brian, if he were here, would give her the same advice. Shelby would make the call for her.

"Time to be a Big Girl," she told herself.

Claude answered on the first ring. "Ingram here."

Indigo cleared her throat. "Good morning, Claude."

"Indigo! How are things? Got good news for me?"

She paused and bit her lip. There was nothing to do but to do it. "Claude, I have glaucoma. In both eyes."

The dead air unnerved her.

"Excuse me?" he finally said. "I thought that happened to . . . older people. My eighty-nine-year-old grandmother was recently diagnosed."

God, please forgive me for the ugly words I want to say to this man right now.

She took a few seconds to gain control.

"Apparently my great-grandmother had it too," she said. She wasn't going into details about her family history. "I saw a specialist yesterday who says it's the most common kind, open-angle, and it's early enough that I haven't lost too much of my vision."

"Won't it gradually get worse, though, Indigo?"

"Not if it's caught early on, Claude. I've been given some prescription eyedrops, but my ophthalmologist is recommending that I have laser surgery to correct the problem, since I'm so young. It won't cure the disease, but it will give me freedom from eyedrops for a few years and allow me to function normally. She's willing to write a letter to you, verifying all of this."

"Glaucoma? At your age? Well, how long would you have to

80

be out for surgery? You only had another six weeks for your internship."

Indigo heard him utter the word "had" instead of "have." She couldn't believe it. He was looking for a way to dump her. Rachelle appeared in the bedroom doorway and waved.

"Claude, I'm here now with my optometrist," Indigo said. "The ophthalmologist is going to perform the laser surgery, but Dr. Covington was there with me yesterday and heard everything. She can give you more details if you want me to put her on the phone."

"Sure," he said. She heard him whacking a pen or pencil on his desk. She extended the phone toward Rachelle and mouthed "thank you."

Rachelle held it to her ear and assumed her professional tone.

"Dr. Covington here. I understand you have questions about Ms. Burns's condition?"

Indigo didn't find any of this funny, but she couldn't help but smile as she watched Rachelle handle her boss's questions.

"The laser surgery actually will be done in the ophthalmologist's office, in the exam chair, and will literally take no more than five minutes. Ms. Burns will be able to return to her regular duties as soon as the day after the procedure."

Rachelle listened for a few minutes before responding.

"I'm not at liberty to discuss her condition in detail because of privacy laws, Mr. Ingram, but I'll repeat that when she has surgery in two weeks, she can return to work the next day."

Rachelle, who clearly had stopped by on her way to the office, plunged her free hand into the pocket of her white lab coat and listened.

"No," she said, "it's not normal for someone this age to be

diagnosed with glaucoma, but it happens. Anyone diagnosed from infancy through age thirty-five is considered to have juvenile glaucoma."

She listened again.

"You are correct—there is no cure, but because we've caught this early on, there's also no reason that further vision loss will occur, and there's no reason she can't have a full life as a photographer, even during this summer internship."

Before he could say more, Rachelle cut him short.

"Thanks so much for your concern, Mr. Ingram. If you need something in writing outlining what I've told you, I'll be happy to draft a letter for you. Have a good day."

She passed the phone back to Indigo and shook her head.

"Hello, Claude?"

"Yes, Indigo," he said. "I'm so sorry to hear about the glaucoma, but it seems like you've gotten a handle on it. Are you sure you want to come back to work? You've got a lot on your plate, with the upcoming surgery and all."

Indigo frowned. What was this really about? "The eyedrops should clear up the blurriness right away and I can be at work this afternoon, or tomorrow, if you prefer," she said. "I'm fine and ready to return to work. There's no reason for me to quit."

"Bring me the letter from your doctor and we'll go from there, okay?" Claude said. "Take today off and I'll see you in the morning, Indigo, and sorry again about your diagnosis."

Indigo hung up and turned toward Rachelle. "I feel like I have a scarlet letter or a contagious disease or something. Maybe I shouldn't have told him."

She flung herself back across the bed and buried her head in a pillow.

"Don't let that man tear down your spirits, Indigo," Rachelle said. "You got some tough news yesterday, especially for someone who will make a living using her eyes. But this is just an obstacle, not a death sentence. You'll be fine, regardless of what happens with this newspaper. That's not the medium you really want to work in, anyway. Let's just focus on getting your eyes in tip-top shape so you'll be ready for grad school in the Big Apple."

Indigo lifted her head and looked at Rachelle. "That's the other thing. Should I be asking my parents to shell out $26,000 a year for a prestigious photography program if I won't be able to work in this field long term? That doesn't make sense. Maybe I need to withdraw from school."

Taryn entered the room and looked around, as if wondering why Indigo hadn't turned on the lights or opened the blinds. But whatever her thoughts were, she kept them to herself as she rested her chin on her mother's shoulder. "Hey, cuz," she said to Indigo. "Yasmin just told me about your eyes. I'm sorry."

The pity made Indigo angry. What was Brian going to say when he found out? Maybe now he'd be willing to wait on the wedding. Who wanted a half-blind wife?

She willed the tears to dry up, but they flowed anyway.

Rachelle pushed Taryn toward the door and looked back at Indigo before leaving.

"It's okay to have a brief pity party, Indigo. This is tough news. But you've got to know that God is in this too. He wouldn't give you dreams just to dash them. You've got to look within and figure out how to keep moving forward, despite the doors that close. That's what the Indigo I know would do. Take some time for yourself today, then get up."

When she was alone, Indigo pounded the pillow.

Life could be so unfair. She knew that, though, didn't she?

The car accident that killed her birth parents when she was

seven and led Yasmin, their brother, Reuben, and her to be adopted by their paternal grandparents wasn't fair; her grandmother/mother's struggle with alcohol that had made living in this house suffocating and secretive hadn't been fair. Now she had to deal with this—an unfair blow to her health at a time when she should be embracing opportunities and living to the fullest.

Despite these issues, she simply was supposed to trust God?

Indigo closed her eyes. She knew the answer to the question even if she didn't want to accept it.

She wasn't just *supposed* to trust him—apparently she *had* to, because everything else in her life that mattered seemed to be shifting like quicksand.

16

*B*rian had never felt the sun's heat like this.

From now on, whenever he heard the term "buzz cut," he would remember that day, one week ago, when he sat in the barber's chair on base to get one. He had zeroed in on the humming of a sharp, electric razor while a stoic, bottle-blonde stylist with designer nails went back and forth across his scalp. He had always worn his hair closely cropped or in a microafro, but now he was a sneeze away from being bald. Friends had teased him for years about resembling actor Boris Kodjoe, and with this cut he could pass for brother man's twin.

Except for the intensity of the sun that he dealt with during outdoor physical training, he didn't really mind his new 'do. Today, though, he was sweating buckets during a brief walk across the lawn from his bunk to the main hall, where he intended to call Indigo for the first time since he'd left Jubilant. He figured excitement fueled his perspiration more than anything else.

He was allowed one five-minute call each week, and he had decided last Sunday, after talking with his folks, to alternate between calling them and his girl. He had so much to tell her.

But then, that must be the point of putting a time limit on the calls. With so few minutes to talk with loved ones, what indoctrination candidate would waste them spilling his guts about the rigors of OCS? It was better to use those precious seconds reassuring their family and friends that they were okay, a candidate officer had advised Brian and his classmates, and to receive some news about the routine happenings at home that might encourage them.

But when Brian dialed Indigo's cell and she answered with some hesitancy, he wanted to do more than listen. If he could have crawled through the phone, he would have held her and told her he'd fix whatever had her sounding so troubled.

"What is it, Indie?"

"Nothing, babe—just missing you," she said, but he knew better. Her cheerfulness was forced. "It's so good to hear your voice. You taking care of yourself?"

Brian snorted. "I'm still standing. How about you? What has you so down? You miss me that much?"

"Yeah, I do," she said. "I'm fine, Brian, I just found out that I need a little laser surgery on my eyes."

"A 'little' surgery on your eyes? What in the world—?"

"I have glaucoma. We've caught it early enough that the surgery should correct the problem and keep it from getting worse. There's no cure, but it hasn't done too much damage. My vision is 20/60, but the laser surgery will reroute some fluid to take the pressure off my eyes and correct the nearsightedness so I won't need glasses. Rachelle is looking out for me."

"When did all of this happen?"

Indigo must have been concerned that the clock was ticking. "I'll give you details later. I don't want to waste the few minutes we have left talking about it," she said. "I probably shouldn't have told you anyway—you'll be worrying about me when you need to be focused."

She giggled. "I just wanna make sure you still want to marry me. I might opt for that instead of grad school, since I could be half blind."

Brian could tell that she had thrown out the idea only half jokingly, to gauge his reaction. His heart softened.

"I love you, babe, bad eyesight and all. If you have to walk down the aisle to become my wife wearing Coke-bottle lenses, I'll take you. Just remove them for the photos—and the honeymoon— okay?"

She laughed and he felt better.

"Seriously though, that's a hard thing to hear. You're really thinking about sitting out of grad school?"

Behind him, a bullhorn sounded, alerting him and the candidates on the other pay phones that they had two minutes left.

Indigo heard it too. She sighed. "I don't know, Brian. Everything is up in the air right now. I don't even know if I'll finish the newspaper internship. I'm just taking it day by day at the moment. I don't want to waste my parents' money if this eye thing is more serious than we think."

Brian heard her despair. "Tell you what—you take me with my nearly bald head and I'll take you, whatever may come. We're still on for August 25. Be there or be square. After I'm commissioned, you can work wherever I'm planted for flight school, and it's looking like it will be Pensacola."

Indigo didn't respond. Brian imagined her sitting Indian style on the floor or sofa, twirling a piece of her dark brown hair and nodding, as if he could see her.

"Whenever they give you a moment, send me a picture of that bald head," she finally said. "If you're all shiny up there, I can't imagine what Shelby looks like."

Brian's eyes darted around the stark white room that held a bank of telephones and a few tables. The space was small, but it was crammed right now with indoctrination candidates who didn't want to miss the opportunity to connect briefly with reality.

He spotted Shelby at the opposite end of the room with her hands jammed into the pockets of the standard olive green jumpsuit worn by every indoctrination candidate on the campus.

Shelby's hair had been drastically cut too. She looked like a puny man without her usual bob or makeup to soften the angles of her face.

"She has two inches of growth left on top, babe, and her perm is sweating out."

"Wow," Indigo said.

Brian barely heard her response. He had a minute left before it was time to end the call, but his attention was drawn to the scene unfolding before him.

Shelby suddenly snapped to attention and assumed the one-thousand-yard stare, while a uniformed man addressed her. She seemed surprised, despite her effort to remain expressionless, and so did the man. Based on his uniform, Brian pegged him as a senior officer candidate, just a few weeks ahead of his and Shelby's class in OCS.

Brian squinted at the officer's profile, wondering why he looked familiar.

"Indie, my time's up. I love you, baby. Don't worry about the eyes. We'll get through this. Keep planning the wedding."

He hung up before she could respond, entranced by Shelby and the mystery man.

Brian's eyes weren't playing tricks. Shelby was talking to Craig Miller.

Craig graduated from Tuskegee a year ahead of him. When had he decided to become a naval officer? What Indoctrination Class was he helping lead?

Rigid orders wouldn't give Brian an opportunity to ask those questions for another few weeks, but it didn't escape his notice that Craig had made a point of seeking out Shelby. Both of them were grown, but Brian prayed right then that these two old friends would remain as formal—and as distant—as possible.

17

"What you need right now is a piece of this."

Yasmin strolled into the family room with two hunks of chocolate cake and placed one on the glass coffee table in front of Indigo. She smiled at Aunt Melba and her mother, who sat nearby, and held out the other piece for them to inspect.

"Would you two like some?"

Mama looked up from *Wheel of Fortune* and frowned at her youngest daughter. "Didn't you have a slice after dinner? You keep on eating like that, talking about you gonna model. For whom?"

Yasmin shrugged and sat next to Indigo on the love seat.

Indigo picked up her plate and took a big bite. She let the taste fill her mouth and gave Yasmin a thumbs-up.

"I'm not trying to be as big as this house by the time Brian gets back, but thanks, little sis."

They ate in silence and tried to solve the puzzles along with the television game show guests who were spinning the wheel and raking in the cash.

"Isn't this what old people do?" Yasmin whispered. "Can you take me to the mall?"

Indigo laughed out loud, but pinched her lips together when Aunt Melba frowned and Mama shushed her.

Her brief conversation with Brian half an hour ago had lifted her spirits. He wasn't going to leave her. At least he hadn't sounded like he had one foot out of the door.

She was nervous about going into the newsroom tomorrow, for the first time since her chat with Claude, but Brian's reassurance had calmed her. As long as the newspaper gave her a chance, she'd be able to do her job despite this minor setback.

She and Yasmin polished off their cake just as the show was ending, and Indigo realized that, like her sister, she was bored.

"Where are your little girlfriends this evening?" she asked Yasmin. "You aren't usually trying to hang out with your older sister. Where's Taryn?"

Yasmin yawned. "Taryn's on punishment for talking on the phone too late last night."

Mama peered at Yasmin over the rim of her reading glasses. "You are too, so why are you making her look bad? I'm the one who caught you guys, remember?"

Indigo tried to suppress more laughter. Mama was more ornery than she remembered from her flashbacks to her teenage years.

"How late were you guys on? Were you talking to each other?"

Mama answered for Yasmin. "I happened to get up at four a.m. to use the bathroom and check on Melba. They had a six-way call going, with another girl and three boys."

"Yasmin!" Indigo said in surprise, and then, under her breath, "We'll talk later."

Indigo saw the look of frustration on Mama's face and felt bad. Mama was doing her best to rein in Yasmin, who thought she knew everything. She needed to be helping, not playing devil's advocate.

"When you do what you're *supposed* to do, little girl, then I'll help you do what you'd *like* to do," Indigo said.

Yasmin rolled her eyes and pushed herself off the sofa.

"Where are you going? To your room to sulk?" Mama asked.

"I have to use the bathroom," the teenager said sullenly, without turning around.

Indigo looked at Mama, whose eyes were following Yasmin down the hallway.

"Don't worry, Mama, you'll get through it with her just like you did with me."

Mama parted her lips to speak, but changed her mind. Melba had put both hands on her walker and had pulled herself into a standing position. Every day she was getting stronger, and her speech was steadily improving too. Indigo was seeing glimpses of humor return.

"See . . . my . . . arms? . . . Angela . . . Bassett . . . arms?" Melba said slowly, between breaths. She looked at Mama and motioned toward the bedroom with her head. "Come on . . . Irene . . . Help . . . Miss Daisy . . . down the hall."

Indigo watched the two sisters move arm in arm slowly toward the bedroom. They had cackled like hens earlier in the day when their brother, Rachelle's father, Herbert, called to check on them. They urged him to come for a visit while the two of them were still under the same roof.

"You can stay with us, and we'll let Charles hang out with his friends," Mama had teased. "It'll be just like old times, when we were growing up and your sisters drove you crazy."

Indigo stretched out on the love seat and propped her feet up on one end. Daddy was out tonight, at a deacon's meeting at St. Peter's Baptist. Besides that monthly commitment, bowling, and an occasional movie, there wasn't much else to do in Jubilant.

She ran the events of the day through her mind, especially Brian's call, and the relaxed evening she'd had with her family. It felt good.

Next week about this time she would be recovering from laser surgery, but she would be okay. In her heart of hearts, she knew it. Otherwise, she was wasting her time in prayer.

She wished, just like everyone else in the world concerned about their future, that she could see how this would all end. Maybe getting married was the path God was nudging her to take after all. The date was already set and Brian was a good man, not to mention all of his other attributes.

Or was God using this minicrisis to test her resolve, to see just how badly she wanted what she always called her lifelong dream?

Indigo was convinced that God didn't always make his children struggle to find answers. Moses's orders were put right in his path. Where was her burning bush?

18

*I*t didn't take a fiery symbol to see that Claude wanted her gone. Even a fourth grader could have read his body language.

Legally, he'd be liable if he forced Indigo to leave because of a medical condition, so there was little he could do. But what he could do, he did.

When she returned to the office two days ago, his disdain had been obvious.

"Let me see your letter," he said and held out his hand. He took his time reading the note that Rachelle had crafted on her optometry practice letterhead. It explained that Indigo's eye issues were being resolved promptly and in a fashion that would not prohibit her from serving as a professional photographer. She noted the brief amount of time Indigo would need to recover from laser surgery.

"This makes it all sound so . . . simple," he said. "I've never heard of a quick fix for glaucoma."

Indigo shrugged. "I don't think laser surgery is a quick fix. It's a temporary reprieve that keeps me from having to use the prescription eyedrops several times a day, or having to wear glasses. It will have to be repeated as the pressure returns, but it's a solid remedy at this point and will allow me to do my job with no problem."

She paused, but continued when Claude looked skeptical.

"I apologize again for not being proactive about the issue with my eyes. I assure you that you don't have to worry about any more issues when you send me on assignments in the future."

But apparently he was worried. Rather than assigning Indigo photos to shoot, Claude had her cropping other photographers' shots. Or she was filling the role of administrative assistant, running between the photo department and various editors' desks, dropping off prints for them to review.

Today was Friday, and all morning she had fielded calls from the newspaper's archive librarian and the general public.

Around lunchtime, when she heard Claude ask photographer Roger Simon for the new cell phone number of a freelance photographer he hired sometimes to cover breaking news, Indigo's radar went up.

"Claude? Is there something going on that you'd like me to shoot? I've got my camera in the car."

Claude glanced at Indigo and looked away. "No thanks, Indigo. You're doing fine."

He turned back to Roger. "Get Max on the phone. I need him to hustle to Fifth and Monroe streets as quickly as possible. There's a water main break and it's causing some problems in that neighborhood."

Indigo bit her bottom lip in frustration.

She did a quick mental calculation—today was the end of her fifth week. She had five weeks left in her internship, but clearly she wasn't going to be allowed to learn anything or contribute to the team.

She was scheduled to be off work on Monday for her laser

surgery and planned to return on Tuesday or Wednesday. It was looking like that needed to be reconsidered.

"I'm taking my lunch break," she said and grabbed her purse.

Indigo left the building by a side entrance and strolled around the block, but her stomach was flip-flopping too much right now to eat.

A small park was located diagonally across from the newspaper, and people sometimes ate lunch there or took breaks to feed the pigeons. She wandered over to a wrought iron bench located under a cedar tree and pulled her cell phone from her purse.

"Hello, Daddy?"

Indigo explained what had happened.

"I don't want to be unprofessional and just walk out," she said. "On the other hand, why stay and be treated this way?"

"The first thing we're going to do is pray," her father said.

Indigo would do whatever might help. She tucked her purse into her body, gripped the phone, and closed her eyes while Charles Burns led their talk with God.

"Give her clarity, Lord, and let no harm come to her for moving on. Let what seems to be her downfall lead to her greatest victory. We ask for it in your name, Jesus, and we believe it is done!"

"Amen," Indigo said and opened her eyes.

Daddy was thorough. "Now, young lady, you remember who you are and do what you would normally do in a situation like this."

Indigo sat back on the bench and thought about it. She knew what she would "normally" do, but could she be that bold today?

"Then," Daddy continued, "you go back in there with a smile on your face and type a nice letter of resignation or farewell, or whatever you want to call it. Bring your camera home and find something more meaningful to do with your time."

Indigo was stunned. This couldn't be coming from the Charles Burns she knew, the one who had worked at the same car dealership for thirty years and took whatever nonsense he had to, to take care of his family.

"I don't know, Daddy . . ."

"You know I'd never tell you to quit a job over some nonsense, or in a rash way, Indigo," he said. "Do what you think is right. But God doesn't want you casting your pearls before swine.

"You're not in a situation right now where you have to support a family or keep a roof over your head," he said. "Your mama and I still have you covered—for now. Don't go in there and burn bridges—you never know who you'll need later. But you can respectfully and humbly tell them you're moving on."

Indigo ended the call and bought a sub sandwich from the only sidewalk vendor she'd ever seen operating in the city. She forced the sandwich down and then crossed the street, strode to the employee parking lot behind the *Herald*, and jumped into her Honda. Since she had nothing to lose, she was going to follow her heart.

Minutes later, she pulled up to a meter on Fifth Street.

Water spewed from an exposed pipe in the middle of Fifth and Monroe and was steadily rising, threatening to flood some businesses. She retrieved her camera from the back of the SUV, along with a pair of socks and sneakers she kept in a gym bag.

When she was ready, she surveyed the area to determine which position might yield the best photos. The three photographers already there—a man holding a black camera similar to hers and the others from two regional TV stations—were positioned across the street from where she now stood, shooting the water as it spewed upward.

Indigo noticed a stairwell off the side of the building behind her that led to a low roof. In downtown Jubilant, this four-story building qualified as a high-rise.

She turned and jogged up the steps. When she reached the landing that led to a terrace roof, she slowly climbed onto the roof and walked toward the edge that faced the flooding intersection.

Perfect. Not only could she see the waterspout, she was able to capture images from a few side streets, where worried business owners huddled and waited for emergency crews to fix the problem. She zoomed in on a kitchen and bath design store, which was already flooding, and showed the water seeping beneath the doorsill.

Half an hour later, Indigo had captured tons of great shots, and she realized she had done it without hesitation. She wasn't sure whether the prescription drops had kicked in or whether her eyes were working properly on their own today. Regardless, she had no problems focusing and snapping image after great image.

Indigo climbed down slowly, no longer doubting what she needed to do.

When she returned to the newspaper, thankfully, Claude and Roger were both out. She positioned herself in front of a computer and quickly downloaded the pictures she had just shot, printing her three favorites—pictures she knew that none of the other photographers could have possibly captured from their positions.

She tucked the images in a folder and resumed her duties for the day—answering calls and assisting Claude however he requested.

About an hour later, just after two p.m., the photographer she had seen standing across the street from the water main break swaggered into the photo lab and sat in front of one of the computers as if he belonged there.

Claude, who was just returning from a lunch meeting, approached him from behind and clapped him on the shoulder.

"Did you get some good stuff, Max?"

So this was the favored photographer, Indigo mused. He looked about five years older than she and wore his confidence like an expensive cologne. His oatmeal complexion and jet black curly hair indicated that he could be biracial, Hispanic, or Native American.

"I always do, Claude. Let me download some of the pictures and let you choose."

While he worked, Indigo began drafting her letter.

Just after six p.m., she packed her plaid shoulder bag and stopped by Claude's desk. He was standing in front of his chair, poring over a series of picture prints spread out before him, chewing on the end of an ink pen.

"Got a minute?" she asked.

Claude nodded. "Come on in."

"I have something for you," Indigo said.

She watched Claude while he read the letter.

```
June 28 will be my last day as an intern
for the Jubilant Herald. I have enjoyed my
tenure and have learned to value various
aspects of photojournalism. Thank you for
this opportunity.
```

When he raised his eyes, Indigo saw the mixture of triumph and relief.

"Some things work out for the best," he said. "Don't feel obligated to work two more weeks. You have surgery next week. Just take this time off to recover. We'll pay you through next week and consider ourselves even."

Indigo wanted to tell him she knew better. But at least she wasn't leaving without her dignity.

"Whatever you'd like, Claude," she said.

Before she turned to leave, Indigo opened her shoulder bag and pulled out the folder holding the photos she had printed from the water main break. She laid them on Claude's desk, next to her letter.

"I took a little time during my lunch break to make sure my skills are intact," she said. "Just so you know, the eyedrops are working, and despite the diagnosis, I'm going to be fine. Good luck to you and your staff. Thanks again for this opportunity."

With that, she left the office and walked to her car without looking back.

Once she had settled into the driver's seat, she sat there for a moment, wondering how, in a matter of weeks, she had gone from summa cum laude graduate to a suddenly unemployed intern with a chronic eye disease.

Her life was just getting started, and already, she felt like a loser.

19

*T*his couldn't count as surgery.

Dr. Yolanda Woodman dimmed the lights in the exam room and scooted her roller seat in front of Indigo. She pressed a floor button with the tip of her shoe that lowered an instrument attached to the ceiling. When it was positioned between the two of them, she sat up straighter and smiled at Indigo.

"Ready?"

Indigo sighed and shrugged.

"Keep your eyes open and hold them steady," Dr. Woodman instructed. "I'll start with the right eye, but I need you to keep both of them open."

A beam of blue light appeared, and Dr. Woodman aimed it at Indigo's dilated pupil.

The only discomfort Indigo felt came from trying to maintain her stare for two minutes.

"There," the ophthalmologist said. She sat back in her chair for a few minutes before positioning the instrument to zap the other eye.

When she was done, she kept the lights low. Dr. Woodman's assistant put drops in Indigo's eyes and gave her a pair of flimsy paper sunglasses to block the light.

"We'll monitor you for about an hour before we send you home," the cheerful young lady said. "Step down from the exam chair carefully and sit in this wheelchair; I'll take you next door to the postsurgery room, where you can stretch out on one of the cots and nap if you'd like."

The wheelchair ride was quick. Indigo climbed onto one of the low beds, with help from the assistant, and lay back. She relaxed and folded her arms across her belly. If this brief, but focused, work paid what Indigo believed it did, she needed to switch careers. Indigo knew the specialized procedure required expertise; still, she couldn't help but marvel at its swiftness.

God, let this work. No more eye problems, please? You said ask and you would answer. I'm begging you to preserve my eyesight.

Those clichés were always true—you didn't miss your water 'til your well ran dry; it was easy to take something for granted if you had no reason to doubt that it would always be there.

She wasn't going blind and prayed that the glaucoma would never get to that point. But the diagnosis alone had been enough to fill her with dread. Getting it at age twenty-two versus sixty-two made a world of difference.

While the laser surgery was a gift that would soon give her freedom from having to use prescription eyedrops, the reality that she had a condition that needed to be managed for the rest of her life was still overwhelming.

Dr. Woodman felt certain that Indigo wouldn't have problems pursuing her photography goals.

"We'll monitor you every six months—every three if that's what makes you comfortable. I'm in this with you," she had promised. "Don't let this little hiccup keep you from living life. I'm looking forward to seeing your photographs in some amazing places."

Yet, as Indigo rested on the thin cot and felt herself drifting to sleep, she couldn't help but fret.

How often would she have to have this procedure to maintain a normal life? What if the doctors were wrong about the disease's progression? Should she get a desk job where her eyes weren't central to her work?

Maybe she should take the bird in her hand—marriage to a man she loved—and let whatever else happened, happen. She wondered what Shelby would advise her to do. But then, Shelby had never been one to make choices based on matters of the heart. She flew through boyfriends the way some women changed shoes.

Indigo felt the knots in her stomach as she tossed around all of her options.

She loved Brian, but she needed to be able to breathe without him. She had learned from the women she cared about most—Mama, Rachelle, Aunt Melba—that life got hard sometimes, and she'd be wise to make sure she could take care of herself.

Before she could wrestle with herself any further, Dr. Woodman's assistant returned and told her she could go.

Mama and Daddy had been watching the clock in the eye clinic's waiting room. They stood to greet her when she emerged from the post-op area and peered at her expectantly.

Indigo shrugged and answered the questions they were asking with their eyes. "I'm okay; no pain or anything. Dr. Woodman says I'll be ready to move forward with life by tomorrow."

She tried not to sound glum, but truth be told, she had only partially pulled herself out of the pity party she had lapsed into a few days ago, when Claude Ingram seemed so thrilled to bid her farewell. It shouldn't have surprised her that he hadn't acknowledged the pictures she'd left with him.

Indigo knew the newspaper would still be produced and photos would still be published, but she alternated between not caring and wanting her absence to be felt. Then she'd pray and ask God to forgive her for feeling that way.

"Ready to go?" Mama asked.

"Sure."

They walked to the hospital garage and climbed into her parents' GMC.

Mama and Daddy were quiet on the drive home. When they were about five minutes away, Indigo brought up a concern that had been worrying her for a couple of weeks now.

"What do you want me to do about grad school?"

Mama shifted in the front passenger seat and turned toward Indigo. "What do you mean? You're still leaving after the wedding, aren't you? I thought that you and Brian had discussed it and agreed."

Indigo tried to gauge by her mother's expression what she was thinking and feeling, but Mama had always been a master at masking her emotions. That skill had contributed to her ability to hide her alcoholism for so long. She'd never been loud and nasty, but shutting down and withdrawing from the family every chance she got over a period of years had caused just as much pain.

"We've discussed it, but I would say the issue is still on the table," Indigo said. "I'm still struggling with what to do, given the glaucoma diagnosis. I just don't know. Should I still try to go?"

"Why are you asking us?" Daddy piped up. "You're all set to go, with a partial scholarship and all, and you've wanted to go for a long time. Why give up now? Dr. Woodman said this surgery should work."

"But what if it doesn't and I've wasted all that money and time?"

104

Mama peered at Indigo. "When did you start letting fear dictate your path? Haven't we taught you that life is a series of what-ifs? Are you going to let your dreams go based on a possibility that things might not work out as planned, when there's a strong chance that they will? Have you talked to God about it?"

Well, yes—she had prayed. She had pleaded.

Mama could read the answer in Indigo's eyes. "Have you been listening?" she asked gently. "When you do that, you'll know what to do. We've been saving money for your education since you were a baby, Indigo, even before you came to live with us. It was already earmarked, so don't get all caught up in that. If you go and you spend it, you will have still learned something and had experiences that God wanted you to have, regardless of what may happen down the road."

Indigo closed her eyes and laid her head back on the seat. Mama was right. Why should she stop pushing forward now, when only God knew what the future held?

If she chose to attend grad school, though, Brian would have to wait for them to live together as husband and wife. She wasn't sure how she would broach that conversation, especially since the last time they talked, she hadn't balked at his plan for her to join him in Pensacola after their wedding.

That led to another unsettling question—would he agree to a long-distance marriage?

20

On most nights, Brian couldn't purge the scene from his mind.

It had been over three years since that romantic liaison, but every time he remembered it, he felt ashamed. His thoughts would float between that pivotal evening and his routine date with Indigo the next day.

She had no clue, and for that, he had been thankful. Nothing was worth losing her. Nothing.

Life was so regimented at OCS that he had not had much time to think about anything but memorizing rules and regulations and barking the required responses to his drill sergeant and commanding officer.

When he wasn't running or swimming or completing some other physical training activity, he was cramming material on engineering and naval equipment into his brain. He prayed daily to master every challenge so he wouldn't get rolled back to another class. That would mean an additional three months here and would throw off plans for his wedding. Indigo would jump on the excuse to move to New York.

In his first few weeks here, Brian had been ready to sleep like a baby by the time Gunnery Sgt. McArthur conducted nine p.m.

taps to make sure all lights were out and that the officers were complying with mandatory silence.

As the weeks wore on, his body adjusted to the rigorous pace and he was able to stay up as late as he wanted in the dark, quiet room.

That left more time for ruminating and dreaming, and fretting over the past, and what the future would look like. If he passed OCS and was commissioned, he would be on the path to become a Navy pilot.

But what was going to happen with his relationship with Indigo if she wasn't ready to settle down? He didn't want to be one of those lonely military men, pining away for a long-distance love and waiting for mail call, and he knew she wouldn't be at a loss for people to see in New York. Or what if the Navy decided he just didn't measure up?

These were the fears that haunted him when he let down his guard. It hadn't helped that he now came in regular contact with his former friend and fellow Tuskegee alum Craig Miller, who had been a superb athlete and academic all-star in the class ahead of him. Craig's presence here at OCS brought back a flood of memories that Brian wanted to stay buried.

He wondered if Craig had matured or whether he still considered himself a master player, who loved and left his conquests without a drop of guilt. He wondered if Shelby needed to be reminded of Craig's reputation, just in case.

The officer candidates were given more freedom around their sixth week of school, because they had passed the room inspection. They could now go out to the local pubs and restaurants on weekends, and they had an occasional evening free during the week.

The downtime allowed them to finally get to know each other.

His roommate, Todd Wayland, was a good guy. Greg Kemper could get anyone riled up.

For Brian, however, the loosened rein was a problem.

Now that things weren't so regimented, Craig could freely interact with him and with Shelby. She didn't seem to mind, but Brian wanted to know why all of a sudden he was "Officer Friendly." The three of them had rarely spoken when they saw one another on campus during Craig's senior year.

"Why is he all in your face now?" Brian asked Shelby one evening, while they played cards in a recreation room on campus.

"It's no big deal," Shelby said, and shrugged. "He just wants someone familiar to shoot the breeze with before he leaves. His class graduates in four weeks."

Brian smirked and Shelby mimicked the gesture.

"Trust me, I have no interest in getting tangled up with Craig Miller, of all people. Why are you so worked up about this anyway?"

Instead of answering, Brian dealt the cards and changed the subject. "Are your parents coming up to visit next weekend?"

Now it was Shelby's turn to be evasive. "I don't know—why? Did your parents want all of us to have dinner or something?"

"Actually, I was thinking about having Indigo come," Brian said. "She's been so bummed out about the eye diagnosis and all that happened with the newspaper job. Plus, I want to see how much progress she's made with the wedding plans."

Shelby nodded.

"So if your parents aren't coming, who is?" Brian asked. "You aren't going to waste a weekend to actually have a good time, are you?"

Shelby pursed her lips. "Actually, I have a new friend, and I was thinking of inviting him," she said, making sure to keep her eyes focused on her cards.

Brian sat up straighter. Why hadn't he heard about this? "So you're keeping secrets now, huh?" he said. "Who is the mystery man?"

Shelby rolled her eyes. "Keeping secrets? You act like you have some say in my decisions. Don't worry about it. If he comes, I'll be sure to introduce you and Indigo. If my parents come instead, you'll just have to wait."

With that, she played her final hand, a Joker, and won the game. She stood up and patted Brian on the shoulder on her way out of the room.

"Good night, Officer Candidate Harper, Indoctrination Class zero-ten, zero-eight. I'm going to bed."

As he lay here tonight, struggling to keep memories from the past in the past, Brian wondered whether Shelby lay awake in her bunk too, and whether her dreams were haunting or hopeful.

21

Family meeting tonight at 7. No excused absences.

Indigo sank to a new low when she saw the note posted on the refrigerator.

Of course, she had nowhere to go, so being there wouldn't be a problem. But the idea of being summoned to a meeting with her parents when she should have been "grown and gone" deepened her self-pity.

It had been two weeks since she'd left the newspaper, and mostly, she spent her days pushing Aunt Melba's wheelchair through the neighborhood on afternoon walks and halfheartedly perusing the bridal magazines Mama and Yasmin kept leaving on the kitchen table.

This morning, she and Aunt Melba started out early to beat the record haze and humidity the weatherman was predicting.

"You're . . . quiet . . . extra," Aunt Melba said five minutes into their usual circuit down tree-lined streets that showcased their favorite houses and flower beds. Indigo knew she meant "extra quiet." Every so often, her aunt's brain still got the words mixed up, and they came out in reverse order.

"No particular reason," Indigo said. "Just one of those days."

"You've . . . had . . . a lot . . . of . . . those lately," Melba said. "It . . . will . . . get better. We . . . both . . . will . . . get better."

Aunt Melba's confidence made her smile.

"You will at a rate faster than me, it appears," Indigo said. "You're doing great, Aunt Melba. It won't be much longer before you'll be walking these blocks with me instead of having to ride."

Aunt Melba nodded. "I've already . . . talked to . . . God . . . about it," she said. ". . . You?"

Indigo pushed in silence for a few more blocks. What about her? She wished she could pour out her heart to Aunt Melba like she used to and get her honest feedback on everything. But she didn't want to burden her ailing aunt with issues that seemed trivial in comparison to the effort to recover from a stroke.

"I don't talk to God like I know I should," Indigo finally said. "I hate to admit it, but I guess I'm frustrated with him. I know I have no right to be. Who am I to be mad because things aren't going so well in my life right now? I don't want to feel this way, but I just don't understand. I've always served him and been faithful." She sighed in frustration. "I don't understand."

Before Aunt Melba could respond, a woman across the street interrupted them.

"Indigo Burns! How are you?"

Indigo raised her eyes and smiled when she saw Vanessa Little-john, one of her girlfriends from high school. She was coming down the walkway from one of the brick and stone mini-mansions that Indigo admired when they walked this route.

Vanessa, dressed in a classic short-sleeved navy pantsuit and open-toed navy pumps, trotted across the street and gave Indigo a hug.

"I haven't seen you in ages! You look wonderful!" she said to Indigo.

"Well, you look fabulous," Indigo told Vanessa, before introducing her to Aunt Melba.

"What are you doing these days?" Vanessa asked. "Do you live in this neighborhood?"

Indigo scrambled for a quick answer that wouldn't require too much detail.

"My parents live here," she said. "I'm home with them for the summer, but I've been accepted to grad school in New York to work on my master's in photography and the program starts in August." She didn't mention Brian, the wedding, or the fact that these days she was trying to keep her head up. "What about you?" Indigo asked.

"My aunt and uncle live here," Vanessa said and waved at the house from which she had emerged. "I'm house-sitting for them while they're in Europe. My uncle landed a new contract for his company and he's working there for six weeks. My aunt's just there to shop! This worked out great for me, because my parents moved to St. Louis a few years ago and sold their home here. I landed a job at IBM and they decided to send me to the Jubilant satellite office until the fall, when they'll transfer me to Dallas. So life is great!"

Indigo mustered a smile and prayed the conversation would end soon.

"It's so good to see you, Indigo," Vanessa said and gave her another light hug. "I always knew you would do great things. You keep up the good work."

Vanessa strode to a red Corvette parked in her aunt and uncle's driveway and jumped in. She waved cheerfully as she sped away.

Indigo stayed put for a few minutes after Vanessa was gone, staring at the house and processing what had just transpired. She wasn't sure what she should be feeling, but she knew it shouldn't be the envy she recognized.

Where was the Indigo she always thought she was?

22

*I*f Indigo didn't have answers, it seemed her father did—for her and for Yasmin.

"Why are we having a family meeting on a Friday night?" Yasmin asked in exasperation,when she, Indigo, and their parents gathered in the family room at the designated time. Aunt Melba had been invited but had declined to participate, citing the need for them to move forward as if she were back in her own home, which she hoped to be soon.

"Tonight was best for my schedule," Daddy said and leveled his gaze at Yasmin, warning her that she was bordering on disrespectfulness. "You got any other questions?"

She shook her head, sat back on the sofa, and crossed her arms.

Indigo sat in a similar position, waiting to hear what her parents had on their minds.

Both of them usually led the discussion, but it seemed that Daddy wanted to have a talk with his daughters tonight.

"I called this meeting because your mama and I have been watching both of you closely, and we're worried about you."

Yasmin frowned. Indigo didn't respond.

"Yasmin, we know you want to be a model, and you have the

114

beauty, the build, and the height to achieve your goal," Daddy said. "But you've begun to play with fire in your quest to have your cake and eat it too. Forgive the pun, but it's true."

Indigo had no idea where her father was going with this. She watched Yasmin's reaction to see if the teenager did.

Yasmin's eyes grew wide. "Daddy, what are you talking about?" she asked. "Can you speak plain English?"

Mama chimed in. "We know you're making yourself throw up after you eat, Yasmin."

The deer-in-the-headlights expression that filled Yasmin's face told Indigo her mother's declaration was true.

"Yasmin!" Indigo said. "What on earth?"

"Bulimia is serious, Yasmin," Daddy said. "You can't keep doing that to your body and think there won't be consequences. You've got to stop or get help to stop."

Scenes raced through Indigo's mind of her sister's recent eating patterns and it all made sense: Yasmin gorging on pancakes for breakfast, eating several servings of cake back-to-back, constantly weighing herself on the bathroom scale, or running to the bathroom after a meal. God help her.

Yasmin lowered her eyes.

"Yasmin?" Mama prodded.

The girl lifted her head and looked at her parents. "I didn't mean to start this," she said as tears spilled down her cheeks. "A girl at school who models in Dallas told me she does it to get ready for auditions and for her photo shoots. She insisted that it beats dieting. I tried it because I was curious, and it just got easier each time. Now I don't know if I can stop."

Indigo reached for her sister's hand.

"It's okay, baby," Daddy said. "We're not asking you to try to do this on your own. We're here to help you. We'll get you professional help if necessary."

Yasmin's tears turned into sobs. She covered her face with both hands and sank farther into the sofa. Indigo slid closer and pulled Yasmin into her arms.

"I'm here for you too, sis," she said and hugged her. "You can beat this, okay? *We'll* beat it."

She held Yasmin until the tears abated and the girl had composed herself.

Mama walked over and held out her arms. Yasmin stood up and towered over her mother. She stooped to wrap herself in Mama's embrace.

When both of them had returned to their seats, Daddy looked toward Indigo.

"We've been watching you and praying for you too, Indigo," he said. "Hearing the news at twenty-two that you have a chronic illness is pretty tough. That's a lot to handle at your age. But I have six words for you baby: Get up and dust yourself off."

Indigo was stunned. Where had that missive come from? "Daddy, what do you—"

"I mean that we've let you wallow in your pity and grief, or whatever you want to call it, long enough," Daddy said. "We understand that you're feeling bad about the glaucoma diagnosis and about what happened with the newspaper internship, but guess what? The world keeps revolving and we have to keep moving with it.

"So you've got a little health issue to contend with—you can handle it," he said. "So you had a minor career setback—minor because it was an internship, not a full-time job—you can get over it. So you're wondering whether to go to grad school, get married, or both—if you get your head out of the sand, God will

116

make his vision for your life plain. You have to be open to hearing from him.

"So buck up and get up. It's time, you know."

Indigo felt strangely calm about being knocked out of her self-absorption. "Yes, I know, Daddy. It's time to be a big girl now. But how?"

He and Mama traded glances before Mama responded.

"We're not going to figure it all out for you, because you're an adult now and you need to learn to make your own decisions, deal with the consequences of your mistakes, and accept responsibility for your life," Mama said.

"That's right," Daddy interjected. "A lot of this you've got to do on your own. We do have one thing lined up for you, though, and that's a job."

Indigo sat up straighter. "You're kidding. Who is going to hire me?"

Daddy smiled.

"Aunt Melba," he said. "She needs help keeping the business side of the salon on track until she's ready to return. We discussed and fretted over who should temporarily take over and whether we needed to find an outside professional when God placed your name on my heart, and your mother's—unbeknownst to either of us until we talked two days later.

"It's time to get out of that bed, Daughter," Daddy said. "You're going to work at Hair Pizzazz. As you know, the shop is closed on Mondays and opens at ten a.m. sharp Tuesday. You need to be there by nine."

23

*S*ix down, six more to go.

Brian kept track of how many weeks he had left in Rhode Island to reassure himself that soon he'd be moving to the next phase of his dream. Not that he was faltering physically or mentally. He was just ready to get back to the real world.

This morning, he and his classmates had been ordered out of bed before dawn to run three seven-minute miles. Never mind that it was Saturday, or that most of them had spent the night before in the city, drinking and picking up women—this was their reminder that they had to be on call, ready to perform well whenever necessary.

Brian had joined his bunkmates, Todd and Greg, for dinner at the Brick Alley Pub before coming back to campus to catch a movie in the rec room. He had spent the rest of the evening on his cell phone, catching up with all that had been going on with Indigo.

He couldn't believe her dad had ordered her to go to work. Then again, Mr. Burns was right—she didn't need to wallow in self-pity the whole summer. She'd never bat another home run if she didn't step up to the plate again. Brian hadn't told her that, though. He had been sympathetic and reassuring.

It didn't escape him that Indigo had failed to mention their wedding. He hadn't prodded. Maybe her going to work would be just the thing to make her feel better and get everything finalized.

This morning's run was nearing an end, and his thoughts shifted to what he would do the rest of today. Gunnery Sgt. McArthur had given the class liberty until Monday morning.

"Are you ready to head back, Harper?" Greg wanted to shower and clean up after their run.

"Yeah, Kemper," Brian said. He fell in step with his bunkmate, and they jogged from the training field to the barracks in less than ten minutes.

"What are you going to do with your free time?" Brian asked.

Greg grinned. "Eat some lobster, meet some ladies, and remember what it's like to party. I hung out a little while last night, but something told me that McArthur was going to pull a stunt like he did this morning. I didn't want to be in too bad a shape to perform. Now that that's over, it's on."

Brian shook his head. "I'm trying to keep my nose clean. I want the leaders to notice me for all of the right reasons. Besides, my girl at home is planning our wedding. Ain't nothing here for me."

They reached the barracks and stopped on the front lawn of the building to catch their breath.

"Come on, Harper," Greg said. "Live a little. You aren't married yet. If you don't have a little fun now, when will you?"

Brian laughed and led the way inside. "Who said fun had to end with 'I do'?"

Greg sat on his bunk and removed his sneakers. "What makes your lady so special?"

Brian sat across from him, on his own bunk, and leaned back to grab a framed picture of Indigo from a makeshift nightstand.

On the photo, they were snuggling, and Indigo's smiling face filled the frame. He passed it to Greg.

"I don't have to explain myself to you, man," Brian said. "Just so you know her when she visits next weekend, this is Indigo."

Greg nodded and passed the picture back to Brian. "She have any sisters?"

Brian laughed and stood up to stretch.

"Too young for you, my friend," he said. "Listen, I'll join you and the guys for dinner tonight and decide what to do from there."

Hours later, they wound up at a restaurant that played live music, and Brian was glad he had come.

The riffs from the reggae band and the camaraderie among senior officer candidates and OCS leaders who were usually stone-faced and barking orders reminded Brian that they were real people too.

Brian enjoyed a plateful of grilled shark, roasted vegetables, and potato salad, and ordered a draft beer to wash it down. He wasn't a regular drinker, but tonight he thought he'd treat himself. Besides, he didn't want everyone ragging on him for guzzling soda instead.

Just as he took his first sip, he looked up and into Shelby's eyes.

She walked in with a group from their class that included two other women and three guys. Brian hadn't had a chance to get acquainted with them outside of their mandatory meal, class, and training times.

They all were dressed casually, and Shelby looked particularly striking in a pair of form-fitting jeans, a black tank top, and black stiletto sandals.

Her eyes widened when she saw Brian. She waved and smiled.

Her group settled in a booth across the restaurant from Brian's and quickly began perusing menus. Brian checked them out, trying to figure out who was with whom.

Why did it matter? he finally asked himself. Shelby was a grown woman, and an officer candidate, at that. She could hold her own.

He turned his attention back to the guys at his table and was trying to decide on dessert when a tap on the shoulder startled him.

He looked up and into Craig Miller's eyes. His stomach fell to his feet.

"Harper, how's it going?" Craig asked, in the deep baritone that Brian remembered from their Tuskegee days.

Brian stuck out his hand and shook Craig's. "It's going great. How you doing, man?"

The guys at his table seemed to be waiting for an introduction.

"Members of Class zero-ten, zero-eight, this is Candidate Officer Craig Miller, an old college buddy of mine."

The men greeted him properly and resumed their meal, but Craig stood there and asked Brian about his future plans and life after OCS.

"I'm hoping I'll get sent to Pensacola," Brian said. He decided to share only what was necessary. "What about you?"

One of Brian's comrades pulled a chair from a nearby table and motioned for Craig to sit, next to Brian.

This is going to be a long night, Brian thought as Craig slid into the seat.

Craig told him he wanted to work in submarines and would likely be shipped to a naval base that specialized in sub training when he completed OCS in another three weeks.

"I can't wait," he said. "This has been a good experience, but I'm ready to move on."

Brian nodded, remembering he had felt the same way just this morning.

He wanted to ask Craig what he had been up to since graduation, and whether he was married or engaged, or if Player, with a capital P, was still his middle name. But none of that was his business.

Craig took the moment of awkward silence as his cue. He stood up and shook Brian's hand again.

"Good to see you, Harper," he said. "You're looking good. Next week you and your classmates will be Senior Candidate Officers, showing some new recruits the drill. Have fun, but don't get drunk with power."

They both chuckled, then Craig strode across the room to join other officers of his ranking. He nodded at Shelby when he passed her table. She smiled at him and looked in Brian's direction.

He read something in her eyes that he couldn't quite interpret. Before he could figure it out, she turned her attention back to her friends and seemed to shut out the world.

24

*I*ndigo slid the key into the lock of Hair Pizzazz's front door and sighed.

Mama's encouraging words rang in her ears: This too would pass; everything happened for a reason and a season, and she was going to have to not just endure, but learn how to thrive despite life's challenges.

Indigo went inside, turned on the lights, and set her purse on the receptionist desk in the foyer.

"Welcome to Hair Pizzazz," she said softly to herself. "Aunt Melba, I'm doing this for you."

The low-heeled black strapless sandals she wore with her dressy blue jeans and black ruffled top created a staccato beat as Indigo walked through the empty salon, eyeing everything as if for the first time. The red leather sofas in the waiting area that had been replaced several times since Melba had made them one of her salon signatures years ago; the original pieces of art from Africa, India, and Europe that graced the walls; pictures of Aunt Melba with some of her famous clients, including Houston's own gospel artist Yolanda Adams.

Indigo returned to the reception area and nearly jumped out of her skin when the door opened.

"It's just me," Rachelle said and stepped inside. She opened her arms to offer Indigo a hug. "I heard that Uncle Charles designated you as the temporary business manager, and I decided to come over this morning to offer my support. You can do this and do it well."

Indigo received the embrace, then stepped back to look at Rachelle.

"I know I can," Indigo said. "This is just a little fork in the road I hadn't anticipated."

Rachelle smiled. "I've learned that sometimes the turns we didn't anticipate can lead us to our biggest blessings." She grabbed Indigo's hands. "Come on, let's pray."

And they did—for Indigo's temporary role at Hair Pizzazz, for Aunt Melba's complete return to health and to the salon she loved, for the salon and its staff to be a blessing to everyone who crossed its threshold, for God to give Indigo the wisdom and the courage to handle whatever life brought her way.

Rachelle was teary-eyed by the time they finished their joint petition. She wiped her eyes.

"What's it going to look like for the optometrist to have red eyes while she's examining patients?" she said and laughed. "Let me get to work. I'll call you later and check on you."

Yasmin was entering as Rachelle prepared to exit. Rachelle gave her a big hug and kissed her cheek.

"You have a wonderful day, young lady, you hear me?"

Yasmin smiled and nodded.

When Rachelle was gone, Yasmin turned to Indigo.

"Well, you've got me most of the day," she said. "Daddy dropped me off and told me to help out with whatever you needed to get settled into a routine."

Indigo smiled. She locked the door to the salon and motioned to Yasmin.

"Follow me," she said.

She led Yasmin to a small kitchen area in the back and handed her a can of coffee.

"Can you make a pot?" Indigo asked. "Now that Jubilant has gone big-time and rated its own Starbucks, I could have stopped there this morning. But given that I'm only temporarily employed, I thought better of it."

The sisters laughed.

When the coffee was ready, Indigo poured herself a cup and offered Yasmin one.

The teenager shook her head. "No thanks. I'm a tea drinker."

"Sorry, there's none here," Indigo said. "Come on, let's get back up front, in case customers decide to show up early."

Indigo unlocked the door again and sat behind the reception desk. She turned on the computer so it could boot up.

Yasmin grabbed a folding chair tucked in a corner and set it behind the desk, next to Indigo. She shrugged when Indigo raised an eyebrow.

"If I'm your assistant, I need to act the part!"

Indigo stared at the girl, then asked the question she had been wrestling with since learning about Yasmin's struggle with bulimia.

"You okay?"

Yasmin shrugged again and looked down at her hands. "This is so embarrassing," she said.

"Everything is embarrassing when you're fourteen, Yas," Indigo said. "Really, though, I need to know that you're going to work through this and get better. Making yourself throw up after you eat may not seem like a big deal, but bulimia can kill you if it throws your body out of whack. Seriously."

Yasmin nodded. "Mama gave me some brochures and a few

websites with information on eating disorders and all that. I don't think I have a 'disorder,' but I know I was headed that way. I want to turn things around, but I don't want to be fat."

"Look at our bone structure, Yasmin," Indigo said. "We're not built to be thick, so I think that should be the least of your concerns. You can monitor what you eat to make sure you're healthy and maintaining a normal weight, but beyond that, you shouldn't have to diet or throw up—not as long as you have that teenage metabolism."

"Mama said she wants me to talk to a counselor, but I'm not crazy," Yasmin said.

"No, you're not, and we want to keep it that way," Indigo teased. "There's nothing wrong with working through your eating and purging habits with a professional counselor who can help you find ways to stop the cycle. If talking to someone opens your eyes to what may be stressing you out or triggering you to hurt yourself in this way, it's worth it."

Yasmin didn't look convinced. "I don't know. All I want to do is model and do photo shoots in cool locations, and walk the runway in the premier fashion shows of each season, wearing clothes so well that people drool."

Indigo contained the smile that she knew Yasmin would consider condescending. If the desire to become a model would motivate Yasmin to get well, she wasn't going to dash her hope.

"Well, why can't you?" Indigo asked. "The only thing that could stop you would be you."

Indigo leaned toward Yasmin and stroked her cheek.

"Tell you what. You work on getting better, on getting well, and when you get a clean bill of health from your doctor or your counselor, I'll take some fabulous photos of you and send them to the top modeling agencies in New York."

Yasmin's eyes widened and she sat up straighter. "Are you serious?"

"As a heart attack." She remembered that her camera was in the back of her SUV. "You know what? I've got my camera with me. Let me take a few practice shots of you now, before this place gets full."

Indigo trotted out to her Honda and retrieved the camera bag from the spot she'd placed it in two weeks ago, just before her eye surgery. On her way back inside, she sent an arrow prayer to heaven.

She didn't know a soul in the modeling industry, but if this would save her sister, she would find a way to make some connections.

25

Half an hour after she began snapping pictures of a regal and sassy Yasmin, Eboni, Carlotta, and Carmen showed up for work.

Yasmin was lounging on a sofa, gazing heavenward when they strolled into the foyer.

"This is still a hair salon, isn't it?" Carlotta asked.

Indigo laughed and lowered the camera.

"Of course," she said. "Yasmin and I are just playing around, that's all. I'll be here most days now, helping with the day-to-day operations for the rest of the summer."

Eboni tucked her purse and an oversized shoulder bag in a cabinet beneath the reception desk.

"Good. We need some help managing the phones and scheduling appointments while we work," Eboni said.

"How's Melba doing?" Carmen asked.

"Better each day, Carmen," Indigo said. "She's fighting her way back here as fast as she can."

Eboni's first customer arrived a few minutes later, and Carmen led her to the back so she could shampoo the woman's hair. The customer was a college student from Oklahoma, working in a nearby law office for the summer.

Carlotta's first client of the day was Mrs. Greer, Indigo's eleventh grade history teacher.

"I didn't know you were a client here!" Indigo said and gave her a hug.

"I didn't know you worked here—weren't you one of my hotshot students?" Mrs. Greer asked.

It struck Indigo how this must look—lauded high school and college graduate with a bright future in photography returns to her hometown to work in a hair salon rather than pursue her dream.

"I'm just helping out here for the summer, Mrs. Greer," she said. "My aunt owns this place, but is recovering from a serious illness. I'll be off to bigger and better things soon."

But that answer wasn't enough for Mrs. Greer. She put a hand on her plush hip and leaned forward on the desk.

"Like what?"

Before Indigo could respond, Yasmin interjected, "Excuse me, Mrs. Greer. I checked the calendar and Carlotta has you down for an eleven a.m. appointment. You're an hour early."

"What?! That throws off my entire day," she said.

Thankful for the shift in focus, Indigo pushed her chair back and trotted around the desk.

"Let me run back there and see what she can do, okay?"

By the time Indigo had resolved the dilemma to Mrs. Greer's satisfaction, Yasmin had rescheduled two other appointments and was preparing to run to the barbershop across the street to get change for a $100 bill a customer needed to break.

Indigo welcomed a woman and a young girl who was the lady's carbon copy. Melba didn't allow customers to bring children to the salon unless they were being served. Indigo smiled at them as she toyed with how to share the news.

"I'm a client of Melba's and this is my regular appointment day, but I'm giving it to Summer," the woman said.

Whew. Thank you, God. No confrontation necessary.

"Your name is Summer?" Indigo said to the child, who looked like she was about five. "That is a pretty name for a pretty girl. What would you like to have done today?"

Summer, who had seemed shy at first, perked up and went into overdrive. "I brought my Barbie to show you," she said and whipped out a brown doll with flowing brownish blonde locks. "See how she has the ponytail on top and it's all curly? Can we do that?"

Indigo looked at the mother and saw that she wasn't the only one stifling her laughter.

"I'm not sure, Summer. That will be up to your mom and to Miss Eboni, the lady who's doing your hair today. I can't wait to see it when she's finished. You make sure you stop by here before you leave, okay? In fact, I have my camera here. I may just take your picture."

Summer jumped up and down in excitement. Indigo looked at her mother.

"That's a lucky little girl. Is today her birthday or something?"

"No," the mother said. "She's competing in the Little Miss Jubilant pageant down at the new performing arts center over the weekend, but she's taking her formal portrait today, to display at the event. So if we like what Eboni does with her hair, we'll probably be back on Saturday to get her to style it again for the big day."

Indigo had never met a pageant mom before. This woman appeared normal, but Summer already seemed caught up in her own hype.

"So much for a photo from an amateur photographer, huh?"

Indigo said and smiled. "Just let me know what you decide about Saturday and we'll put it on the books for you, okay?"

Before Indigo could process that encounter, another client was standing before her. This was a face she knew, despite the scarf covering the woman's head.

She leaned over the desk and hugged Mrs. Bernard, the mother of her best friend from elementary school. She and Audrey had been tight from first through fifth grades, before Audrey's family moved to a neighborhood in another school district. They saw each other occasionally, but their friendship had never been quite as solid again.

"How are you doing? How is Audrey?" Indigo asked.

Mrs. Bernard shared the bright, welcoming smile that Indigo still remembered. "We're all doing okay," she said, but the smile faltered, and she abruptly changed the subject. "I don't have an appointment, but I don't need to have much done. I was hoping Melba could see me really quickly?"

Indigo explained that her aunt was home recovering from a stroke.

"I had no idea," Mrs. Bernard said softly. "Will she be able to come back? Is she doing okay?"

Indigo nodded. "She's doing extremely well. We're hoping she'll be able to come back before summer's over, at least to run the business side of things."

"I'll be keeping her in my prayers, then," Mrs. Bernard said. She stood there for a moment and turned to leave.

"Could someone else help you?" Indigo asked. "Eboni and Carlotta have back-to-back clients, but if you don't mind waiting a little bit, I'm sure one of them can fit you in. They're both really good."

Mrs. Bernard hesitated, then walked closer to Indigo so she could lower her voice.

"What about you? Do you have any experience? Actually, it doesn't take much. Can you use a razor?"

The questions caught Indigo so off guard that she nearly choked. Mrs. Bernard saved her the task of asking why.

"I have cancer and I'm undergoing chemo, Indigo," she said. "My hair has begun to fall out and I was planning to have Melba shave the rest of it off. I know she has a private salon area in the back—that's why I came here. I've made peace with cutting it all off, but I still want some privacy, and I didn't want just anyone doing it."

She sighed and squared her shoulders. "I suppose I could have Audrey do it for me, or my husband, but they are so frightened by all of this. I'm trying to be strong."

Indigo grabbed Mrs. Bernard's hand. "Just tell me what to do, and I'll do it. I'm not a pro by a long shot, and I might not cut it as low as you'd like, because I don't want to nick your scalp, but I'll do my best."

Mrs. Bernard smiled. "Thank you."

They waited for Yasmin to return from her errand so she could man the phones, then Mrs. Bernard followed Indigo to a miniature salon area in the rear of the building that featured a shampoo bowl and styling chair. Aunt Melba had a set of supplies already waiting, including clippers and a razor.

Indigo had shaved her father once, about five years ago, when he decided to take off his beard and asked her if she wanted to help. She had done okay, but still, that was five years ago, and it was a beard, not someone's lovely locks.

But if Mrs. Bernard was brave enough to ask her to try, she was going to pray her way through this.

"You won't be upset if I don't get this quite right?" Indigo asked.

"I just need to get it off, because it's coming out in clumps," Mrs. Bernard said. "I know you'll do your best, and that's all that matters. I don't want to wait."

Indigo nodded and asked Mrs. Bernard to sit in the black swivel chair.

She slowly pulled Aunt Melba's clippers from the clear plastic box in which they were stored, along with a small tube of oil. She squeezed a drop of the oil over them, plugged them in, and briefly switched them on to make sure they worked. The soft hum of the electric blade made her heart beat faster. Could she really do this?

Find your strength in me.

God's unbidden voice startled her. Where had that come from? Regardless, she knew it was him.

Indigo draped a black cape around Mrs. Bernard's shoulders and removed the peacock yellow scarf from her head.

She caught the gasp before it left her throat, but she couldn't control the tears. They slid down both cheeks as she ran her fingers through Mrs. Bernard's once lush black hair. It was still thick—in patches—and bald in others.

She switched on the clippers again and the soft hum filled the air while she zigzagged back and forth across the scalp.

At some point, the monotonous sound was overshadowed by Mrs. Bernard's humming, then her humming turned into a full-fledged song: "His strength is perfect, when our strength is gone. He carries us when we can't carry on . . ."

Indigo was nearing the end of the ordeal. Hair was all over the floor and her heart was heavy. But Mrs. Bernard, in contrast, seemed lighter and fuller, with each swipe of the razor and each verse she sang. Indigo knew they were more than just words to her; Mrs. Bernard believed them.

"That is a beautiful song," Indigo said when she had finished shaving the woman's head. "Who sings that?"

Mrs. Bernard ran her hands over her now bald scalp before replying.

"CeCe Winans," she said. "That song has been my mantra these past few months. When I haven't known what to pray, I've hummed or sang the words to this song and trusted that God already knows what I need."

She turned toward Indigo and wiped the tearstains from Indigo's cheeks.

"Thank you for doing this for me, dear," she said. "I know it was hard, but you've given me a gift. Can I ask one more favor?"

Indigo waited, not knowing what to expect.

"I saw a camera out there on the desk. Would you mind taking a picture of me with my new 'do? I want a copy for my scrapbook, so I'll always remember where God has brought me from."

Indigo's heart leapt. "Let me go get it now. The camera is mine, and taking your photo will be my real gift to you."

26

*B*rian excused himself from the table around midnight when the reggae band took a break.

The male officers he'd been hanging with were beginning to pair off with female officers and local women who had come in looking for dates. He wasn't even tempted.

He had driven his car so he could escape when he needed to, and now was the time. He saluted his friends.

"Good night, guys," Brian said. "See you on base."

Most of them were so wrapped up in each other that they hardly noticed his departure. He looked over at the table Shelby had been occupying and saw that she and her friends had already left.

In the parking lot, the warm breeze from the nearby ocean was welcome relief from the stuffy air and body heat in the cozy restaurant. He walked the few feet to his car, which was parked against the eatery's brick wall, in partial shadows, and jumped when he saw someone leaning against the driver's door.

Craig Miller smiled at Brian's shock. "I figured we should finish our chat when we were alone."

Brian wasn't going to let this jerk see him sweat. "Whatcha talking about, man?"

"That's *Candidate Officer Miller*, to you, Harper," Craig said.

Brian smelled the liquor on Craig's breath.

The shame and temptation he'd held at bay for so long swelled. He knew what he'd be dreaming about tonight, whether he wanted to or not.

"You missed me, didn't you?" Craig asked and sneered at him.

Brian didn't answer. When Craig moved toward him, he took a step backward.

"What are you doing?" Brian asked. "You could ruin both of our careers. What happened between us was a long time ago. And it was a mistake."

Craig paused and emitted a laugh that sounded more like a bark. "Nothing I ever do is a mistake," he said. "Try to fool yourself if you want, but you know you enjoyed it."

Brian tried to walk past him and open the door of his Saturn.

Craig grabbed his arm. "Where you going, Harper? Didn't I say I wanted to talk?"

Brian yanked his arm free. "Talk about what? The past is the past, and the past was a mistake. I don't know what you're doing these days, but I don't roll like that."

"Like what?" Craig said. "Why do things have to be labeled? It is what it is. So what—you some holy roller now? You got a girl or something?"

Brian faced Craig. "I have a life and I'd like to keep it that way."

Understanding flickered in Craig's eyes. He grinned.

"Oh . . . so this is about a girl. Are you still dating Indigo?" He shook his head. "Wonder what she'd say if she knew her Tuskegee Man wasn't into only her?"

Brian took a swing, but Craig grabbed his fist and leaned in, until he was inches from Brian's face.

"Careful—I'm a senior candidate officer, remember? You don't want to get yanked from your class this close to becoming an officer."

A chill coursed through Brian's body. *Please, God, don't let him destroy my career and my life. Not after all I've invested.*

"Look, Craig," Brian said, "I'm sorry about all of this. You just caught me off guard. I'm glad you're doing well, but I've moved on."

He read the disbelief in Craig's eyes.

"Have you really?" Craig asked. "Or are you trying to convince both of us?"

Brian had been praying for God to cleanse him and forgive him since that senior year encounter with Craig, and he had believed it was working until he got to Rhode Island and ran smack-dab into the source of his sin.

Tonight, he called on the heavenly Father and all of his angels. He needed every ounce of support he could rally to keep moving forward.

27

Indigo checked the time and willed herself not to pick up the phone and call Yasmin.

Where was that girl? It was four p.m. and Indigo had an appointment. So what if it was at the salon, with Eboni? If she wasn't sitting at the shampoo bowl in another five minutes, Eboni's next client would show up and Indigo would either have to stay later than she wanted or miss getting her hair done altogether.

Visit Brian with some jacked-up hair? That wasn't going to happen.

In the meantime, she couldn't leave the reception desk un-manned, so she sat here answering calls, trying to remain pro-fessional.

She was scheduled to leave for the airport first thing in the morning and wanted to make sure she didn't forget anything. Plus, she needed to get to bed at a decent hour. Dark circles and bags under the eyes did not equal fabulous.

Indigo pulled a magazine out of her bag and chuckled. Shame on her for fronting. She hadn't picked up this copy of *Bride* since Yasmin brought it home two weeks ago. She was going to read through it while she sat under the dryer today, so she'd have some idea of what to say when Brian began peppering her with questions about their wedding.

Truthfully, she wasn't feeling as resistant to the idea as she had been. She loved this man. Getting married didn't have to be equated with a death sentence, just like ending her summer internship early hadn't been.

She had seen a lot by working at the salon for just these few weeks. Everyone had a story behind her smile, and often, it wasn't pretty. Some of Jubilant's most successful women, with thriving careers, beautiful families, and respect in the community, would sit in the private salon area and weep (from stress, they insisted), while Eboni or Carlotta styled their hair. Or sometimes they just wanted to talk, to get things off their chests.

Somehow Indigo had found herself serving as the salon's "mini-Melba"—listening when clients wanted to share a heartfelt need or prayer request, calming frazzled or hurried clients, and even taking photos of the more interesting customers who happened to explain why they were getting their 'dos done on a particular day or share something else special about their lives.

The practice had become so routine that now many of the regulars would ask where the camera was if they didn't see it in its usual spot on the reception desk. Today, she had snagged photos of a new mother and baby when the woman came in to introduce her six-week-old son to Carlotta and the rest of the staff.

Then Ms. Harrow had surprised her by showing up with an oversized arrangement of red, yellow, and purple cut flowers.

"When I heard you were here helping Melba these days, I decided to stop by with this dose of sunshine," she said. "Thank you so much for the lovely spread of photos in the newspaper. I've had neighbors come by just to talk and sit in the garden ever since they were published. In no time at all, we wind up praying to the great Creator of it all."

Indigo had taken Ms. Harrow's picture with her gift of flowers and made a mental note to print and frame a copy for Aunt Melba to hang in the salon.

This afternoon, as she waited for her workday to end, she pulled the camera out of the bag and scrolled through the digital images, pleased with the range of what she had captured.

Mrs. Bernard and her newly shaven head. Summer and her fancy pageant hairdo. Cara, who brought along her wedding veil so her hair could be styled for her prewedding photo shoot.

Indigo admitted it: maybe her reconsideration of her own wedding plans stemmed from seeing Cara's enthusiasm. Cara had just completed her master's in biology at the local Everson College and was marrying her college sweetheart, a certified professional accountant.

Whatever the motivation, she was finally inspired. She knew Brian would be thankful.

Indigo checked the clock again—4:14 p.m. Before she could pick up the phone to call Yasmin, Nizhoni walked in. She had become a regular of Yasmin's, getting her long ponytail braided once a week.

"Hi there," Indigo said. "Yasmin is not here yet; I apologize—she's usually punctual. Sit tight a few minutes while I try to get her on the phone."

Nizhoni smiled. "That's okay; I'll wait for her."

"Are you getting your hair rebraided in the same style today?"

Nizhoni nodded. "Yep—the braid again."

Why was this beautiful girl continuing to tuck her hair into this bland style? The question must have clouded Indigo's face.

"There's a good reason, you know," Nizhoni said.

Her directness caught Indigo off guard. Nizhoni was quiet, but there was something no-nonsense about her that Indigo liked. The two women were about the same age, and they always chatted when she walked in to see Yasmin. This was her third time visiting the salon since Indigo had joined the staff, and last week she had actually made an appointment for today.

"You don't have to explain," Indigo said.

Nizhoni shook her head and hinted at a smile. "I've told you before that my dad is African American and my mom is a Navajo Indian," she said. "It is a belief in many Indian tribes that when you have problems, you braid them up to contain them. When I'm braiding my hair, I'm braiding up my worries. That allows me to release them and go on, because I know they are contained and the proper solution eventually will surface."

Indigo was intrigued. "Is this sort of like prayer? You tell God what is bothering you and you're supposed to leave your burdens there?"

Nizhoni shrugged. "I just know that it helps. When Yasmin is shampooing my hair, I am talking to myself throughout the process about everything that is troubling me, and when I leave here with a fresh braid, those problems are tucked away. Out of sight, out of mind."

"But you keep coming back," Indigo said.

"Yes," Nizhoni said. "I will keep coming back until the problem has been resolved."

It was killing Indigo not to pry for more details.

"It's a physical act and a visual reminder that helps me actively let go of the issue," Nizhoni said. "That way, I'm not carrying it around in my mind and my heart all week. I allow myself to think about it when Yasmin takes the braid down, but as she's braiding my hair up again, I'm letting go again."

"That's powerful," Indigo said. "It *is* the same concept as prayer, which I do. But because you can see an end result, the feeling of giving up the burden must be especially strong."

Nizhoni nodded. "It's not a perfect cure—I mean, it's just a cultural tradition. But it definitely helps, given the alternative— fretting and worrying."

Indigo thought about how she had been taught to cope with problems. She didn't always do it, but her family had a tradition too.

Trust in the Lord with all your heart and lean not on your own understanding.

To someone like Nizhoni, reciting a Scripture might seem trite, but when Indigo rested in the truths of God's Word, she found that life did go smoother. Talking with Nizhoni about other ways of facing life's challenges was making her value her method all the more. She glanced at the clock on the computer and shook her head.

"You've been waiting almost twenty minutes," Indigo said. "Let me call and see if I can get Yasmin on the phone."

The call went straight to Yasmin's voice mail and Indigo left her a message.

"Nizhoni Witherspoon is here. She's waiting to get her hair braided. Can you please call and let me know how soon you'll be here?"

Indigo hung up and apologized again.

"No worries," Nizhoni said. "It's not like I have a hot date tonight or something."

Indigo laughed. "What type of work do you do?"

"I'm a bridal consultant at Brides Central, on Dixon Street downtown."

Indigo had left her post to pour a cup of crangrape juice for

Nizhoni from a small refrigerator located a few feet from the reception desk. She stopped in her tracks.

"You're kidding."

"Why?" Nizhoni asked.

Indigo strode over to the desk, lifted her *Bride* magazine, and waved it at Nizhoni.

"My fiancé thinks we're having an intimate church wedding with close friends and family in about eight weeks. This is the first magazine I've looked at."

"*You're* kidding," Nizhoni said. "Have you chosen a dress?"

Indigo shook her head.

"They take at least four weeks to be custom fitted," Nizhoni said. "I'll help you if you'd like. Have you confirmed a place for the ceremony and reception?"

Indigo shook her head again.

Nizhoni frowned. "Are you sure you want to get married?"

They laughed in unison.

"That's a long story," Indigo said. "But I love my fiancé very much. That I can tell you with no hesitation. Timing is the issue."

Indigo's cell phone rang. She handed the juice to Nizhoni and dashed around the desk to grab it. She picked it up and saw her mother's cell phone number.

"Hey there," she said, then strained to maintain her professionalism. "Umm . . . How can I help you?"

"It's Mama, Indigo. I'm at the hospital with Yasmin. I came home to pick her up and get her to the hair salon and found her passed out on the bathroom floor. She was vomiting again."

Indigo's heart sank. Her sister was sicker than she thought. "I'm on my way," she said thickly and hung up.

She was shaking as she turned toward Nizhoni. "I'm sorry. Yasmin is not feeling well. She's not going to make it in today.

Can we reschedule? Better yet, let me just give you a call. Write down your number?"

Nizhoni scribbled her phone number and email address on a notepad at the desk and hugged Indigo.

"This braid will do for a while. I'll be thinking of Yasmin and pulling for her to get better. You stay strong, okay?"

Indigo nodded, afraid that if she tried to speak, she might lose it. She grabbed her purse and, by the time she reached the door, found the strength to yell to Eboni and Carlotta that she had an emergency.

"Can you listen for the phones? I'll check in with you later."

Nizhoni walked out with her. "Do you want me to drive you somewhere?" she asked Indigo.

Indigo took a deep breath. "Thanks, Nizhoni. That's kind of you, but I'll be okay. I'm just a little rattled, with Yasmin being my baby sister and all. She's going to be fine."

Nizhoni squeezed her hand. "Yes, she is."

Indigo climbed into the car and sped off without looking back.

Thank God Brian's parents had decided to fly up to Newport tomorrow to see him too. She wasn't going to make it.

28

By 4:55 a.m., Brian was awake and terrified.

He had been looking forward to Indigo's visit for weeks, but after the encounter with Craig, he had spent the days leading up to her arrival trying to come up with legitimate excuses to keep her away.

"What—you don't want me to see the ladies you've been dating?" she teased him two days ago. "I thought you didn't mind that I was half blind."

Brian tried to laugh along. It had been good to hear her being lighthearted about her condition. If he had his way, though, his parents wouldn't be coming, either. The president would have to shut down the airlines and the interstates for that to happen. Mary and Otis were not going to allow another week to pass without seeing their only child.

"Besides," Indigo had told him, "I'm not going to give up a chance to spend some time with you *and* Shelby. It's been pitiful not having either one of you to talk to."

Indigo and his parents would be flying into Providence from different airports, but all three of them were scheduled to land around noon. Indigo was going to ride with his parents to Newport Naval Base in the car they rented.

Already, he knew it wasn't going to be the experience he had planned.

A week ago, he had been confident and self-assured, ready to give them a tour, introduce them to his classmates, and boast about the uniform he'd soon be wearing.

Now he could barely function. He didn't hear instructions for some of the physical training drills. He passed the endurance tests with little or no room to spare. He zoned out in classes and missed information that would more than likely show up on his academic quizzes. Even when he and his classmates were gouging, or memorizing, information from the manual that they were supposed to provide upon immediate request from an officer or gunnery sergeant, Brian responded seconds too late—at a snail's pace in OCS time.

Gunnery Sgt. McArthur had pulled him aside yesterday.

"That liberty last weekend was a bit much for you, Harper?" he growled. "Get your head back in this game or you're out of here."

This wasn't good. He was as distracted as if he had contracted some form of attention deficit disorder.

What if someone had seen him and Craig outside the restaurant? What if Craig decided to confront him while his parents and Indigo were here? What if he told someone else?

Brian rarely saw Craig during the week, but he hadn't taken his threats lightly. Craig could very well pull rank and get him demoted.

In the rec room last night, he had jumped as if he were in a combat zone when Shelby approached him and touched his shoulder.

"Brian, are you okay?"

He had been staring at his Navy manual but not really reading it. Worry lines creased Shelby's forehead. She sat next to him.

146

"What's going on? You nervous about Indigo's visit?"

Brian looked at her, but didn't answer, knowing she couldn't help, but wishing she could. He tried to smile.

"You could say that. I'm just having a rough week, that's all."

She laid her hand on top of his. "Brian, you're the reason that I'm here," she said intensely, peering into his eyes. "When you started talking to me about flight school and being a pilot and even Tuskegee, you gave wind to my dreams. You've been my guide as I follow in your footsteps. You can't flake out now. We're in this together. If I'm going to be an officer, you're going to be an officer.

"I don't know what's going on, and I don't need to know," Shelby said and stood up. "If you're nervous about something you've done since you've been away from Indigo, deal with it. But don't let it steal your dream. I know this is your dream. Fight for it."

Brian watched her leave as the truth sank in. He was usually the one giving the pep talks, but today Shelby had taken the lead. She was an officer in the making. And she was right: he had too much at stake to crumble now.

He had gone to bed last night with a new resolve to focus on the future and let Craig take care of Craig.

Then sleep came, and he couldn't control his thoughts. His dreams traveled back to Tuskegee, to the night of that fateful decision and to the realization that he had new demons to wrestle with.

He had kept them caged this long with a lot of effort, because that's where he knew they belonged, and because he truly loved Indigo. She was his light.

Now this.

Now what?

Help me, Lord.

Brian lay awake, tossing and turning and pleading with God, until about six a.m. When the hallway phone rang, he had an excuse to get up.

Since officer candidates couldn't have cell phones and there were no phones in their individual rooms, there was no telling whom this call was for. Just about everyone had visitors coming for the weekend, so he'd have to figure out whom to wake up to take a call.

When he picked it up though, it was Indigo, asking for him. He thought he was still dreaming

"Indie? Where are you? Was your flight delayed?"

He half hoped for a yes.

"It left about an hour ago, babe, but I'm not on it," Indigo said. He heard the weariness in her voice.

"What's wrong?"

She hesitated. "Yasmin has an eating disorder, Brian, and she had a pretty bad episode yesterday."

The words were tumbling from Indigo's lips so fast that Brian struggled to keep up.

"What do you mean?" he asked.

Indigo slowed down. "Yasmin is bulimic, Brian. She has been gorging on food, then making herself throw it up. Yesterday she bought some over-the-counter medicine that induces vomiting and apparently drank half the bottle.

"Mama found her on the bathroom floor and called an ambulance. When she got to the hospital, they were able to stop the vomiting and get her hydrated. She's stable now, but very weak, and I just don't think I can leave her. I'm sorry."

Brian felt a pang of guilt. He had wanted her to stay home, but not under these circumstances. Not because her fourteen-year-old sister was seriously ill.

"You know I understand, babe," he finally said. "You tell Yasmin I want her to get well, and I'm pulling for her. I love you."

Indigo started to weep.

"I love you too, Brian, and I'm sorry."

"For what?"

"I haven't been planning our wedding," Indigo said. "I was going to get started on the way to Newport so I would have something to show you, but I don't have a thing—no dress for me, nothing for a bridesmaid or two, no flowers, not even a reception hall."

Brian's heart ran cold. What did all of this mean? Was God telling him to back off? Was Indigo pulling away on her own?

He needed her.

"Brian, you still there?" Indigo asked.

"Yeah," he said. "The question is, are you? I thought you wanted this too."

Indigo sighed. "I love you, Brian, and I want to be your wife. But I have been struggling with the timetable. I've already been accepted into grad school and it's just two years. I'm not understanding the reasoning behind rushing."

And he sure wasn't about to tell her. At least this missed opportunity to see each other meant he didn't have to worry about Craig staking them out to offer his opinion.

"Indigo, we can work through this," he said. "I want you to be happy too, and I want you to be my wife. I don't care if we go down to the Jubilant courthouse when I get back, or if we stand at the St. Peter's Baptist Church altar with just your parents and mine.

"I want you with me, but if you need to go to grad school to feel complete, I'm not going to stand in your way. I love you too much to lose you."

And he meant it, with every fiber of his being.

29

Craig stayed out of view until evening.

Just as Brian and his parents settled at a corner table in an oceanside restaurant located off of the base, he strode over, in full uniform.

"Officer Candidate Harper, how goes it?"

Brian tried to remain cool. "Aye, sir," he said to Craig and assumed the one-thousand-yard stare required when an officer candidate addressed someone superior in rank.

"At ease," Craig said.

He turned to Brian's parents and shook his father's hand.

"Mr. and Mrs. Harper, you have a fine young man here," Craig told them.

Brian's dad chuckled. "You sound like you're thirty years older than my son . . . son," he said. "Looks like you are just as wet behind the ears as he is, if you don't mind me saying so."

Craig smiled, but Brian noticed that the warmth didn't travel to his eyes.

"Your son would know, right, Brian?" Craig patted Brian's back before walking away.

Brian's mom turned toward him and frowned. "What was all that for?" she said and peered into Brian's shifty eyes. "He must need that uniform to feel important. Don't you be like that, Son.

You remain humble and remember that without God's favor and blessings, you wouldn't have anything to be proud about."

Brian nodded and turned his attention to the menu. He felt seven years old again, but he couldn't climb into his mother's lap and tell her all of his secrets anymore. Some of them might kill her.

He looked up and saw that she was staring at him. She held his gaze for a few minutes and blew him a kiss.

Embarrassed and unsettled, he looked toward his father. "So what's going on back home?"

They chatted about the latest news in Austin, including recent sightings of Hollywood star Matthew McConnaughey, his girlfriend, and their new baby. His dad talked to him in detail about the riding lawn mower he had just purchased, and a new barbecue joint in town that was pretty good but had nothing on his "skills with a grill."

Brian's mom listened as her two men bantered back and forth and joined in occasionally. She was unusually quiet, though.

Brian paused and grabbed her hand. "What's on your mind, young lady?"

She laughed. "I wish I *were* still young. When I was, I used to keep your daddy in a tizzy, panting behind me. But these days, he can't keep up with me now."

"TMI, people," Brian said. "That is entirely too much information. I keep telling Dad what you two do behind closed doors needs to stay there."

His father doubled over with laughter.

"Sit up, old man," his mother teased him.

She grew serious. "So tell me about these wedding plans," she said to Brian and pursed her lips. "How am I going to buy a mother-of-the-groom dress when I have no clue about colors, a theme, or a location for the reception? Indigo needs to get on the ball—or have you two decided to wait?"

Brian took a bite of his steak and hunched his shoulders. "We were going to discuss all of that this weekend, while she was here," he said. "I've been caught up in candidate training so I've pretty much left everything to her. We talked this morning and she admitted that she wasn't ready to get married in August—neither logistically or emotionally. Before we got off the phone, we decided that we'll have a small ceremony in December, when she's home from grad school for the holidays and I can get a few days of leave. I'm surprised she hasn't been in touch with you at all, but then again, she's had a lot going on."

He thought about her glaucoma diagnosis and Yasmin's illness, but didn't mention either.

"I know she's been helping out at her aunt's hair salon," his mom said. "The last time we talked, she mentioned that the internship hadn't worked out, but didn't say why. That was surprising for Miss Indigo. She's usually a go-getter. And what's going on with her sister?"

His parents watched him and waited for replies. Brian could tell that they'd had long discussions about these issues on the way up.

Shelby walked into his view just then, sparing him from having to talk about things Indigo might not be ready for him to share. She came up behind Brian's mother and hugged her from the rear. When she turned and saw Shelby, she stood and gasped.

"Shelby? Is that you? You've lost twenty pounds *and* all of your beautiful hair!"

Shelby hugged her tightly, while her parents moved past her to greet Brian with similar enthusiasm.

"It will grow back, Ms. Mary," Shelby said and laughed. "I'm not complaining about the weight loss, though. You don't know how good it feels to eat whatever you want, knowing that the way they train you, it's not going to show up on the hips. How are you?"

Brian's mom hugged her again, then Brian's dad had his turn.

"How's my girl? You doing good?"

Shelby laughed and saluted him. "Yes sir! I've never been better."

At that moment, Brian noticed someone else standing off to the side, taking in the whole scene, waiting to be invited into the group.

Shelby followed his gaze, then walked over and grabbed the man's hand. She led him over to Brian.

"Brian, this is my friend Hunt Pappas. He lives in New York City and flew in to meet my parents this weekend."

Brian stared until his mother coughed. He shook himself back to reality and extended his hand.

"Nice to meet you, Hunt."

No other words would come.

"Likewise," said the man. "Shelby's told me all about you and how you helped her dream her way here. I can't say I like the idea of her flying fighter planes or living all over the world while I'm stuck in New York City, but I'll get used to it."

His piercing blue eyes penetrated Brian's. He ran a massive hand through his dirty blond hair and shifted from one foot to the other.

He was nervous, but Brian was in shock. How long had Shelby been hiding this . . . friend? Why hadn't she told him she'd fallen for a Brad Pitt look-alike with a Greek last name?

He asked her silently, with his eyes. The defiant answer she returned with hers told him to mind his own business.

Brian saw Craig lurking in the background, standing near the restaurant door with his eyes fixed on him, and realized that Shelby's unspoken advice was dead-on: Tending to his own business had to be his top priority right now.

30

I'm not keeping my promise until you keep yours."

Indigo folded her arms and bit her lip to defuse some of her anger. She knew Yasmin couldn't help it, but it was so frustrating to see this beautiful girl losing herself in a sickness that was so unnecessary.

She didn't have a weight problem; she was naturally tall and willowy. And yet, here they sat, in a professional counselor's office, trying to convince this child that if she didn't work hard to get well, she wouldn't be coming home for a while.

"You want pictures to go to the top modeling agencies in New York? Prove that you can handle it," Indigo challenged.

The hospital psychologist, Dr. Danvers, shook his head and raised his palm to silence Indigo.

"You can't bribe her into doing this," he told Indigo. "This is more than just a conscious choice at this point. It started out as a way to control her environment, to maintain some sense of equilibrium, and now it has overtaken her will. Yasmin has to work really hard to get healthy, and it will happen only if she wants it to."

The news was hard to hear.

Yasmin didn't react. She sat between Mama and Daddy on Dr.

Danvers's office sofa, which was covered with an outdated baby blue checkered pattern.

"What does she need to control?" Daddy said and leaned forward, shaking his head in frustration.

Dr. Danvers leaned forward too and looked at Yasmin. "Can you tell them?"

She lowered her head and sighed. "I don't know. Everything. Me. Something."

Dr. Danvers nodded. "Good."

Mama and Indigo looked at each other, puzzled.

"That was good?" Mama said. "What did it mean?"

Dr. Danvers sat back and weighed his words.

"It means . . ." He paused before resuming his explanation. "Yasmin was nearly a year old when she came to live with you after her parents were killed in the car accident, Mr. and Mrs. Burns.

"You two were grieving the loss of your daughter and her husband, and suddenly, you went from being doting grandparents to daily caretakers of Yasmin, Indigo, and Reuben. Then, apparently a hip injury caused you to become dependent on alcohol, Mrs. Burns?"

Indigo winced as Mama nodded. This had to be painful.

"That period was tough for Yasmin, because there was a sense of chaos in your home, a sense that nothing was predictable and safe. Everyone deals with issues like this differently."

He leaned forward again and Indigo saw the sympathy in his eyes. "When was the last time Reuben came home?"

Silence served as his answer.

Reuben had flown from Seattle to Tuskegee for Indigo's college graduation, but she still was smarting over the fact that he had declined to come home to Texas for her party.

"He seems to be coping by staying away, by creating a life outside of the pain of losing his parents and watching his grandparents deteriorate in other ways," Dr. Danvers said.

Mama began to weep. Indigo left her seat and walked over to rub her shoulders. But this was about helping Yasmin, and apparently Dr. Danvers wasn't going to dance around feelings.

"Indigo, how do you think you're coping? What are you afraid to tackle? Whom do you push away? What do you avoid?" he asked. "When you can answer those questions, you'll understand how, in your own way, you are controlling, or trying to control, your environment to compensate for the period during your youth when nothing was in your control.

"For Yasmin, this has manifested as a desire, a need, to control her body image and her weight. Some people become anorexic, and some eat and purge. Plus the fact that she wants to model means she's seeing the images in the media of stick-thin women, and that has validated or at least given her an excuse to do what already brings her comfort."

Indigo felt as if the wind had been knocked out of her. In a matter of minutes, Dr. Danvers had laid out her and her siblings' dysfunctions, when they hadn't really known they were there.

Was this the real reason she was postponing her wedding? Was this why her photography meant so much to her? If she couldn't hold onto anything else, she would always have the images she created and the memories that came along with them.

She wanted to run outside so she could use her cell phone and call Brian to apologize. But he wouldn't be at the barracks on a Tuesday afternoon anyway.

Indigo pulled herself back to the present when Yasmin wrapped her arms around herself and began rocking back and forth.

"I want help. I don't want to stay like this."

Yasmin's whimpered declaration made Indigo's heart leap.

Dr. Danvers's expression didn't change. "That's easy to say, Yasmin, but it's going to take a lot of work. Not only for you, but for your family. You can't heal and go back into an environment where no one understands the journey you're on. In order for you to get well, the whole family has to embrace hard truths and make a commitment to understand each other better so you can all heal—starting today."

Indigo looked at Daddy. He sat up straighter and seemed resolved. He wasn't a Navy man like Brian, but tell him how he could fix something, and you could count him in.

"Starting today," Daddy repeated.

Mama nodded and wiped her eyes. "The past is the past. We will heal, starting today."

She reached for her purse and searched through its contents until she found her tiny black cell phone. Despite the fact that they were still in session, Mama dialed a code programmed into the phone, then put the receiver to her ear. Her face fell as she listened.

"Hello, Son."

Indigo realized that Mama was trying to reach Reuben, and as usual, her call was being routed to his voice mail.

"Check your schedule and see when you can come home. It's been a long time, Reuben. We need you."

31

It was Saturday morning, and for a change, Indigo got a chance to sleep in. She stretched, then smiled when the aroma of Daddy's pancakes and bacon wafted across her nose.

Normally about this time she would already be at the hair salon, welcoming Eboni's and Carlotta's early morning clients, but Rachelle had called yesterday and offered to fill her shoes.

"You've got a lot going on. Take a break," Rachelle had advised.

Indigo was grateful for the support and eagerly accepted the offer. She needed a weekend off, and today, she was going to be productive.

She climbed out of bed and slipped into a robe before padding down the hall to Yasmin's room. She suspected Yasmin wouldn't want to join them at breakfast and be tempted by all that she smelled, but she thought she'd at least try.

"I'll eat something a little later," said Yasmin, who was awake, but still under the covers, flipping through TV channels with her remote control.

Her spirits had remained low since she had been rushed to the hospital and had entered counseling. Her friends called constantly, asking her to come over or meet them at the mall. But since coming home two weeks ago, she mostly avoided them.

Rachelle's daughter, Taryn, had been coming over quite a bit to hang out with Yasmin, and she seemed to be trying to get her cousin back in the swing of things.

This morning, Indigo invited Yasmin to join her when she met Nizhoni at the bridal shop in a few hours to try on wedding gowns.

"Maybe I will," Yasmin said. "That sounds like fun."

Indigo left the girl to her teenage pastime and headed toward the kitchen. Aunt Melba was in the hallway just ahead of her, moving in the same direction.

Indigo felt like cheering. It was so wonderful to see her walking, without any assistance.

Indigo cruised alongside her and gave her a hug. "How are you doing this morning?"

Aunt Melba smiled. "I am . . . blessed and . . . highly . . . favored."

Both women roared with laughter. Long before her illness, Aunt Melba used to mock her customers who'd come into the salon and respond with that phrase.

Now that her speech had mostly returned to its normal pattern and she was able to be more physically mobile, she seemed to grasp and appreciate its full meaning.

"How . . . are you doing? I see that you took . . . the morning off," Aunt Melba said.

Indigo paused and faced her, remembering that Aunt Melba was technically her boss.

"Is that okay? Rachelle is filling in for me."

Aunt Melba waved Indigo away. "That's more than fine. I didn't make the comment . . . because I was worried. I only mentioned it because now that I'm feeling better, I'd like to start going to the salon with you . . . a couple of days a week, to get back in the swing of things."

159

"Really?" Indigo didn't conceal her excitement. She had been praying for this day. "That would be wonderful, Aunt Melba."

Aunt Melba nodded. "I know. God . . . is really good."

They entered the kitchen and found Mama and Daddy already eating. Both of them smiled when they saw Melba making her way to the table. Mama got up, fixed Melba a plate of pancakes, bacon, and eggs, and set it in front of her.

Aunt Melba bowed her head in prayer, then picked up her fork. "I'll eat this today . . . but how about some oatmeal and fruit . . . next time? I keep . . . telling ya . . . all of y'all in here . . . are going to end up with . . . stroke risks if you keep this up."

Daddy chuckled. "We eat healthy most of the week," he countered. "Can't we splurge on the weekends? Eat up and be happy."

"Feel up to going wedding gown shopping with us, sis?" Indigo's mother asked Melba.

Melba took a few bites, then eyed Indigo. "You are the most . . . unenthusiastic . . . bride I have ever seen."

She stared at Indigo and awaited a response.

"I'm glad you're back, Aunt Melba," Indigo said and patted her hand.

Mama looked from one to the other. "What do you mean, Melba?"

Aunt Melba set down her fork.

"Do you remember . . . how excited you were when Charles proposed? You drove me crazy . . . for six months . . . planning your wedding, talking about your wedding . . . dreaming about your wedding," Melba told Mama. "That's the kind of . . . excitement . . . you expect to see . . . in brides, but I don't see it in . . . Indigo . . . that's all."

Mama nodded politely. "Well, they've agreed that Indigo will start grad school in August and they'll move the wedding back to December, so it's not as urgent as it once was," she said. "But you're right—it's July now, so we need to start planning in order to get the location we want for the reception."

But Aunt Melba wouldn't relent. "If you aren't ready, Indigo . . . that's okay. Why rush it?"

Indigo felt her defenses rising and tried to stay calm.

"You are . . . one of the most . . . awesome young ladies I know," Aunt Melba continued. "You knew as a child . . . that you wanted to be a photographer . . . and by ninth grade . . . had mapped out a plan . . . to become one. You received . . . early acceptance letters . . . to college and grad school . . . and landed internships . . . at some of the nation's top companies. How many people . . . can say they were summer interns . . . for *Time* magazine or a national foundation?"

Aunt Melba shook her head. "But on this? You seem to be . . . as cool as iced coffee . . . when it comes to talk . . . of being Mrs. Brian Harper. What gives?"

Indigo sighed and sat back in her chair. She had lost her appetite and was tempted to join Yasmin in bedroom seclusion.

She looked at Mama, who seemed pensive. "Go ahead, Mama," she said. "You can let me have it too."

Mama shook her head. "I'm not quite as convinced as Melba that getting married is a tragic mistake. Brian is a good man. You don't want to lose him just because you've had a rocky summer and things haven't gone as planned. It wouldn't be a big wedding at this point, anyway. Don't let go of a good thing."

Indigo's eyes swung back to Melba, to hear her next volley, but Aunt Melba seemed to have decided not to bicker with her sister.

"I know I've procrastinated," Indigo said. "Brian and I were going to map everything out a couple of weekends ago, when I was scheduled to visit him in Newport. With all that has gone on with my eyes, then taking over the salon, and now Yasmin, I've put my planning on the back burner. It's not like me, but this summer hasn't been typical."

She looked at Aunt Melba. "Thank you for your concern. I know it's out of love. But I love Brian, and I do want to marry him. He's a great guy, and I know that he'll find a way to support my photography."

Aunt Melba peered at Indigo over her coffee cup as she drank the last few drops. "What about . . . grad school?"

"We've talked about that, and he's not happy about having a long-distance marriage until I finish, but he's willing to do it for my sake," Indigo said. "We also decided that we do want a small wedding at this point—just friends and family. If we can get Reuben here from out of town, that would be enough for me."

Mama and Daddy looked at each other.

"We hope we can get him here," Daddy said.

"We'll talk more later," Aunt Melba said. "I'm here for you . . . whatever you need." She changed the subject. "Irene, are you going . . . to let me cut your hair . . . into a cute style . . . when I'm back . . . at work?"

An hour or so later, after she had showered and dressed for the day, Indigo strolled into the family room to wait for Mama so they could meet with Nizhoni at Brides Central. She plopped on the sofa next to her aunt, who was flipping through a stack of magazines.

She wanted to ask the question that had been nagging her ever since Aunt Melba had the stroke: what advice had she been planning to give regarding marriage when she fell sick? But Indigo didn't ask, out of fear that Aunt Melba might not even remember the conversation and might be upset by that fact.

"You're ready to go home, aren't you?" Indigo asked Aunt Melba instead.

"Yep," Aunt Melba said, without taking her eyes off of an article in *O Magazine*. "My doctor says . . . I should be able . . . to live independently soon . . . but I don't know . . . what his definition . . . of 'soon' is."

Indigo rested her head on her aunt's shoulder. "I'm so happy you're better, and that we can talk again. But I'm going to miss having you here."

Aunt Melba patted her head and smiled. "You'll know where to find me . . . and now that you know . . . all of my business secrets . . . and practices . . . you can keep me in line."

Indigo raised her head. "No need to do that. You had everything in order. All I had to do was come in and keep things moving."

Aunt Melba held the magazine article closer, then tapped at the page. "You need to do this."

Indigo peered over her shoulder. "'Photography contest,'" Indigo read aloud. "'Send us your three "slice-of-life" photos that best represent people in your community and win a temporary slot on the *O Magazine* photography team. No manufactured poses or formal studio shots. We want everyday people in their daily settings, living and loving life.'"

Aunt Melba put the magazine on Indigo's lap.

"Do this. Today. The deadline . . . is Monday."

"In two days?!" Indigo shrieked. "I don't have time!"

Then she remembered where her camera was now. Locked in a desk at the salon, waiting for everyday people to come in and prepare to look their best for the people and the activities they loved. Maybe she would give this a try.

Indigo's eyes wandered to the digital clock on the fireplace mantle. She jumped up from the sofa.

"Let me call Nizhoni," she said. "I'm going to be late getting to the bridal shop today."

32

rian couldn't believe he had fallen for the lie.

```
Meet with me on Saturday and we'll
hash this out. I'll move on and so
can you. CM
```

The note that Craig had slipped him one evening after dinner shook him and gave him hope at the same time. Meeting with this guy was dangerous—there was no telling what Craig might have up his sleeve. But he was being commissioned next week; maybe he really wanted to put all of this behind him.

That's what Brian had been praying for, for weeks now. Keeping Craig quiet was the only way to make sure he'd have a solid career in the Navy and a solid marriage with Indigo.

The military's "Don't ask, don't tell" policy concerning gays was still in effect. Not that Brian considered that to be his sexual orientation at all; but any hint or doubt on the part of his comrades or superiors would mean he'd never go as far as he'd like up the career ladder. He would be ostracized and worse.

The flip side of that was that Craig would be too. So why would he risk it all?

Maybe this face-to-face discussion would put to bed the demons Brian still wrestled with every night. He couldn't take this into his life after OCS, or into his marriage. What would Indigo think?

Now here they were on Saturday evening, at a cozy restaurant half an hour away in Providence, having dinner and drinks. Brian knew better. Alcohol had gotten him in trouble the first time. He swallowed his second sip of bourbon and set the glass aside.

The waiter arrived with their lobster and crab cakes.

They ate outside, on the restaurant's deck, and talked little while they consumed the meal.

Brian didn't want to provoke Craig, but he had to ask.

"So what's this all about—taking me to dinner? The drive to Providence?"

He stared at Craig and waited for his answer.

Craig put down his fork and wiped his mouth. "What do you think?"

I think you're stone crazy. Brian wanted to say it aloud, but didn't want to get left in Providence. Instead, he shrugged.

"Come on, man. If we're here to talk, let's talk."

"We don't have to talk, if you prefer to do something else," Craig said and smiled.

Brian rolled his eyes. He understood now how stupid he had been. If he'd stayed in Newport, he could have walked out. This way, he was at Craig's mercy—a captive audience.

He sat back in his chair, folded his arms across his chest, and waited.

"I want to know what you remember about our . . . encounters at Tuskegee," Craig finally said.

"Why?" Brian asked. "If I can tell you nothing else, I can tell you they were a mistake. The first time I was drunk and out of my mind. The last time, I was reeling from what happened the first time, and I wasn't thinking clearly.

"I know who I am—a heterosexual man. What happened was out of character and out of the norm for me, and it hasn't happened since. I've repented and asked God to cleanse me, and he has. So whatever you thought was going to happen tonight, you can forget it and take us back to the base."

"You had your speech prepared, huh," Craig said and took another sip of his drink. "If you weren't worried about losing control, would that even be necessary?"

Craig was playing with him. Brian inhaled and exhaled slowly to keep his cool. He was way too old to have been this stupid.

Craig squinted and leaned toward Brian. "You know what? You aren't even my type anymore. Besides, messing with you isn't worth risking my career. I receive my commission next week. I'll be an officer and I'm outta here. Heading to Connecticut to do my thing, buddy. That's all that matters."

"Okay . . . ," Brian said. "And the reason for bringing me here?"

"You and I both know that if anyone in the Navy or at OCS suspects we go both ways or to the far left, we're dead in the water," Craig said in a near whisper. "Getting commissioned will be a waste of time for both of us if they stall our careers because of questionable sexual orientation. I hear you're getting married— good. I'm looking for someone too."

Brian shook his head. "What—you think my relationship is a front? Come on, man. I'm for real. I'm not on the DL."

Craig shrugged. "Whatever you have to do, do it, that's my motto. There's a little problem, though, and I need you to help take care of it."

Brian frowned and leaned forward too. "What—?"

"Shelby knows, Harper. You've got to keep her quiet."

33

*I*ndigo slipped into her fifth dress of the day, and she knew, before even turning to face the mirror, that this was the one.

The strapless, satin gown had a fitted, crisscross waist, a modestly full skirt embellished with crystals and beads, and a sweeping train. She was in love.

Nizhoni pinned Indigo's hair up in a mock French roll to give her a different effect, then turned her toward the mirror.

Indigo gasped.

"It's beautiful," she whispered, drawing out the word. "Can I have it?"

Nizhoni laughed. "For $3,995 plus tax and custom fitting fees, it's yours."

Indigo stopped and looked at her. "Tell me you're kidding."

Nizhoni shook her head. "Unfortunately I'm not. It's made by a popular designer and has hundreds of hand-sewn crystals and beads on the body of the skirt."

When Indigo didn't speak, Nizhoni grabbed her hand.

"Come on, let's show your mom and Yasmin and see what they think."

Mama saw Indigo coming through the door and began to tear up.

"You didn't do that when I came out in the other ones, so I take it that this one is a winner?"

Mama gave her a thumbs-up.

Yasmin sat there wide-eyed.

"You look like a princess, Sis," she said. "Brian is going to cry when he sees you in that."

Indigo's grin stretched from one ear to the other. Then she pouted.

"There's sticker shock, though."

Nizhoni shared the price of the dress and Mama covered her heart with her hands.

"Do you have a bridal sale coming up anytime soon? We've got a little time to order, since the wedding has been pushed back to December." She looked at Indigo and smiled. "You look beautiful in it, baby. I want you to have it, if we can manage."

Now it was Indigo's turn to get weepy. "Thank you, Mama. I do love it."

Nizhoni went into her office to check the calendar and returned a few minutes later.

"There's nothing on the books now, but we usually have a fall sale, just before the holidays," she said. "I can't guarantee that this dress will be included, but usually the wedding dresses are 15 percent off during that time. The other issue is that it takes ten to twelve weeks to get a dress back after custom changes have been requested, so you don't want to wait too close to December to be doing this.

"Let me go talk to my manager too, and see if there's anything she can do, since you guys are friends."

Nizhoni trotted off and Yasmin rose from the cushioned chair and approached Indigo.

"You look beautiful," Yasmin said. "You're doing great things with your life—I'm just proud of you."

Indigo leaned down from the pedestal she stood on in front of the three-way mirror and stroked Yasmin's face.

"I'm proud of you too, baby sis," she said. "You're going through a rough patch right now, but like I learned when I found out about the glaucoma, you just have to pick yourself up and get back in the game. You're doing great."

Yasmin nodded. "I am, aren't I? Dr. Danvers is helping."

"Good," Indigo said. "Because once we get this dress squared away, it will be time to look for yours and Shelby's. I'm going to have two maids of honor, you know, so by December 15 you've got to be fabulous and healthy."

Yasmin smiled.

"I'll be ready."

34

If Shelby knew, Brian was as good as dead.

She could tell Navy officials, and Indigo, what she had seen and end his future in one fell swoop.

Brian fretted all the way to the base. As Craig rounded the curve and prepared to drive up to the security gate to enter Naval Station Newport, he asked Craig to recount for him one more time why he was certain she had the goods.

"You think I'm making this up?" Craig asked in frustration. "Just take care of it, okay?"

"Tell me again. I want to have my facts straight when I talk to her," Brian said.

"The second time you and I were together, she saw us embrace and she saw me kiss you," Craig said slowly.

"But we were away from campus, at a park, and it was dusk," Brian said. "How was she so sure it was us?"

"You'll have to ask her why she was there; all I know is that she was," Craig said. "She knew what we looked like, of course, and she recognized my car and license plate, because I dated her for about a month the semester before you and I hooked up."

"You didn't tell me that part!" Brian yelled. "Great. She might want to out you 'cause she's feeling played."

Craig kept his eyes on the road. "You know her better than I do. That's why I'm asking you to handle it."

But that was the problem. Brian thought he knew her well enough to think she'd never keep something like this from him for so long. She hadn't said a word in three years.

Had she told Indigo? Was that the reason Indigo was so hesitant to get married?

He rid himself of that thought. He did know Indigo well enough to know that she would have questioned him by now.

They stopped at the security gate and were waved through. Craig dropped Brian off in front of one of the administration buildings, so he could walk to the barracks and not be seen fraternizing with a Candi-O—a candidate about to be commissioned.

Brian turned to him before walking away. "Look, man, let's really just get past this. I wish you the best on your assignment when you leave here. I'm going to talk to Shelby, but if she's the person I know her to be, she won't use this against us."

Brian read the skepticism in Craig's eyes.

"I hope you're right," Craig said. "Like I told you earlier tonight, she's a tough girl. I didn't know that she knew about our connection until she said something in passing two weeks ago. If it comes down to getting ahead or watching you rise faster than she does, she could let the chips fall where they may."

Brian shuddered at the thought. He strode to the barracks without telling Craig goodbye.

Too bad he didn't have his cell phone. He would call Shelby now and ask her to meet him somewhere. They had liberty tonight and most of tomorrow, but it was back to the normal routine by six p.m. Sunday.

He wondered what she'd say and whether Craig was right to be so worried. He wondered what Shelby thought of him. But

171

then, he really didn't know what to think of himself these days. He just wanted to get his commission and conquer the next step toward his dream.

If his skeletons were going to come out of the closet, better now, when he could handle them privately, in his own way. He just hoped that Shelby was still his friend, and that she would agree.

35

Brian knew where he'd find her on Sunday morning.

He rose early as usual, slid into navy slacks and a white collared shirt, and arrived at the chapel on base just as the eight a.m. service was beginning. He scanned the tiny sanctuary and surmised that most of the officers and other OCS residents must have had late nights; there were plenty of seats.

Shelby sat in the middle of a center section pew. Brian slid in beside her and pretended not to notice when she did a double take.

The base had several chaplains from different denominations, and this morning, an Episcopal priest was leading the service. His teaching was from 1 Samuel 25, which described how Abigail begged David for mercy after her foolish husband, Nabal, insulted David.

"Consider the courage and humility this woman must have possessed to approach the king of Israel and beg for forgiveness for something she didn't do," the priest said. "Or, even better, consider the fact that she did so to save the lives of her people. What are we willing to sacrifice for the greater good? What are we willing to give up so that others can live more fully?

"In our society, the focus is on 'me, me, me,'" he said. "But the

Bible indicates that when we take care of others and consider their needs above our own, then God will take care of us."

Brian wanted to look at Shelby, but was afraid. *Please, Father, let her hear this message in the context of what I need to talk to her about.*

"Now I can guarantee that most of you sitting here listening to this sermon are thinking of someone you wish were here to hear it." The priest chuckled. "Or maybe you're glad the person *is* here to hear it."

Brian felt sheepish.

"But I also guarantee that since you are here receiving this word, it was meant for you too. You may not understand why or in what context, but ask God to reveal to you what you need to be doing along the lines of Abigail's sacrifice, and he will make it clear to you."

Brian heard, but he didn't hear. At least, he didn't process that last part of the message. This wasn't about him; it was about Shelby being a real friend.

After service, they rose from their seats and hugged.

"Fancy running into you here, Candidate Officer Harper," Shelby said and punched his arm. They hadn't talked since the night she'd seen him fretting over his OCS manual in the rec room.

Brian wondered if she had an idea about why he was here today. "Want to join me for lunch, Candidate Officer 'homegirl' Arrington?" he joked.

She nodded and linked her arm through his as they left the sanctuary. "Sure, where to?"

They chose a spot off base that served breakfast all day.

As Shelby dug into her omelet, he watched her. She was a beautiful girl, even with her Navy buzz cut. Her cocoa skin, dazzling white smile, small build, and outgoing nature had made her a perfect Tuskegee cheerleader. It was no surprise that she had been elected the campus queen their senior year, or that she'd broken a string of Tuskegee hearts before she graduated.

Brian found it funny that when she finally seemed ready to get serious, it was with someone of another race.

"Tell me about this Hunt Pappas," he said. "Where did you meet him? Does Indigo know about him?"

She took a bite of food and nodded. "Yeah, I've mentioned him, but I haven't made a big deal out of it, so she probably didn't think it was worth discussing with you."

Brian raised an eyebrow. "It's a pretty big deal when he comes to see you during visitors' weekend and meets your parents, isn't it?"

Shelby smiled. "You're right. I met him last summer when I was interning at Kennedy Space Center down in Florida. He's an engineer too, and had just landed a job with Lockheed Martin. We went out a few times over the summer and clicked. He kept in touch and we started seeing each other again, albeit long distance, about six months before I graduated."

"Seems like it would be hard enough to maintain an interracial relationship when you're in the same city, let alone long distance," Brian said. "How's that working?"

Shelby glared at him. "You don't have to be so pessimistic. He's special, but he's just a friend, anyway. We'll see where things go."

Brian leveled his gaze at her. "Are you trying to convince me or yourself?"

Shelby sighed. "I just know a relationship like this isn't easy. I care for him deeply. I spent the summer getting to know him and I love so many things about him. He's funny, he has a deep faith in God, and he has a good heart. But I just don't know. I want to take it really slow. Plus, I'm about to ship off to flight school and he'll be working in New York on a federal contract."

Brian smiled. "That's the most I've ever heard you talk about a guy. You love him."

Shelby dropped her head and blushed. When she looked up again, she shifted the focus to him. "What's up with you? Why did you track me down this morning?"

Where should he begin? He took a deep breath.

"I know you've been talking to Craig, and I need to know what the deal is."

Shelby sat up straight and put her fork down. Her expression grew somber, but she didn't respond.

"What do you think you saw?" Brian asked.

Shelby shook her head. "I don't think anything, Brian," she said softly. "I had been biking along one of the trails at the park and had just parted ways with Danica, one of the other cheerleaders, so I could go to my car. I was parked a few feet from where Craig's car was, and I saw you two sitting inside embracing. I saw him kiss you full on the mouth. And you didn't pull away. I wasn't hallucinating."

The memory of it all came rushing back to Brian as she described the incident, and he felt his face growing warm.

"I . . . it was all . . . you don't understand," he said.

"What is there to understand beyond what I saw? You and a guy I used to date were locking lips in what you thought was a private spot," Shelby said. "It was an intimate moment. And the next day you went on your usual date with my best friend, like nothing happened."

Brian's heart stopped. "You didn't tell her?"

Shelby sat back and folded her arms. She looked angry.

176

"Believe me, I came close many times," she said. "I still struggle with the fact that I haven't told her, especially now that you are engaged. But I prayed about it—in fact, I continue to pray about it.

"Every time I take it before the Lord, he tells me to let it go," Shelby said "He tells me that you are the one who has to own your truth and live it out in a way that doesn't destroy others.

"If I were to tell her, there's no guarantee that she would believe me. If you didn't confess, she might just cut me off and continue on with you anyway. At least this way I'm here for her, no matter what happens."

She waited for Brian to say something, and when he didn't, she continued.

"Why are you asking me about this now? After all this time?"

"You've been talking to Craig," Brian said. "He's worried that you'll spread rumors. I told him you're not like that, but I still wanted to talk with you about all of this. And I want to reassure you that whatever happened back then, it was a stupid mistake."

Shelby didn't look convinced.

"I got drunk at one of the fraternity parties and Craig offered me a ride home and . . . some things happened that I hadn't expected."

Shelby held up her hands and turned her head. "Please don't give me details, Brian. I'm already disgusted."

"I want you to know that I'm not . . . *gay*," he said in a hushed voice. "You know I don't drink. That night I got a little crazy and one thing led to another."

"What about when I saw you in the park?"

Brian lowered his eyes. How could he explain that away? He got caught up in the moment? His body betrayed him? She was right when she said he hadn't ignored Craig's advances.

177

"I don't know, Shelby," he said. "But it never happened again. I promise before God. Right after that, I started going to church with you and Indigo, remember? I asked God to forgive me and to take away whatever was in me that had tempted me to go in that direction. I got baptized that year, remember?"

"So you haven't dated any other guys since then?" she asked.

"Not a one, Shelby. Nobody but Indigo. I love her."

Shelby leaned forward and searched his eyes. "But this is the reason you've been hounding her to get married, isn't it? You're trying to convince yourself that you're not only a Navy man, you're all man. And you need her help to prove it."

Brian felt like a child caught red-handed with a pocketful of forbidden candy. Craig was right—Shelby might be dangerous.

36

*O*ndigo settled at the Hair Pizzazz reception desk with a cup of coffee and rifled through her bag.

It was filled with unopened mail from several days ago that she needed to review. With Aunt Melba coming into the salon one day a week to man the reception desk, she had a little more time on her hands.

Her aunt wasn't styling hair yet; but she was thrilled to be back in her business, which was like her second home, and Melba's clients who were temporarily visiting Eboni or Carlotta were overjoyed to see her.

Aunt Melba was here this morning, reading her bank statements and answering the phone.

Indigo pulled out a small stack of letters and began sorting through the information from her graduate school, credit card offers, and other junk mail. She got to one envelope though, and paused.

It felt pretty thin, so she wasn't expecting much. But when she opened it and read the first sentence, she jumped up from her seat next to Aunt Melba and started dancing.

Indigo waved the letter in the air. "It's a letter from *O Magazine*,

Aunt Melba! The three photos I submitted are going to be featured in the magazine's December issue."

She wanted to pinch herself to make sure she wasn't dreaming. Better yet, she should stop dancing and peruse the letter again, just in case she had read it wrong. She held it in front of her and read aloud to Aunt Melba.

"'Dear Ms. Burns, It is with great pleasure that I write to inform you that you are one of ten photographers from around the nation selected as a winner of the *O Magazine* Everyday Life Photo contest. Congratulations—you're coming to New York!'"

By the time Indigo made it to the end, Aunt Melba was clapping.

"Isn't . . . that . . . something! Praise . . . God!"

She stood and held out her arms to give Indigo a hug.

Indigo's tears of joy mingled with giggles at her aunt's enthusiasm. Aunt Melba's speech had improved greatly, and sometimes she didn't stutter or experience delays at all. But when she was excited, the words seemed harder to form.

She sat down and read the letter again.

Eboni came around the corner and smiled at them. "What's going on up here? Why weren't we invited to the early morning party?"

Aunt Melba pointed at Indigo's letter. "Indigo's pictures. . . . will be . . . in *0 Magazine!*"

Eboni seemed surprised. "That's great—when have you had time to take pictures, though?"

"While I was here working," Indigo said. "When you finished with a client, sometimes she came to me to get her picture taken."

Indigo was still beaming and still in disbelief. "I sent in three shots from my first week working here—a picture of little Summer getting ready for her pageant, a picture of Mrs. Harrow and the flowers she dropped off, and a picture of Yasmin striking a pose. I just can't believe it."

Aunt Melba grinned. "Get ready, baby. Bigger . . . and better things . . . are coming for you . . . and for Yasmin. Call her now . . . call your parents."

Indigo did, and the shrieks from Mama and Yasmin on the other end were nearly deafening.

"When are we going to New York?!" Yasmin yelled.

"I'm going to accept an award and finalize a thirty-day internship in two weeks," Indigo said. "It doesn't say anything about the models coming along. Sorry!"

Indigo's cell phone rang, and she rushed Yasmin and her mother off the salon phone so she could answer it.

"Indigo, it's Claude Ingram. With the *Jubilant Herald*."

She paused. Why was he was calling now?

"Congratulations! The city editor received a press release this morning announcing that you won an *O Magazine* photography contest. Wow. I guess your eyes are doing okay?"

"Wonderful," Indigo responded, trying to remain gracious. "I'm doing great, and as you probably know from the press release, all of my photos featured Jubilant residents, which means I'm helping put our town on the map."

"Would you be willing to share them with us?" Claude asked hesitantly. "The executive editor thought it would be neat to run your pictures with the press release."

Indigo remained quiet as she tried to process it all. Claude Ingram, who wouldn't send her out to a water main break to shoot photos, wanted to publish her pictures.

She was seeing firsthand how God redeemed his children, and she was glad to be in that number.

37

Not only did the *Jubilant Herald* want to publish her winning shots, they also wanted to feature her.

Claude called back an hour after their initial conversation to ask if he could send a photographer to take her picture.

Mama, Daddy, Yasmin, and Taryn had joined Indigo and Aunt Melba at the hair salon for an impromptu celebration. They were enjoying coffee, tea, and doughnuts when the second call came.

Indigo motioned to them as she listened to Claude.

"He wants to take my picture," she mouthed to her parents.

Daddy nodded and mouthed, "Go for it."

"Sure, Claude," she said. "That would be fine. I'm at Hair Pizzazz, on Column Parkway. This is the place where I've taken most of my photos all summer, so it's fitting to do it here anyway."

"You have more photos?" he asked.

"I have plenty more," Indigo said. "I take candid shots of clients who frequent the hair salon and strike up a conversation with me. It's fun and it's different: think about coming to a hair salon to get beautiful and then taking a photo when you're feeling just that.

"I was doing it so frequently that I started asking customers to sign photo releases." Indigo laughed. "I don't know what I'll do with all of the images, but it was great to have something ready to submit for the magazine contest at the last minute."

Claude was quiet for so long that Indigo wasn't sure he was still there.

"Hello?"

"I'm here," he said. "I'm glad your summer has turned out okay. Seems like leaving the newspaper was the best thing that could have happened to you."

Indigo didn't respond. Telling him that God would work everything out for your good if you loved him would sound like she was preaching. Instead of uttering the words, she asked God to deliver that message to Claude in a way that he could receive it.

"Things are going well, and I'm happy—actually overjoyed—right now, having just received this news," Indigo said. "My eyes are doing well, my photos are being recognized, my family's doing great, and I'm getting married in December. I couldn't ask for more.

"I'll look forward to seeing one of the newspaper's photographers, okay? I'll be here until about four today."

Half an hour later, in strolled a handsome brother with hazel eyes and naturally curly dark hair. He had two cameras slung over his shoulder and he was holding the press release about Indigo.

Yasmin was manning the reception desk when he entered.

"Are you here to take my sister's picture?" she asked.

"Depends on who your sister is," the man said lightheartedly. "Indigo Burns?"

He nodded. "That's who I'm looking for."

Indigo emerged at that second from the private salon area, where she had been getting a client settled for Carlotta. She was about to offer pleasantries and welcome the man to the salon, but stopped in her tracks.

It was Max Shepherd, the freelance photographer who had come strolling through the newsroom on her last day there as if he were a company stockholder and God's gift to photojournalism.

He was taking her picture? Great.

She approached him and extended her hand. "Good morning; welcome to Hair Pizzazz. I'm Indigo."

She wondered if he would remember her.

"I know who you are," he said and smiled. "You were in the newsroom the day I came in to develop some breaking news photos. You were the cause of me almost not getting paid."

Indigo frowned. "Excuse me?"

"Apparently you went out on your own and covered the water main break, after the paper had hired me to do it. When the editors saw the shots you had taken from the roof of one of the nearby buildings, my shots looked amateur by comparison.

"They wound up using mine, though, because you had just resigned and you hadn't been officially asked to shoot the pictures. I was impressed, though, to almost be upstaged by a new college graduate."

"What does my relative youth have to do with anything?" Indigo teased.

"Clearly nothing!" Max said and laughed. He set his camera bag on the reception desk and unpacked one of his lenses. "I'm still stringing for the newspaper and operating my own photography studio, but *O Magazine* isn't pursuing me!"

Indigo relaxed and allowed herself to admit how handsome he was.

"Where would you like to take my picture?"

Mama and Daddy had taken Aunt Melba to lunch. While Yasmin and Taryn manned the phones, Indigo gave Max a brief tour of the salon so he could decide where to position her.

He chose one of Melba's red sofas.

"Grab your camera for me and set it next to you," Max suggested. "And do you have prints of any of the other photos you've taken?"

"Sure," Indigo said.

She got up and grabbed her camera and the folder that held the images she printed. She gave them to the featured salon client the next time she came in for her appointment.

Max flipped through the photos and selected five. He laid them, and Indigo's camera, on the seat of the sofa.

"Now, you go stand behind the couch, perch your elbows up on the back, and put your chin in your hands," he told Indigo. "I want to get a shot of you leaning over these images, which I'll spread out in front of you."

Indigo was impressed. She did as she was told and waited for him to give her further instructions. She understood now why he was a little cocky. He was good and he knew it.

"How long have you been a professional photog?" she asked him, between shots.

"About five years," he said. "I moved down here from New Jersey to attend Everson College for undergrad and fell in love with the area. I went to grad school in New York at the School of Visual Arts, but wound up coming back here to open my own studio and freelance."

Indigo broke her pose and stared at him. "You went to SVA? I start there in late August."

He nodded. "I know. I get the alumni newsletter and they list incoming students from various regions so you can connect with them or support them however they need. I saw your name on the list and remembered it from the newspaper. It's a great school. It will expand your horizons and open up opportunities you never could have imagined—although this *O Magazine* gig ain't bad at all."

They both laughed and worked together in silence for the next few minutes.

When Max was done, he pointed to her photos on the sofa.

"Those are really well done," he said. "It would be cool if Claude would run them in the *Herald* as their own feature. Mind if I borrow them and show him?"

Indigo hesitated. She didn't know this man or what his true intentions were. Why was he being so friendly?

He smiled at her. "I'm not a thief or conspirator. I really just want to show Claude. But if you feel more comfortable doing it yourself, consider setting up a meeting and taking them in, okay?"

Indigo nodded. "Sorry—you know how possessive we artists can be about our work," she said.

Max packed up his camera. "I understand. Don't worry about it."

He turned to go, then stopped and walked over to shake her hand. "Congratulations again, Miss Indigo Burns. I look forward to seeing more great things from you."

He held her gaze, and her hand, for a few seconds longer than necessary.

Indigo became flustered. "Um, thank you, Max. I'm honored to have you take my picture. You take care."

When he was gone, she sat on the sofa and fanned herself with her hand. What was that all about? Her heart hadn't fluttered like that since she first met Brian.

38

The day had finally come and Brian felt overwhelmed. He stood in front of the mirror flecking imaginary dirt from the shoulder of his white uniform and tried to control the emotions that swung from elation to weepiness to relief. He had made it, by the grace of God, and today he would be commissioned into the United States Navy as an officer.

His bags were packed and stored in the trunk of his car, ready to go. He had exchanged contact information with his bunkmates and a few other classmates.

His parents had flown in for the ceremony and would be driving back to Austin with him tonight. Indigo was here too, wearing his engagement ring and looking beautiful and happy. She had flown in with her parents and Yasmin.

This was his day.

Brian grabbed his black-and-white cap and turned around to take one last look at his tiny room. He snapped a mental picture, hoping he would always remember this space and what he had endured.

His roommates seemed to be doing the same.

Todd and Greg hugged him and slapped his back.

"This is it, men," Brian said. "Godspeed to both of you."

Todd was going to be a Navy weatherman and would be shipping out to Virginia Beach, Virginia, for service. Greg was an engineer like Brian, but wanted to work in intelligence. He was headed to Washington, DC. Brian had received orders, as he had expected, for flight training school in Pensacola, Florida, and he was excited.

The men fell into single file formation, as if their gunnery sergeant were watching, and walked out of the room.

"Thank God that's over," Todd said and sighed.

The men crossed the campus and joined other members of their class on the lawn in front of the base gymnasium, where the ceremony would be held because of the sweltering heat.

Brian saw his family and Indigo's and acknowledged them with a short wave and nod of his head. As excited as he was, it wasn't supposed to register on his face.

He spotted Shelby a few feet away and could tell by the twinkle in her eyes that she too was working hard to contain herself. She would leave here today and head to flight training school in Corpus Christi, Texas, after a brief visit home to Austin.

Wherever they wound up long term, Brian knew that she would always be his sister-friend, despite the concerns Craig had raised before he graduated and went on to Naval Submarine School in Connecticut. Shelby hadn't made any promises, but he knew that her love for Indigo would keep her from being vindictive. That revelation had comforted him when he realized that Indigo and Shelby would soon be back to their every-other-day telephone chats, talking about him and anything else that mattered to them.

Gunnery Sgt. McArthur approached the members of Class 10–08 and ordered them to fall into formation. There was a parade and a drill show and a formal speech to the graduates from the base commander.

Half an hour later, Brian managed to maintain his composure when he was called forward and asked to take the Navy pledge:

"I, Brian James Harper, do solemnly swear to support and defend the United States against all enemies, foreign and domestic."

When the base commander officially congratulated the new officers, they turned away from the audience and flipped their caps in the air before catching them.

Friends and family cheered, clapped, and whistled. Brian looked toward the stands and spotted his crew. Indigo waved and blew him a kiss. He grinned and motioned for her, his mother, and the rest of the family to join him.

When she reached him, Brian gathered Indigo in his arms and gave her a long kiss, unconcerned about who might be watching.

Greg came up behind him and slapped his back. "The picture didn't do her justice, Harper," he whispered in Brian's ear. "You two will make a beautiful family."

Brian grinned. He was looking forward to it.

His father and Indigo's dad approached him and shook his hand. He gathered his dad into a hug and thanked him for all of his support. Brian's mother and Mrs. Burns were next, and then Yasmin, who looked more and more like Indigo each time he saw her. She was still a shade lighter and two sizes smaller than her older sister, but they were the spitting image of each other.

"You looking good, girl," he told her, and she did. She had put on about five pounds, but on her thin frame, even that small amount made a difference. "Are you taking care of yourself?"

She nodded. "I'm getting ready for your wedding—big brother," she said and smiled.

Those words made him feel almost as good as being commissioned. He was starting a new chapter today, and he was thankful.

This morning, he had asked God to purge his temptations and to help him leave them here in Newport, along with his civilian status, his ties to Craig, and anything else that might hinder him.

He was Officer Brian Harper now, and life was good.

39

With all of the talk and laughter, the two-hour drive from Jubilant to Houston seemed to take just half an hour.

Brian had driven back to Austin with his parents last week, but was spending this weekend in Jubilant, visiting Indigo and helping with wedding preparations. He was staying with Gabe and Rachelle, and they had offered to treat him and Indigo to dinner.

On a whim, Gabe and Rachelle decided to take the young couple to one of their favorite spots in Houston. Gabe made the reservation and steered them toward his SUV. Brian sat in the front passenger seat so he and Gabe could chat while Gabe drove.

"I'm telling you," Gabe insisted, "engineering is the career of the future. Tate said just yesterday that he wants to be a doctor and I tried to talk him out of it."

"Gabe!" Rachelle leaned forward and lightly spanked her husband's shoulder. "Don't do that to your son. If he wants to follow in your footsteps, you're supposed to encourage him."

Rachelle shook her head and looked at Indigo. *Men!* she mouthed.

Indigo chuckled. It was funny to see their dynamic as a couple and how, despite the fact that they loved each other deeply, that didn't necessarily translate to agreeing on everything.

"You know I love what I do, Rachelle," Gabe said as he weaved in and out of traffic in downtown Houston. "But having to deal with these insurance company rules and treating patients based on what their plans allow or don't allow is nerve-wracking and, in some instances, borders on making me ineffective as a surgeon.

"If I can't, as the expert, determine what type of care or testing my patients need based on the gravity of their condition versus what the insurance company is going to approve, then my hands are tied. It strips me of the power to 'first do no harm,' in many cases," Gabe said. "An engineer can do well and not have to deal with all of that. That's all I'm suggesting to Tate."

Gabe pulled in front of Pesce Restaurant and the four of them climbed out of the Range Rover so the waiting attendant could valet park it. Once inside, they were ushered to a corner table with a candlelight view of the city and an interior aquarium.

"This is beautiful," Indigo said. "Thanks for treating us. You guys are something else."

"No, you guys are." Gabe looked at Brian. "Graduating from Officer Candidate School with honors—congrats, man."

Then he looked at Indigo. "Winning a photo contest in *O Magazine* that comes with a monthlong internship. How often does that happen?"

Indigo and Brian smiled at each other. Their mutual pride was evident.

"How are you going to fit in an internship with grad school—and a wedding?" Rachelle asked.

"I've talked to the magazine's photo editor and we've agreed that I'll do the internship in New York, working about ten hours a week, around my grad school courses," Indigo said. "I'll get settled into grad school, get the wedding behind me, and start the internship in March or April of next year. They're really flexible."

Rachelle shook her head. "I can't believe you're doing all of this. Remember how torn up you were about learning about the glaucoma and about leaving the newspaper? Do you see how God works?"

Indigo laughed. "You should hear Aunt Melba walking around the house preaching about it. Between her recovery and all the exciting things going on with me, she's beside herself. And there's more."

Rachelle raised an eyebrow. "You won a Pulitzer Prize?"

They all laughed.

"No," Indigo said. "Even better. Claude Ingram, the photography editor at the *Herald*, called last week and asked if I would be interested in a photo column that would feature the pictures that I've been snapping at the salon all summer, and any future shots of local residents that would be fitting. He'll pay me a freelance column fee and run the photos once a month, on Sundays."

"Did you accept?" Rachelle asked.

"Of course," Indigo said, and dug into the calamari appetizer the waitress brought to the table. "That'll cover my meals while I'm in grad school.

"But what's even better is that *Reader's Digest* called. They want to reprint my photo of Ms. Harrow delivering flowers to the salon."

Indigo laughed as Rachelle covered her mouth with her hand to contain a mock scream.

"*Reader's Digest*?!" Rachelle said. "Are you sure you need to go to grad school? You're on your way."

Rachelle leaned across the table and grasped Indigo's hand. "I'm only kidding about ditching grad school—you get all of the education you can," she said. "But this is so exciting, so blessed. I'm just thrilled."

Indigo nodded and grinned. "I know—and there's more."

Rachelle sat back and put her wrist in front of Gabe. "Check my heart rate, Doc, I don't know if I can stand any more."

"A staff photographer for *O* who helped judge the contest mentioned to a friend of hers—a recruiter for Ford Models—that one of the photos I submitted was a picture of an aspiring model—Yasmin. The agency wants to talk to Yasmin about doing some work for them."

Rachelle bowed her head. Indigo wasn't sure if she was praying or crying, but when she lifted her eyes, Indigo saw that she had been doing both.

"God is doing some amazing things in our family right now," she said softly. "We need to be sure to remember this season. What does Aunt Irene say about Yasmin possibly modeling?"

Indigo took a sip of water. "She's a little nervous, but she's willing to go along with it, as long as Yasmin's counselor gives her the okay. We're all concerned about Yas lapsing into the bulimia. Mama and Daddy are willing to let her try this, as long as she continues working with Dr. Danvers and as long as one of them can be with her at all times. Right now, though, everything's still in the talking stage. When they take me up to grad school, they'll take Yasmin for a visit with the model recruiter. Yasmin is about to die from excitement. I *told* her my photos would take her places."

Gabe leaned forward and raised his palm so Indigo could give him a high five.

"Anything else—from either of you—that we need to know about before we order all the champagne in this place?" he asked.

"I'm done!" Indigo said and laughed. Gabe knew she didn't

drink, but she appreciated his enthusiasm. "I'm still pinching myself about it all too."

Brian looked at her and smiled. "There's no way I can compete with all of that. I'm just getting ready to go to flight school so I can become a little old Navy pilot. No excitement and glamour there."

He laughed, but Gabe looked at him soberly.

"I know you're joking," Gabe told Brian, "but a lot of this is unfolding just as you two are planning to become husband and wife. That's a lot to consider. These changing dynamics can have a big impact on your relationship."

Indigo hadn't told anyone she'd been troubled by the same concerns. It was one thing for the husband to be the top dog, but what happened if she outshone him and gained more notoriety for her work than he did for his? She didn't want to be like Whitney Houston at a long-ago awards show, trying to make her man feel better by declaring to the audience that he was the king. She was thankful to have the issue raised by someone else, and a man at that.

"What do you mean?" Brian asked Gabe. "I do what I do and she does what she does. We're in two different worlds so it's not like I'm competing with her."

Rachelle looked him in the eyes. "I'm glad you see it that way, Brian, but our society operates differently. It was okay for me to be Mrs. Gabe Covington, wife of a renowned heart surgeon. But it took some of the polish off his brass buckle when my title changed to Dr. Rachelle Covington. You can have the best of intentions, but you need to be honest with yourself, in your heart, about what you want in a wife and what your expectations are from Indigo, given that she's already locked into a career that she loves."

Brian and Indigo looked at each other.

"You need to be careful too," Rachelle told Indigo. "I can tell you from experience that it's easy to set aside your goals and dreams and dismiss opportunities that come your way because you don't want to make your husband feel insecure or inferior.

"That seems noble and all, but that's not what love is about," Rachelle told both of them. "At the end of the day, the key to a solid marriage partnership is not just love. You also have to be with someone who respects you deeply and who is looking out for your best interest. If you connect with someone who makes those two qualities a priority in your relationship, you'll be okay."

Indigo wanted to ask a question but hesitated.

Rachelle noticed. "Go ahead. Let's get it all on the table. We love you both and want you to succeed. If our being honest helps you get there, we're willing and ready to listen or talk."

"What about you and Gabe?" Indigo finally asked. "I know you struggled for a while. What was missing and how did you get things back on track?"

Gabe looked at Rachelle. "You go first," he said.

"I got married for the wrong reasons," Rachelle said. "I wanted to please my parents and I was looking for security, and it just happened to come wrapped in a handsome and successful package named Gabe.

"When we started out, we were very much like you two. I was beginning my work as an optometrist and he was finishing a residency. We both were on track to pursue our dreams. But at some point, *my* dream got lost in *our* dream."

Rachelle took a deep breath, as if the memory of that period still weighed her down. "Gabe kept his individual goals—to become a heart surgeon, to work at a leading hospital in Houston, to become a valued member of the community. He also was committed to our goals as a family. When we had Tate and Taryn, he wanted them to be exposed to certain things and be educated a certain way. I became the facilitator for making him look good and helping him reach his goals, and making sure the kids got everything we had agreed upon. There was no time left for me to pursue the things that had once mattered to me."

She looked at Gabe. "He loved me, but I'm not sure that the respect was there or that he had my best interest at heart, especially when my needs competed with his. I have to be honest about that. Things started turning around for us when I decided to stand up for myself and make myself a priority again. I realized, in doing that, I was also helping him be less selfish and teaching our children that everybody's needs matter."

Gabe sat forward. "Rachelle's version is correct. But I have to say for my part, I had to realize that the world didn't revolve around me and my needs. That was huge, because at work, it did. In the community, it did. Even at home, Rachelle made sure that it did."

He reached for Rachelle's hand and smiled at her. "So when she had this 'early life crisis' and decided to change the terms of our unwritten contract, I wasn't too happy. Two things happened. I went on a mission trip to Uganda with a Christian friend and his wife and saw the beauty in a relationship that didn't require either partner to be subservient. And I felt a connection with God, for the first time ever. Both of those experiences were humbling. I realized that it didn't matter who I was back in Houston, on paper or in the hospital. What mattered was who God said I was, and who Rachelle needed me to be."

He looked at Brian. "It's sounds easy, right? But trust me, it hasn't been. I came home from that trip really afraid to let go of the way life had been. I had promised Rachelle before I got home that I was willing to change and do better, but when I walked into my home in a suburb not far from here, the old Gabe came back. I was in charge and that was the way it was going to be.

"When I realized that I might lose my wife, though, I finally woke up. We went to counseling for about a year and worked through some of the things we've mentioned tonight. But the most important thing I took away from that time was exactly what Rachelle first pointed out—I couldn't *say* that I loved her if I wasn't going to treat her with respect and do whatever I could to help her reach her highest potential.

"And ultimately," Gabe said, "it all boiled down to facing truths. I had to take a long, hard look at myself and accept that I was arrogant and selfish. Until I did that, there was no hope of me changing for the better."

Rachelle nodded. "And I had to be truthful with myself and own the fact that I had married him for prestige and security, and on the rebound from a first marriage that my parents had not approved of. I had to look at myself and honestly determine if I was a gold digger or manipulator or what. Acknowledging what had led me down the path to becoming Gabe's wife and accepting life on his terms instead of our terms freed me to make new decisions that were better for me, and to be okay with that."

Indigo was speechless. Her cousins had bared their souls, without making it pretty. She was grateful. It hit home that marriage wasn't about the beautiful dress she had ordered or the logistics of where she and Brian would live or even whether they'd support each other in their individual endeavors.

Brian said it before she could formulate the words. "This all boils down to truth, doesn't it?" he said pensively. "Being honest with ourselves and with each other."

"With nothing held back," Gabe said. "Truth has to be your foundation. If you can reveal your flaws and mistakes and misgivings to each other honestly, and sometimes even painfully, and still look into each other's eyes and want to be together, there's nothing that, with the help of God, you can't overcome."

Brian and Indigo smiled nervously at each other.

"This must be called Premarital Boot Camp," Indigo joked. She looked at Rachelle. "You two get the Aunt Melba award for candidness. Thank you. From my heart."

Indigo smiled at Rachelle and Gabe and at Brian, who planted a light kiss on her lips, but inside, she felt like jello. Everything was quivering, from her heart to her stomach to her beliefs about who she was as an individual and in relation to Brian.

Rachelle and Gabe had toppled her fantasy. She had been preparing for a wedding, when she needed to be deciding whether she was ready for a marriage.

40

*I*ndigo's graduation party had been special, but tonight was spectacular.

The Burns family had rented the ballroom in the city's newly renovated performing arts center and it seemed like half of Jubilant was there to celebrate Aunt Melba's return to her salon. Melba was a friend to many, from the mayor and police chief to the single mother who owned the cleaning business that kept Hair Pizzazz in tip-top shape.

Aunt Melba wasn't moving as fast as before, but she wasn't shy about getting on the dance floor with her brother, Herbert; with Indigo's dad, Charles; with Gabe or with Brian.

After the fourth song in a row, Mama instructed Indigo to intervene. Indigo danced over to Melba and urged her to take a break.

"You won't be able to move anything tomorrow if you keep this up," Indigo teased and led her off the dance floor.

Aunt Melba laughed and relented. She joined Indigo at the table where Indigo sat with Brian, Shelby, Shelby's friend Hunt, and Nizhoni. Each had plates filled with hors d'oeuvres, and the wait staff kept circulating and offering more.

"Thank you, guys, for coming and helping make this night

special," Aunt Melba said above the overamplified live band. She turned to Hunt and looked from him to Shelby. She gave Shelby a thumbs-up.

"Care to introduce me, or are you afraid I might take him?"

Shelby laughed and grabbed Hunt's hand.

"Aunt Melba, this is someone special—Hunt Pappas," Shelby said.

Aunt Melba shook the hand he extended and reached across the table for a hug.

"Everybody who knows me knows . . . I'm everybody's aunt, including yours . . . young man," she said. "I hope you're . . . enjoying the party."

Hunt smiled and looked at Shelby.

"I'm having a great time," he said. "I'm honored to help you celebrate your recovery. You've had a long fight, Shelby tells me. You're looking wonderful, and I'm praying that God will keep you going strong."

Aunt Melba sat back in surprise. "Well, now . . . where did you find him?" she asked Shelby. "Smart . . . handsome and . . . God-fearing too? Order me one up!"

Everyone laughed.

"Seriously, though," she said, "he's right. God has kept me strong. I . . . wouldn't be here . . . without his grace and mercy. Strokes don't come . . . with warnings. At least . . . mine didn't. But . . . while God had me off my feet . . . leaning on him . . . and on my family . . . for support . . . he drew me closer to him and deepened my love . . . for him. I have to say . . . that has made it all worth it."

Everyone at the table fell silent, including Indigo. To be thankful for an illness that could have taken your life, cost you your business, and limited your chances of taking care of yourself ever again was deep.

Yasmin danced over and hugged Aunt Melba from behind. "The guest of honor is needed at the podium. Sorry to steal her away, guys."

Yasmin escorted Aunt Melba to the microphone and raised a hand to quiet the music and the crowd.

"Good evening, everyone," Yasmin said into the microphone. "Thank you all for joining us tonight. We're going to start our formal program now with an introduction of my aunt Melba by her friend Dr. Cynthia Bridgeforth."

Cynthia looked regal in a semiformal black chiffon top and flowing black slacks. She trotted across the stage and gave Melba a lingering hug, which the audience applauded.

"Some of us hadn't expected to be here on a night like this, for this occasion," Cynthia finally said into the microphone. "Melba was sick. Really sick. She couldn't work, she couldn't take care of herself, and at one point, she could barely talk. But what we see standing before us—and what you saw dragged off the dance floor a few minutes ago—is the goodness of God.

"Melba is proof that nothing is too hard for him, if we will just trust and believe."

The crowd erupted into shouts of gratitude and applause.

Indigo looked at Hunt and winked. "Welcome to the black Baptist church," she said and laughed.

Hunt furrowed his brow.

"I'll explain later," she said and smiled.

Cynthia continued when the guests settled down. "Melba owns a hair salon, but any of you here who frequent the place know that she's more than just a stylist and she's more than just an entrepreneur. She is a mentor and a counselor and a prayer warrior when you need it the most. Her salon is part of the heart and soul of the Jubilant community.

"I think I'd be accurate in saying that's why most of us are here tonight—to honor a woman of God who has allowed herself to be his vessel, in whatever facet is needed. She is a gift to her family, a treasure to the community, and a friend to anyone in need of one."

Cynthia turned to Melba. "Melba, I thank God for you. Welcome back to Hair Pizzazz."

The crystal ball suspended from the ceiling began to swirl, and confetti showered everyone on the dance floor.

Aunt Melba took the microphone from Cynthia and waited for the commotion to die down. Tears were streaming from her eyes.

"Believe it . . . or not . . . I don't have much to say," she said. "I want to thank . . . Carmen, Eboni, and Carlotta . . . for carrying their load and mine . . . just days after Eboni and Carlotta agreed to work in my salon. I'm sure it was much more . . . than they . . . expected . . . to tackle. Carmen, thanks so much for staying on board and helping everything run so smoothly. You've been a great help to these two ladies as they took care of their own clients as well as mine."

She turned toward Indigo's parents and passed the microphone back to Cynthia, who pulled out a piece of paper.

"As you all see, Melba is doing fabulously well, but her speech still can be labored. She had so much to say that she realized it could take all night."

The crowd erupted in laughter.

"So," Cynthia continued, "she wrote the rest and asked me to read it to you, which I'll do now, on her behalf."

Melba stood beside Cynthia and read along as Cynthia shared her sentiments.

"'I can't say enough about my family, especially my sister, Irene, her husband, Charles, and their children, Indigo and Yasmin,'" Cynthia read. "'They took me in and nurtured me and never made me feel like a burden.

"'Indigo joined my staff and kept the business running like a pro, Rachelle and Yasmin chipped in often, and all I had to do was focus on getting well. Thank you, guys, I love you.'"

Aunt Melba clasped her hands and closed her eyes while Cynthia continued.

"'And what can I say about my almighty Father? There aren't enough words.'" Cynthia's voice quivered as she read. "'So I'll simply say thank you, for the good and the bad, because all of it drew me closer to you.'"

When Cynthia was done, Ms. Harrow approached Melba onstage with a massive, multicolored bouquet of flowers. Melba's eyes widened and a smile stretched across her face.

Suddenly, Indigo saw a flash. She had her camera tonight, but it was on the table. She scanned the crowd behind her to see who else had decided to capture memories. Her eyes landed on a suited-up Max. He was focusing his next shot and didn't notice her. She wiggled through pockets of people to reach him.

He grinned when he saw her and gave her a light hug.

"What are you doing here?" she asked.

"Nice to see you too, Ms. Burns," Max teased.

Indigo blushed. "I'm sorry—that was rude. It's nice to see you. How have you wound up at my aunt's party?"

"Melba Mitchell is well regarded and tons of people are here tonight," Max explained. "It's the social event of the month, and the *Herald* editor wants something for the society page. They called me up this morning and asked if I'd do it. Plus, it gives me an excuse to see you."

Before she could respond, Brian walked up behind her and

rested his hands on her shoulders. Indigo jumped and turned toward him.

"Um, Max, this is my fiancé, Brian Harper. Brian, this is Max Shepherd, the *Herald* photographer who took my photo for the newspaper's article on my *O Magazine* award."

Brian shook Max's hand, but didn't smile or speak.

Indigo was surprised.

"Nice to meet you, man," Max said. "You've got a gem here. Keep up with her."

"You can bet on that," Brian said. "Nice to meet you, Max."

Brian led Indigo away, to the dance floor. The DJ was playing Leona Lewis's version of "The First Time Ever I Saw Your Face," and he pulled her close.

"Should I be jealous?" he said in Indigo's ear.

Indigo smiled. "That would be cute, but unnecessary."

When they were done, Indigo noticed Max talking to Nizhoni. She was tempted to approach them and join in, but thought better of it. Instead, she sat next to Brian and watched them from afar. Maybe the real question was why was *she* jealous.

41

Indigo and Shelby were long overdue for some girlfriend time, and if they had to steal away after Aunt Melba's party to get it, so be it.

The celebration wound down around eleven p.m., and Hunt and Brian went to Gabe's to shoot pool. They would stay there for the night, in Gabe and Rachelle's guesthouse.

Aunt Melba had moved back home a few days earlier, so Shelby was staying with the Burnses, in the bedroom Melba had been using.

The room was Indigo's teenage bedroom, and she and Shelby sat on the floor now, remembering the times they had spent there during weekend visits from college.

Suddenly, though, the conversation took a turn.

"So do you love him?" Indigo had been dying to ask her friend.

Shelby had been talking about Hunt for about a year now, and yet, she'd still been cagey. She had told Indigo from the beginning that he was white, but she'd never really shared whether that made her hesitant to get serious about him.

In recent weeks, though, since her graduation from OCS, Shelby mentioned him when she talked about long-term career decisions.

They had visited each other's parents more than once, and Hunt was considering a job transfer from New York to his engineering firm's Fort Worth office, so he'd be somewhat closer to Shelby while she was in flight school in Corpus Christi.

Shelby sighed and hugged the fluffy purple pillow she had snagged from Indigo's bed.

"I do love him, Indie," she said. "But you know what? I'm scared."

"Why? You don't think he feels the same?"

"I know he does," Shelby said. "He asked me to marry him last week."

"What?" Indigo sat up straighter and stared at her friend. "Why am I just hearing about this? What did you say?"

Shelby looked away. "I didn't say anything because I'm scared. I'm scared to say yes and try to live in a world that won't accept us as an interracial couple. And I'm scared to say no because I love this man more deeply than I've ever loved anyone, and I don't know if I can breathe without him. He makes me a better person."

Indigo thought about the advice Rachelle and Gabe had given her and Brian last week and her heart sank.

Here she sat, wearing the beautiful engagement ring, with the gorgeous wedding dress on the way, and she felt nowhere close to what Shelby was describing about her feelings for Hunt.

She wanted to weep.

Shelby noticed. "What is it?"

Indigo shook her head and took a deep breath. "The way you feel about Hunt is love, Shelby. That's not how I feel about Brian. Intellectually, I know he's a good catch. In my head, I know that I would be foolish to let him slip through my fingers. I love him and care for him deeply, but I don't know that he completes me or that I do that for him.

"We're almost like two really good friends cruising in different directions. I want to focus on my photography career and he's going to be in the Navy, traveling and focusing on what he needs to do to rise through the ranks. He needs a wife by his side to help him succeed. I don't know that I can fill that role and do what my heart is calling me to do. I don't know that I love him enough to even give it a try."

Shelby sat there, wide-eyed.

Indigo continued. "But you, girlfriend, are smitten." She laughed. "Any man who can come to a Burns family party and hang like Hunt did tonight, and propose to you, and take you to meet his family, he's not playing."

Shelby smiled. "I know, Indie. I love him for that. He's so . . . he's just so . . . wonderful. Why couldn't he have been born with a permanent tan!"

They both roared with laughter.

"He probably wonders why you *were* born with a permanent one," Indigo said. "In an ideal romantic world, both of you would be black or both of you would be white. Isn't it funny, though, that love is color-blind? You can't help that the person who feeds your soul is very different from you in some ways. You went to a historically black college and dated just about every fine man on campus until you uncovered his flaws so you could dump him."

Shelby kicked Indigo's leg in jest.

"Then you go off to Florida and fall in love with a beach boy." Indigo laughed heartily at her own joke. "I'm not mad at you, Shelby. I'm not mad at all."

"I'll have you know that he's not a beach boy," Shelby said. "Hunt grew up in Cincinnati, thank you."

"Whatever," Indigo said. "How did he take it when you didn't respond to his proposal?"

"He got quiet and he said he knew I needed to think about it, and to let him know when I was ready to talk," Shelby said. "Then he gave me this amazing kiss that left my heart pounding and got in his car and drove back home."

Indigo fanned herself with her hand. "Shut up, girl! You gone make me find him and marry him!"

Shelby looked at her pointedly. "But you already have someone, remember? Your big day is just over four months away."

Shelby leaned back against the bed and looked at her friend. "Your aunt Melba was making her rounds tonight, making sure she talked to everyone she could. She pulled me and Hunt aside and told us that we should not let the world tell us who we are as individuals or as a couple, and if we decide to be together, let it be because we have decided that weathering the storm together is better than weathering it separately.

"Now that I think about her advice again, I realize that I shouldn't be afraid. I already know in my heart that I'd rather face the stares, the ugly comments, and the reality that some people will ostracize us, if I can be in his world. Otherwise, I'll be flailing about trying to find Mr. Right and working overtime to make him fit some set criteria."

"Like me," Indigo said softly.

She began to weep, because the message Aunt Melba shared with Shelby provided the answer she had needed all along. Now the question became, what was she going to do about it?

42

Brian hadn't slept well since his visit to Jubilant, and his mother had noticed.

"What's with the bags under the eyes, Son?" she asked one morning over breakfast. "You aren't in officer training anymore—you can sleep in as much as you'd like."

She sipped her coffee and watched him.

Brian squirmed under her gaze. He had always believed she had a built-in lie detector with his name emblazoned on it.

"Everything okay?" she asked.

"Why wouldn't it be?"

"Only you can answer that," Mary Harper said. "You're the one looking run-down, not me. How's Indigo?"

Now she was probing, trying to determine what could be stressing him out or keeping him awake at night. If she really knew, she'd be repulsed. Brian was.

He smiled at her and stroked her cheek. "I'm twenty-five years old, but I'll always be your baby, won't I? Even when I'm forty and balding."

"Even then," she said. "Nothing you can tell me, or do, will ever change that."

Nothing?

"I'm going away for a few days this weekend," he said suddenly, changing the subject. "I leave tonight."

Mom seemed surprised. "You were in Jubilant just last week. Are you going back already?"

Brian shook his head. "I'm meeting a Navy buddy in New York. We're going to catch a show on Broadway and just hang out. You know—kind of a bachelor thing before I get tied up in flight school and come back for the wedding."

Mom looked pensive. "No, I don't know. Who is this . . . friend? Why aren't you taking Indigo to the theater?"

"Why do you look so worried?" Brian asked. He shifted his deep brown eyes away from her matching ones. She didn't need to know that he hadn't mentioned the trip to Indigo. Indigo had been tied up with helping Aunt Melba settle back into her home, and was busy this weekend squaring away everything she'd need for grad school. He hadn't wanted to bother her. At least that's what he convinced himself.

"Are you meeting that guy Craig?" Mom asked.

Brian stopped breathing. "Why . . . why did you bring him up? How do you even remember him?" he stammered.

"I met him when we came up to Newport for visitors' weekend, remember?" she said. "I pegged him then for someone who had an interest in you. So what is this weekend about, Brian? Is there something that you need to tell your dad and me? Or Indigo?"

Brian averted his eyes again. His mind traveled back to the dinner two weekends ago when Rachelle and Gabe talked about the importance of living in truth. He wasn't sure he had that kind of courage. Then again, that's really what this trip to New York was about. He wanted to find out once and for all what was going on with him. He needed to discover the truth for himself before he could think about sharing it with Indigo, or anyone else.

Mom sat there waiting and he remembered she had hurled a series of questions at him.

"Everything is okay, Mom. Indigo and I are trying to get plans finalized for December. She's got a lot of great things going on between now and then, and so do I. I'm just letting my hair down with a friend."

But in his mother's eyes, he saw a truth that he wasn't ready to accept. She knew, or at least thought she knew, something about him that the rest of the world didn't. The revelation he saw there wasn't accompanied by anger, pain, or shame. He still saw his mother's love, mingled with a little pity, perhaps, for the fact that he felt the need to run from himself.

She reached for his hand and covered it with hers. "You're right, Son, you're twenty-five, and it's time that I let you grow up. You have a great weekend, and just know that I love you and I'm praying, as always, for God to guide you and bless you."

She pushed her chair from the table and headed upstairs, but not before Brian saw that her eyes were moist.

His heart stung. That alone should have led him to cancel this trip, but he didn't.

He couldn't.

Mom dropped him off at the airport at 4 p.m. so he'd have plenty of time to catch his 5:30 p.m. flight. He kissed her cheek before stepping out of the car and grabbing his bag. Her eyes raised the question he knew her heart was asking: Would he come back the same?

As he waited to board the plane, he prayed.

Show me what's what, God. Help me figure out whether I'm doing right by Indigo or whether I'm being selfish. Help me see the truth and give me the courage to accept it. Most of all, help me to please you.

Brian was afraid of this prayer, even as he uttered it. What if the truth were too ugly?

The answer that sufaced in his spirit settled him. If he were going to trust God in other ways, he had to trust him in this too.

43

*S*o why did you want to meet me? I thought you were done with me," Craig said as he and Brian walked through Times Square, on their way to Virgil's, for a late-night barbecue dinner.

The city that never slept was as busy at nine o'clock tonight as most other places were at noonday.

"I don't know," Brian said. He stuffed his hands deep into the pockets of his jeans, and looked everywhere but at Craig.

Craig stopped abruptly and blocked Brian's path, oblivious to the rush of people who were forced to navigate around them.

"You had me take the train to New York to meet you, and you don't know why we're here? My time is valuable. I'm heading back to Connecticut tonight."

Brian's stomach flip-flopped at the anger etched into Craig's features. His nostrils flared, his eyes were bulging, and a vein in his right temple pulsated rapidly.

"Come on, Craig," he said. "I'm just trying to figure things out, and I knew I could talk to you about it, because you've been there. Shelby's cool—she's not going to say anything. I made sure of that. I thought I could get your help working through some things."

"What?" Craig yelled. "I'm not a psychologist! I don't want

to get into your messed up mind. You need to grow up and stop playing games, man."

Brian stood there and took in Craig's fury. Craig was right: Brian couldn't expect a quick fix or answers to come from someone else. He had to look inside himself and honestly examine his thoughts and feelings.

"I'm sorry, man, you're right," Brian said. "I shouldn't have had you come here. I'll pay you back for your ticket."

With that, Craig's anger deflated. He led Brian from the middle of the sidewalk and they leaned against the side of a building. Brian watched yellow taxis squeeze into impossible spaces between cars and wondered how one learned to maneuver that effortlessly through life.

"What is it, Brian? Why are you fighting so hard with yourself?"

Brian looked at Craig. "I want to know why you aren't fighting. Have you accepted that you're . . . gay or bisexual?"

Craig frowned and shifted from one foot to the other. "Why do we have to label everything? Isn't that what women do? I haven't 'accepted' anything. I just live from day to day and do what feels good and most comfortable. I don't have a problem with experimenting with whoever happens to have my attention at a particular time.

"I'll probably settle down at some point and get married and have a few kids. I see that in my future. But until then, I'm okay playing both sides of the field."

"Would you tell your wife?"

"Why would I? What I've done in the past wouldn't affect her. She'll have a history too. We won't have to 'tell all' to build a future," Craig said. "When did you become so Goody Two-Shoes?"

Brian looked him in the eye. "I don't know, Craig, but I guess that's what has happened. I gave my life to Christ after my encounter with you, and I've been trying ever since to figure out what led me down that path with you. I don't know if I naturally have those tendencies, or if I was drunk and just yielded to what my body felt.

"I truly don't know, and I want to figure it out as soon as I can," he said.

Craig's eyes widened with recognition. "You're getting ready to marry Indigo, aren't you? And you want to know the real deal before you lock her down. Well, isn't that noble. Let me remind you—you weren't drunk the second time we hooked up."

Brian stared at Craig and fought the urge to beat him down. What came to mind was the Scripture his mother sometimes quoted when she found the need to distance herself from someone who wasn't being fair or good.

Don't cast your pearls before swine.

That's exactly what he was doing. He had flown all the way to New York to seek guidance from someone who didn't have a moral center or a desire to get at the truth.

Craig had always bragged about using any means and anyone to get what he wanted, like his father had taught him. Despite his dad going to prison for embezzlement Craig's senior year, Craig clearly still followed that advice. He had been ashamed of his father's conviction, but he was still determined to make his dad proud, and he hadn't changed his tactics for achieving that goal.

Another realization struck Brian: just because he was ready to explore these questions didn't mean he could force Craig to do the same. He was treading into areas where Craig wasn't yet ready to go. For Craig, this was still about the thrill of the moment, the rush of the conquest.

Brian could kick himself. How much more foolish could he have been?

And yet, as Craig moved in close to him on this bustling New York street and brushed his lips against Brian's, Brian was horrified to feel himself getting aroused.

Father God, relieve me of this . . . this curse!

That desperate prayer caused him to push Craig away and break into a sprint.

He heard Craig laughing as he got farther away.

"There's your answer, Harper!" Craig called after him. "Stop running from what you want!"

Brian turned into the narrow alley between two buildings and fell to his knees. Tears overtook him and he didn't try to stop them.

The problem was that he didn't want this; he didn't need this. But he was in a fix—he couldn't run away from his own life and he couldn't keep living a lie.

Finally, in this dark and dirty New York City alley, he had come face-to-face with his truth.

Now he needed to know what God wanted him to do with it, and what this would mean for his soul.

44

*I*f Yasmin grew any more excited, Indigo decided she'd take her to the Toys"R"Us store in Manhattan and let her entertain the throng of customers.

The two of them and their parents had landed at LaGuardia Airport an hour ago and were in a taxi headed for Ford Models.

Yasmin was all dolled up, with her long hair flowing down her back in spiral curls, deep pink gloss covering her lips, and the matching black jacket and jeans that Rachelle had bought her from a Houston boutique hugging her lanky frame.

Indigo felt dowdy in comparison, but she kept reminding herself that this afternoon wasn't about her. They would go apartment hunting for her tomorrow; today was about the family supporting Yasmin's dream.

Indigo offered to wait in the lobby of the modeling agency so they wouldn't look like a bunch of hillbillies from Texas, coming in four deep. But Mama insisted that she sit in on the meeting.

"You're almost a New Yorker—you can help your daddy and me figure out if they're trying to get over on us."

From what Indigo could tell, however, everything was on the up-and-up. Sasha Davies, the modeling scout who requested the meeting, reviewed the portfolio that Indigo had helped Yasmin develop and seemed impressed.

"I like the range of poses and settings," she said. "You have good form and great bone structure. Have you had any modeling training?"

"No, ma'am," Yasmin responded.

Sasha looked up at the girl, over her horn-rimmed glasses.

"Just 'no,' will do, sweetheart," she said. She looked at Indigo.

"I know you took the photo that drew our attention to your sister. Did you shoot these images as well?"

Indigo smiled. "Yes, I did."

Sasha seemed impressed again. "These are really good. You have a great eye and solid technique."

"Thank you," Indigo said. "I start grad school in another month at the School of Visual Arts, and I'm looking forward to learning as much as I can."

Sasha made a note in her file, then turned her attention to Mama and Daddy. "We'd like to sign Yasmin to a limited contract, which, for a fourteen-year-old who lives outside of the New York area, means we'll call her on a regular basis for jobs in the Dallas/ Houston area and occasionally for anything that requires travel. Unless you're planning to relocate to New York."

Mama's eyes grew wide. "Oh no," she responded "But as Indigo said, she'll be moving here in late August for grad school, so technically Yasmin would have somewhere to stay if she needed to be here for a stretch of time. Of course, my husband or I would want to be designated as her permanent companion."

Sasha nodded. "I understand. Parents often sign those rights over to a modeling agent or manager, but you're saying you'd like to retain those?"

Daddy spoke up. "If it's in her best interest to have an agent or a manager overseeing her career, that's fine. What we're talking about is the chaperone piece. We've decided that since she's still a minor, one of us will travel with her at all times. We're both retired, so that's doable for us."

"Okaaay." Sasha made another note in her book. Indigo wanted to laugh. This woman thought they were prudes, but so what—they were and it worked.

Sasha switched gears and turned her focus back to Yasmin.

"Stand up, Yasmin, and walk the length of the room for me," she said.

Indigo sensed her sister's nervousness, but Yasmin confidently followed direction.

"We need to work on your gait and your form a little bit, but you'll get there."

Sasha looked at the Burnses. "Would you be willing to let her attend a model training camp for preprofessionals in Upstate New York? It's held the third week in August and lasts for a week. Parent chaperones aren't allowed."

Mama and Daddy traded questioning glances.

"What's the curriculum, and who are the chaperones?" Daddy asked.

Sasha outlined the sessions that would be offered by some of the world's top-rate models and industry professionals, including a class on etiquette, money management, the price of fame, and the threat of eating disorders.

"We're serious about avoiding that with these girls, because an eating disorder can quickly derail their careers," Sasha said. "We have counselors there to work with girls already struggling with this issue to ensure that while they're working for us they receive regular support, and assistance, if necessary. We want them to be thin, but we also want them healthy."

Indigo and Yasmin eyed their parents. Indigo was relieved

when they simply nodded, without revealing what Yasmin had already been through.

They turned to Indigo, though, to get her thoughts about the camp.

"What do you think?"

"I think she should do it," Indigo said. "If you're going to allow her to launch a modeling career, this sounds like a great opportunity to learn about the pros and cons and what to realistically expect. It also would help her meet and befriend other girls her age who are doing the same thing."

Daddy pursed his lips for a few minutes before responding. He looked at Yasmin. "Can you handle it?"

Indigo knew Yasmin understood the question he was really asking.

"I'm ready, Daddy," Yasmin said. "I won't let you down."

Forty minutes later, a contract had been signed and it was official: Yasmin Burns would soon be gracing magazine spreads and advertisements across the southern region of the United States and occasionally other parts of the country.

When the family left Sasha's office and stood alone on the moving elevator, Indigo gripped Yasmin in a fierce embrace.

"I'm so proud of you! This is exciting!"

Indigo turned toward her parents and saw that they were holding hands and speaking a silent language with their eyes.

"What?" she asked.

Mama looked at her and at Yasmin and smiled. "Nothing. We just can't believe that both of you are growing up and finding your way in New York City, of all places. We've been preparing you for this day, but it's still bittersweet."

Yasmin leaned over and hugged Mama's neck. "Like you told Sasha, where I go, you go, so we're in this big city together. I'm still your baby, Mama. I don't mind if you want to tuck me in at night every now and then."

They laughed and departed from the elevator, all smiles.

Indigo had booked the family a hotel room in Lower Manhattan so they wouldn't be far from the subway line they would ride to apartment hunt tomorrow, or from the heart of the city if they wanted to catch a show.

The price hadn't been pretty, but Daddy had been willing to splurge.

"You're getting married soon, Indigo, and Yasmin's about to become Miss Cosmopolitan." He laughed. "Let me treat you girls with what I can afford while it still means something to you. I'm guessing both of you will be rolling in more dough than I've made my whole career."

The Burnses checked into their suite and relaxed for about an hour before Indigo got antsy.

"We should head over to the Theatre District and catch a show tonight," she suggested. "I'll go downstairs and see if they have any playbills."

When Indigo reached the lobby, she strode to the brochure rack that contained theater information and perused the offerings. After a few minutes, she decided to take one of each pamphlet so the family could review them together and make a decision.

On her way to the bank of elevators, she looked toward the hotel entrance and did a double take. A man with a build, complexion, and haircut similar to Brian's was leaving. He was casually dressed and rolled a suitcase behind him.

Indigo stopped and stared until he was out of sight. He never turned around, so she didn't see his face, but for as long as she had dated Brian, wouldn't she know him anywhere? And shouldn't she also know if he had come to New York?

45

Things hadn't been the same since New York.

More than once, Brian's parents, friends, and Indigo had told him he seemed lost in his own world. He consistently deflected their concern by questioning if they had secret fears about his joining the military in wartime. While he wouldn't be required to participate in ground combat in Iraq or Afghanistan, there was a good chance that as a pilot he could be assigned to serve somewhere near there. Instead, he insisted, preparing for flight school and the looming wedding had him distracted.

But every morning and then again at dusk when he left home for a seven-mile run to keep in shape for flight school, his thoughts would wander. Sometimes he wished he could shut them off.

The next best thing to do was to drown them out with prayer. And he did, fervently asking God to change him, to heal him, to give him a solution.

He loved Indigo, but he hated himself. He wanted a wife and children—a normal life. But he didn't want to live a lie.

For as long as he could remember, he had dreamed of becoming a Navy pilot and someday applying for astronaut status. That was still his goal, but if word leaked out about his college transgressions, or his recent temptations, those aspirations were as good as dead.

His mom and dad hadn't said much, but he could tell they were worried. He knew that his mom was praying on his behalf, asking God to take care of whatever was troubling her son.

His dad was watching him closely, trying to make sure he kept a handle on his future.

"Pace yourself, Son," he'd said more than once. "No need to burn out when you're just getting started. You've got dozens of years to get it all done. Slow and steady still wins the race."

Brian really didn't know what his father meant by all of that, but he was grateful for any sort of pep talk.

This afternoon, he took the first exit into Jubilant and looked at the phone number and address scrawled on the piece of paper in the passenger seat. Aunt Melba had given him Ms. Harrow's contact information, and he had called to ask her permission to cut some fresh flowers from her garden.

Five minutes later, her white brick rancher with green shutters came into view. He pulled into the driveway and followed the rose trail up the sidewalk. Before he could ring the doorbell, she opened the beveled glass outer door and welcomed him inside. She served him a glass of tea and told him the story behind the garden and how she had come to know Melba and eventually Indigo.

Indigo had shared the same details months ago, which was why he knew she'd appreciate these flowers versus a dozen store-bought roses, but he listened anyway.

"I'm honored that you want flowers from my garden for Indigo," Ms. Harrow said when she led him outside to the vast backyard. She gave him a pair of garden shears and fanned her arm out. "Take your pick." She also handed him a glass vase, with a white ribbon tied around the body.

223

Seeing Brian's surprise, she laughed. "Yes, I keep a supply of vases and ribbons—you never know when you want to give someone a gift from the garden. I do that often, so I finally decided to stock up and stop running to the store every week."

"You're amazing," he said.

Ms. Harrow blushed. "Thank you, dear. It's not often that I hear such kind words from such a handsome man."

She stood next to him as he surveyed the reams of flowers of all hues and heights, and struggled to decide what he wanted. She patted his arm and smiled at him.

"Take your time, dear," she said. "I'm going inside to get supper started, but don't feel rushed. I want you to pick what's right for you and for Indigo—she's a special girl.

"And while you're here, take some quiet time for yourself. I know Melba and Indigo have told you this is a prayer garden too. I know for a fact that God dwells here—this has become my sanctuary."

Brian watched her stroll into the house and waited to see if she would peek at him in a few minutes from the kitchen window. She didn't, and when he turned his attention back to the view and space before him, he felt as if he were indeed in a sanctuary, a private garden in which he could meet God.

A sweet silence enveloped him, and he felt his heart rate slow. Brian realized in that moment that he had been doing all the talking in his prayers. Now it was time to listen.

He sat on the C-shaped stone bench near a bed of tulips and lowered his head to his knees. He closed his eyes and waited. No need to say a word. No need to cry. He just listened with his heart and with his soul and allowed God to pour the answers into him.

Half an hour later, Brian raised his head, inhaled deeply, and stood up to cut his beautiful Indigo some flowers. Four years ago today, they had officially become a couple, and he wanted to give her something special.

He picked four pink roses and a handful of purple daisies to complement them, knowing she'd be happy to receive something in her favorite colors. He also took a single red rose, to symbolize his never-ending love.

Brian pulled a $50 bill from his pocket and placed it on the stone bench under a small rock from the garden. He found one of his business cards from his engineering days in his wallet and scribbled a brief note on the back for Ms. Harrow, telling her to consider the money an offering for the upkeep of this special space, and thanking her for her kind heart and generosity.

He walked to his car with the vase of flowers and uttered another prayer.

Thank you.

Regardless of what loomed, God had shown him during that quiet time that he wasn't alone, and he never would be, as long as he listened and obeyed.

46

Oasis was a new, fine dining restaurant in Jubilant, owned by two Everson College professors, and it was the perfect place to celebrate an anniversary.

The soft lighting created a romantic ambiance, and the live piano music was engaging. Formally dressed waiters discreetly hovered and appeared trained not to eavesdrop on their diners' conversations.

If Indigo weren't already engaged, she would have considered it the perfect spot for Brian to propose.

She looked at him now, sitting across from her, smiling at her. She cried earlier, when he gave her the flowers from Ms. Harrow's garden. The fact that he had been thoughtful enough to find out where Ms. Harrow lived and to pick the flowers himself touched her.

She had so much to be thankful for. Her glaucoma wasn't bothering her, she had a regular photo column in the local newspaper, her work would soon be featured in *O Magazine*, and she was heading off to the grad school of her dreams.

Life was so good, and so full, and she was blessed to have this wonderful man to share it with.

In the weeks since her late-night chat with Shelby, however,

Indigo had realized a pivotal truth: Brian was good, kind, and faithful, and he was everything a woman could want in a partner; yet he didn't rate a mention on her list of the primary things that she couldn't live without. She loved him, without question. But she had been asking herself lately if she loved him like Rachelle loved Gabe, or like Shelby loved Hunt, or like Mama and Daddy loved each other—hard and long, through thick and thin.

Rachelle and Gabe had overcome the rocky foundation upon which they began married life. Shelby and Hunt were navigating their bond through the rough winds that still caused turbulence among blacks and whites. Daddy had stuck by Mama when alcohol had its grip on her life, and she sometimes spoke of weathering the year he had a midlife crisis and seemed to forget he had a family.

Brian was her safety net, and ultimately, that was why she couldn't marry him.

Not when she was surrounded by people who exemplified the beauty of a union formed with care. Not when God was showing her that if she trusted him instead of always doing what was safe, he would take her places and give her experiences more awesome than she could fathom.

She looked at this man now, whom she had loved since she was nineteen, and she didn't want to let him go. But because she loved him, she would.

She and Brian chatted over dinner about nothing in particular—the training he had been doing to stay in shape for flight school, the exciting things on the horizon for Yasmin, Aunt Melba's gradual return to styling hair, the apartment her parents had leased for her in New York.

"It's about the size of a doghouse, and costs as much as a penthouse, but I can survive in it," she said and laughed. "Speaking of

New York, I've been meaning to tell you that I saw your twin at the hotel we stayed in during our visit."

The waiter appeared with two forks and the miniature chocolate lava cake they had ordered.

Indigo dug in, but Brian seemed to have lost interest.

"What did you say?"

She swallowed her bite and resumed the conversation. "We checked into a Marriott hotel in Lower Manhattan and I went down to the lobby to get theater brochures, and a man was leaving the hotel who looked just like you."

Brian frowned and looked sick. He took a deep breath and bit his bottom lip.

"You okay?" Indigo asked.

Brian nodded and motioned for her to put her hands in his.

She laid her fork down and complied, not sure where this was going.

"Indigo, that was me you saw that day. I was in New York and never told you."

"Okaaay . . . ," she said, trying to keep her mind from racing with all kinds of scenarios. "Why didn't you tell me? We talked that weekend. You didn't tell me you weren't in Austin. That whole time, that's where I thought you were."

"I went to New York for a personal reason and I wanted to get the answer before I told you," he said.

Indigo was getting impatient. He could stop using code language and spell it out, or she would strangle the truth out of him.

"Keep talking, Brian," she said.

"Indigo." He looked around to make sure no one was nearby, then sat back and folded his arms. "You know what? I really need to talk to you about this, and this isn't the place. Let's finish dessert and go."

This sudden mystery had killed her appetite. If the Brian she'd felt bad about not wanting to marry was a cheat and liar, she was going to hurt him. With her bare hands. Forget the lava cake. It was time to go.

"Why don't you just get the check, Brian," she said. "You can take the cake with you. You've got me too curious to wait."

They left as quickly as Brian could pay the tab, and he drove to downtown Jubilant and parked in front of the public library. The parking lot was empty and the steep stairs leading into the building were as impressive as those leading to the White House.

The night wasn't too humid; it was perfect for a walk.

"This isn't the lake or the beach, but do you want to get out and sit on the steps?" he asked. "It's still our anniversary, you know."

Indigo, tense from all of the suspense, remained silent but climbed out of the Saturn. She followed him up the stairs and took a seat on a step halfway from the top, where she waited for him to finish what he had started. The full moon provided some light, as did the city streetlights lining the sidewalk below them.

He sat next to her for a while without speaking.

When he faced her, there were tears in his eyes. "Indigo, I love you with all my heart, and because of that, I can't marry you."

She gasped. Forget that she'd come to the same conclusion herself earlier tonight; what had he been wrestling with?

He looked away and then squared his shoulders before facing her again. "I've been running away from myself for a long time, and I was fortunate to run right into your arms. I'm not going to label myself, but I've realized recently that I have certain feelings for men that aren't appropriate for someone who is planning to get married."

Indigo stood up and inched away from him. "Are you telling me that you're gay? I've been in love with you and you've been using me as a cover-up?! YOU—"

She had to be dreaming. This was horrible.

Brian approached her and grabbed her by the arms so she wouldn't flee. "You are not a cover-up, Indie. I'm telling you that I have these tendencies, that have surfaced out of nowhere, and it wouldn't be fair for me to marry you and live a lie. I want to marry you, because I love you, and I want to be the father of your children. But I can't force you to deal with the demons I'm still confronting."

He released his grip on her and sat on the step. Sobs began to wrack his body so furiously that Indigo thought he would lose his meal.

She was angry and embarrassed. Stunned and deeply hurt.

But suddenly she was filled with compassion for him, and she began to weep. The Brian she knew would never deceive her on purpose. He had always been her protector, her friend, and her advocate. She had never seen him this broken, and she knew the revelation pained him more than it wounded her.

Indigo knelt beside him and hugged his neck, until he lifted his head and looked into her eyes.

"You don't hate me?"

She wiped his tear-streaked face with her thumbs.

"I don't hate you, Brian," she said and sighed. "I'm furious with you, but I don't hate you."

47

*W*hat pierced her heart more than Brian's revelation was discovering that Shelby knew.

"You are my sister! How could you!" Indigo whispered vehemently into the phone. She was talking softly because she didn't want anyone to overhear. Besides, she was in so much pain that the sound of her own voice grated her spirit.

While she had determined before his confession that she and Brian couldn't marry, hearing his reasons for reaching the same conclusion had left her shell-shocked. To learn that Shelby had kept his secret all these years was like a knife in the heart.

Both of them were crying as they held the phone.

It was Saturday morning, the day after Indigo's dinner with Brian, and she hadn't slept all night. She kept reliving their conversation on the library steps and all that he had told her about his encounters with Craig, his trip to New York, and the realization that he wasn't fit to be her husband.

He had dropped her off at home around midnight and walked her to the front door. She was carrying the vase of flowers he had given her before dinner, and before he turned to leave, he pulled a single red rose from behind his back.

"I saved this for last," he told her. "Whenever you see a red rose, always know that wherever you are and whatever you are going through, your Brian loves you."

Still hurt and angry, she had taken the flower, but hadn't responded. She entered the house without telling him goodbye.

By six a.m. she was dialing Shelby's number, and her best friend's silence after hearing the news let her know that Shelby wasn't surprised.

"You're too quiet," Indigo said. "How long have you known Brian went both ways?"

When Shelby didn't answer, Indigo wanted to scream. She paced her bedroom floor, cradling the cordless phone with one hand and clinching the other to keep her composure. The two people she thought she knew best were turning out to be the biggest strangers.

"I didn't want to hurt you, Indigo," Shelby finally said. "And I kept praying that Brian would work it all out, that what he had done was nothing more than college experimentation. Shortly after I caught him and Craig, Brian joined church and got baptized, remember? I thought his heart was all yours at that point."

"But you had to question whether something was going on between them while you were at OCS, after he had asked me to marry him," Indigo said. "I'm not understanding, Shelby, and maybe I never will."

Indigo hung up on her friend and flung herself across the bed. She cried herself into a fitful sleep, thankful that she had taken the day off from Hair Pizzazz, anticipating that she would be out late with Brian.

Mama knocked on the door around noon to check on her. "You okay in there, Indigo? I haven't seen you since you left yesterday with Brian. Don't you want lunch?"

Indigo wasn't ready to tell Mama everything was over. Brian

hadn't asked her to keep his revelation a secret, but he had explained that life in the Navy would be unbearable if word got out. His dream of becoming an astronaut would be dust. She was wrestling with how to handle this.

"I'm not feeling well, Mama," Indigo said weakly. "I may not get up today."

At three p.m., Yasmin came in to check on her. She was sleeping when she felt her sister's hand on her forehead.

"No fever. No vomiting. Do you have a bug or something? Mama thinks you and Brian must have had a fight," Yasmin said. "He hasn't called today."

Yasmin perched herself on the end of the bed and waited for an answer.

Indigo knew she must look as bad as she felt; therefore, she wasn't lying. She *was* sick. Heartsick.

"I'll be fine, Yas," she said, dodging the question. "Just let me rest."

The next knock came at seven p.m. Indigo rolled over to glare at whoever was about to enter.

When the door crept open, though, she sat up in shock. Shelby turned on the light and closed the door behind her. She walked over to the bed and stood before Indigo.

"I drove down as soon as I could get out of Austin," she said. "You are my sister and I couldn't leave things like this between us. I am sorry. I apologize for not telling you what I knew, but I honestly didn't want to cause trouble if Brian was going to do right by you."

Indigo stared at her. The fact that Shelby had come said a lot. Still, how could she forgive her?

"I had decided I wasn't going to marry him, before he even told me," Indigo said.

233

Shelby moved closer to the bed, but remained standing.

"I came to that conclusion over dinner, I guess around the same time he was finding the courage to tell me the truth." She motioned for Shelby to sit on the bed, which her friend did. "I'm not so mad at the fact that we didn't work out, or that he dumped me before I could dump him. It's the fact that I was in a relationship with him for all of these years, and his heart and soul weren't really mine. Does that make sense?"

"Maybe what you're really angry about is the fact that you came so close to marrying him, and if he hadn't decided to tell you the truth, you could have been his wife and have never known," Shelby said.

Indigo nodded. That was it exactly.

"And you would have helped facilitate the sham, Shelby." Indigo glared at her. "I can't get over that, either."

Shelby looked away and then heavenward. "I've been praying about this all the way here, Indie, and I don't know. I don't know whether I should have told you or let Brian come clean on his own. I've been praying for him to do that for years, or to purge that side of himself so he could be the husband you needed him to be."

She leaned forward and locked eyes with Indigo. "Tell me—what would you have done if this were Gabe, and Rachelle didn't know? Would you tell her?"

Indigo formed her lips to utter a defiant yes, but hesitated. Would she?

She pictured Gabe and Rachelle dancing at her graduation party and counseling her and Brian over dinner. She saw them lounging around their backyard pool, shooting the breeze with Tate and Taryn, and making eye contact every so often.

What if Gabe had a heartbreaking secret that would devastate Rachelle if she knew? Would she be the one to tell or would she encourage Gabe to do the right thing? Indigo realized that she didn't know.

She shook her head and swiped a fresh flow of tears with the back of her hand. "I see how that could be a hard call to make," she said. "But it doesn't hurt any less. Just know that from this day forward, you have my permission to tell me anything, even if it's just a suspicion. You kept this stuff about Brian to yourself because you didn't want to hurt me, but do you see me now? Even after I knew I wasn't going to marry him, the revelation still broke my heart. You see?"

Shelby was crying too. "I see. And I'm sorry."

Indigo sat back on her pillow and pulled her knees up to her chest. She rested her chin there and let her thoughts wander. "I have a wedding to cancel," she said softly.

Shelby squeezed her hand. "Tell me what you need me to do. I'm here."

Indigo stared at her friend, willing herself to trust Shelby and forgive her, despite the inclination to push her away. Intellectually, she knew that Shelby hadn't meant to hurt her; now her heart had to catch up.

"I need you to do two things for me," Indigo said. "Don't tell a soul—not even his parents or mine—about the reality that's only Brian's to share, whenever and however he wants. I owe him that much."

Shelby nodded. "Of course. I love Brian, too, remember?"

Indigo glanced at Shelby's hands and noticed that her fingers were bare.

"What else?" Shelby asked.

"Take my custom-ordered wedding dress off my hands," Indigo said. "I can't send it back and I can't use it now. Get it tailored to fit your petite frame and marry that man who loves you."

48

It felt good, but strange, to be sitting in this chair again, with Aunt Melba standing behind her, blow-drying her hair.

"Don't have another stroke while you're working on us," Indigo teased above the roar of the heat.

Rachelle, who was waiting to get her freshly washed hair blow-dried and styled, chuckled. "Don't give her any ideas, Indigo. You know this woman likes drama."

Aunt Melba thumped Indigo's shoulder, then wagged her finger at Rachelle. "I'm not thinking about you two. God has been too good to me to turn back now. Aunt Melba is back, badder than ever, ladies. Ya better watch out!"

They laughed and waved goodbye to Eboni, who had finished her last customer for the evening and was heading home.

Aunt Melba yawned and grabbed the flatiron to curl Indigo's hair. Indigo knew she must be tired; she had manned the reception desk all day. Rachelle and Indigo were her only clients, and she had agreed to see them after hours so she wouldn't miss calls.

Now that she was styling more customers and Yasmin was gone to modeling camp, Taryn had been serving as the receptionist a few hours a day, between her summer camp sessions. But she would be starting school soon, and Melba needed assistance on a regular basis.

"I'm meeting with a few people from a temp agency tomorrow, but I'd prefer someone I know, or a referral that I'm confident will do a professional job."

She paused and peered at Indigo.

"You sure you want to go to grad school? I offer good benefits."

Indigo rolled her eyes. She would suffocate if she stayed in Jubilant after all that had transpired.

It had been two weeks since she and Brian had broken up, and she was finally beginning to feel like herself. With the time to leave for grad school quickly approaching and positive feedback from her photo column in the *Herald* continuing to come in, she had been less depressed than she had expected.

She and Brian had told her parents together that they had decided to end their engagement and remain friends. Daddy and Mama were stunned. They loved Brian as if he were their son. They wanted a legitimate explanation.

Indigo had led the conversation and told them that the timing wasn't right, they were going in different directions, and they had decided to call things off and wish each other the best.

Brian told his parents on his own, and later assured Indigo that a similar conversation had taken place. She wondered whether he would ever tell his parents the truth. Nevertheless, she was thankful he had bared his soul to her.

Aunt Melba didn't scold her this evening for the unbecoming eye gesture. She patted Indigo's shoulder.

"How are you doing?"

Indigo knew this question would come as soon as the salon was empty. Rachelle hadn't asked much either, so she was waiting for an update too.

"I'm fine," Indigo said. "Believe it or not, we went to dinner on the night of our dating anniversary and both of us were sitting there trying to figure out how to break up with the other person. Brian went first, and that hurt, but . . . we just couldn't go on.

"I've been angry at him, and truthfully, I'm still upset about some things he should have shared with me a long time ago. But I'm working through that, and I'll be okay."

Rachelle nodded. "Yes, you will. Broken hearts do mend. The scars remain, but the healing will begin soon, and hopefully you can focus on the positive things Brian brought to your life. The most important gift he gave you was the freedom to find someone who will love you better than he could have."

Indigo tried to smile. "I hope you're right. But it's hard."

She twisted her head and looked up at Aunt Melba. "I've been meaning to ask if you remember what you were going to share with me the day you had your stroke. You had noticed some doubt when I got engaged, and you were going to offer some advice."

Melba put a hand on her hip and smirked. "I lived with you for months and you never asked—now you expect me to pull that information from my memory bank?"

Indigo chuckled. "Sorry. I guess it doesn't matter anyway, now that we're not getting married."

Aunt Melba resumed curling Indigo's hair. "I think I was going to tell you not to compromise your happiness to make someone else happy. If your decision didn't sit well with your soul, that was God telling you to wait. When it comes to major life decisions like marriage or your education or your career, if you sacrifice so deeply to please others, your needs stop mattering—to you and to them. You can lose the power of being you. I was worried that might happen when I saw you accept the proposal halfheartedly, just to avoid controversy."

Indigo nodded. "You were right on the money, as usual. I guess there's something to be thankful for, in all of this. And to be honest, if you had shared that advice with me back in May, I might have brushed it off. I wasn't ready for it then."

Rachelle leaned forward in her chair. "The most important thing you can do now, Indigo, is forgive yourself and forgive Brian. Whatever happened or didn't happen between you two, give yourselves credit for doing the best you could at the time. Forgive and move on, or it will gnaw at your insides and keep you from receiving all of the beautiful things God has in store for you."

"I'm trying," Indigo said. "It's hard, but I'm really trying."

Her cell phone rang just as Aunt Melba grabbed an oversized mirror to show Indigo her hairstyle.

"Just a minute, Aunt Melba," Indigo said. "It's Nizhoni. Let me see if it's urgent."

Seconds later, she turned toward her aunt. "Nizhoni wants to know if she can come by to get her hair rebraided." Indigo glanced at the clock. It was seven p.m. "Want me to tell her to come tomorrow?"

"If she comes right now, I'll fit her in," Aunt Melba said. "It shouldn't take long."

49

*N*izhoni wasn't her usual chipper self.

She hugged Indigo, Rachelle, and Aunt Melba and thanked Melba for agreeing to take her on such short notice.

Aunt Melba surveyed her head. "That braid looks nice and neat to me; what are you tampering with it for? Because your hair needs to be washed?"

Nizhoni looked at Indigo, who understood immediately.

"Something happen today?"

"Brides Central isn't doing well this quarter—too many brides going to Houston to pick out their gowns," Nizhoni said. "I got laid off today. I need to get my hair rebraided to keep myself from fretting."

Aunt Melba and Rachelle looked confused.

"What?" Melba said, her hand on her hip. "What does braiding have to do with losing your job?"

Rachelle closed the magazine she had been reading while Melba curled her hair.

Indigo explained about the Native American practice of braiding up one's problems to tuck them away and how Yasmin had been braiding Nizhoni's hair for a while now.

"Obviously, then, other things were troubling you before this layoff," Aunt Melba said. She looked at Rachelle. "Mind if I get her started and come back to you?"

Rachelle shrugged. "No problem."

Indigo smiled at Rachelle and Rachelle winked. Both of them knew Aunt Melba had something to share.

Carmen had left for the evening, so Melba led Nizhoni to the shampoo bowl and loosened the braid. She leaned Nizhoni's head back and washed her flowing hair.

Nizhoni was silent for a while, but as Aunt Melba massaged her scalp, she visibly relaxed.

"Yeah, I got troubles." She sighed. "When I first started coming here to get my hair braided, I was living in my car. I had just landed the job at the bridal shop, but things were really tight. My parents back in Oklahoma weren't getting along and, in their tug-of-war with each other, couldn't help me.

"Braiding the troubles up helped me push forward and go to work with a smile every day. I managed to get a nice apartment after I worked for a few months and even opened a bank account. I have some money saved and I'm hoping it will tide me over until I get another job."

Nizhoni's head still rested in the shampoo bowl, but she turned her eyes in Indigo's direction. "They're great people at the bridal shop and said I can come in occasionally to consult with clients who personally request me, so if Shelby needs my help with your . . . uh, her wedding dress, I'm happy to do it."

Aunt Melba listened and slathered conditioner on Nizhoni's hair.

"I'm so sorry, Nizhoni," Indigo said. "All this time we've been building a friendship, I had no idea what you were going through. If I had known, I would have helped."

Aunt Melba sat Nizhoni upright and put a shower cap on her head so the conditioner could soak in for a few minutes.

"I wouldn't have burdened you with that, Indigo," Nizhoni said. "I decided before I moved to Jubilant that I was going to be a responsible adult, unlike some of the ones who 'graced' my life when I was growing up. I had to deal with the good and the bad on my own to prove to myself that I could make it. I made it through that rough patch, and I'll make it through this one."

Melba rinsed and blow-dried Nizhoni's hair with a deftness that Indigo viewed as a gift. It would have taken her hours to manage that much length. Indigo realized Nizhoni hadn't been joking when she said she could sit on it.

Instead of parting it like Yasmin usually did, however, Aunt Melba grabbed her flatiron.

"What are you doing?" Nizhoni asked.

"You just sit back and trust Aunt Melba, okay?"

Nizhoni looked skeptical, but she didn't argue.

Fifteen minutes later, Indigo was speechless. She had watched her friend be transformed from a subtly attractive woman to a beauty with tendrils and curls framing her face in all the right places.

"You look amazing," said Rachelle, who sat transfixed as Aunt Melba worked.

But Nizhoni wasn't happy. She was near tears.

"Thank you," she said to Aunt Melba, "but you don't understand. I need my braid. Can you please just braid it for me?"

Aunt Melba came around the chair to face Nizhoni and grasped her hands.

"Baby, you don't need that braid to help you, you need God to walk with you," she said softly. "I'll braid it back up if you want me to. I want you to leave here comfortable. But I also want you to know that braid is serving as your anchor, as your safety, when the answers and the strength and the wisdom you have needed to succeed already lies within you. You just need to pray to tap into it. Pray and ask God to guide your heart and spirit and to help you bear your troubles. That's the same thing as tucking them away—you just don't have the visual reminder."

Nizhoni bowed her head and removed her hands from Melba's. She wouldn't look in the mirror.

"I'm sure it's beautiful," she said, "but could you please braid it for me?"

Aunt Melba looked at her and patted her knee. "If that's what you'd like, sweetheart, I'm happy to do it."

Indigo and Rachelle looked on as Aunt Melba combed out the waves and curls and brushed Nizhoni's hair back so she could braid it.

When she was done, Nizhoni seemed to exhale.

Aunt Melba handed her a mirror.

"Thank you," she said and hugged Aunt Melba's neck.

She quickly paid her and hugged Indigo and Rachelle goodbye. Before she reached the door, Aunt Melba called after her.

"Nizhoni, this place is not quite as fun as working in a bridal shop, but if you want, you can start here on Monday as my receptionist. Call me tomorrow and we can talk about compensation."

Nizhoni's eyes widened. "I love this place, Melba. I would be honored."

Aunt Melba smiled.

"So would I, baby. God sent you at the right time."

50

*B*rian felt like he was five years old again.

He sat in the church in which he and Shelby had grown up, with Mom and Dad flanking him.

He would be leaving in two weeks for flight school, and Pastor Richardson wanted to have special prayer for him this morning and next Sunday. He was thankful; he needed it.

He hadn't known how he would feel coming into this sanctuary after all that had gone on the past few weeks, but he realized as he joined in with singing the morning hymn that, just as the lyrics professed, he had "come this far by faith."

He had been baptized here, received his Eagle Scout badge as part of the church Boy Scout troop, and even snuck his first kiss with a cute girl in his Vacation Bible School class. This place was part of him. It had helped shape him into the man he had become.

He looked to his left and smiled at Dad, who nudged him with his elbow, and then to his right and smiled at Mom, who patted his hand. That was the hazard of being an only child, he guessed. Once their baby, always their baby.

As Pastor Richardson prepared to deliver his sermon, Brian recalled the last time he had been in this church, right before he left for Officer Candidate School. What had been the beginning of a promising adventure, leading him to indeed become an officer, also had caused his life to change forever. He couldn't have predicted that he would confront his past and alter his future over the course of the summer. He wondered this morning, if he had known the twists and turns he would take, would he still have gone?

But the past was the past. It was part of his truth and he had to live with it. His special time with God in Ms. Harrow's backyard garden had helped him understand that and accept that God loved him no matter what.

He glanced at his parents again. Mom had already pledged her allegiance without knowing any details, but what would Dad say if he knew? Dad was a Navy man through and through. Could he handle this kind of truth?

Brian had come to realize that really, the only one who needed to handle it was him, and if he did, he'd be able to hold his head high.

What saddened him most was the pledge he had made to God that would keep his wonderful parents from ever having biological grandchildren. He wasn't going to marry someone, start a family, and live a lie. Maybe he would adopt someday, but certainly not while he was jet-setting around the world with the Navy.

He also wasn't going to live a life that displeased God, if he could help it.

Brian had been reading 2 Corinthians in recent weeks and studying how Paul struggled with a problem, a thorn in his side that caused him to fail and wrestle with his human weaknesses. Brian had concluded that he wasn't any different. He had to wrestle with a temptation he didn't want to yield to, so he could give his best to God.

245

A wife? Probably not. No children? An even harder reality to accept.

But the alternative right now seemed much worse. He could have been selfish and married Indigo, but in the end, he would have tainted her life and damaged his soul.

Brian shook himself back into the present and realized he had missed most of the sermon. He hoped God would appreciate that his heart and spirit were vested in this worship service.

Shelby wasn't here this morning, but her parents were, and when he looked their way, they acknowledged him with a pride that was as joyful as if he were their son.

The members of Grace Temple loved him, and that was gratifying. Shelby loved him too; she had told him so. Their friendship was solid.

Indigo? He didn't blame her for not returning his calls or responding to his emails. He would have to live with that and keep forgiving himself for hurting her until he was at peace.

But today, he felt good about embracing his truth, and he trusted that because he was being obedient, God would not allow him to wallow in sadness and loneliness for the rest of his days. Single men and women across this land thrived and had full lives. He would learn how to be one of them.

51

Indigo was glad Shelby hadn't insisted they go to church. She couldn't have sat in the same sanctuary as Brian without turning into a sobbing mess.

Instead, the two of them had played hooky this morning and were sitting in front of the computer, viewing screen after screen of bridesmaid dresses.

Shelby repositioned herself in the leather chair and leaned her head back. She closed her eyes and sighed. "You know what? I want to marry Hunt, but I don't want to do this."

Indigo scooted her folding chair closer and poked Shelby's shoulder. "Stop being a wimp, Shel. You've described your dream wedding to me a thousand times. Now that your groom is going to be a few shades lighter than you had imagined, you feel the need to change everything?" She sat back and folded her arms. "Wish I had your problems."

Shelby opened her eyes and looked toward her friend. Indigo recognized the pity that filled them. Every little bit of compassion helped as Indigo still struggled to forgive her.

"This is really selfish of me, isn't it?" Shelby said. "I asked you to come up and spend the weekend with me and here we are looking at wedding stuff when you're still nursing a broken heart."

Indigo shook her head. She had to man up and quit wearing her sadness on her sleeve.

"This is what we need to be doing. I'm leaving for grad school soon and you'll be in Corpus Christi, wrapped up in flight school training. I know your older sisters and your mom will do whatever you need, but I want to make sure you and I nail down your preferences first. You deserve to have a beautiful wedding."

Shelby hugged her neck. "If nothing else, I have a beautiful friend," she said softly.

Shelby's parents sauntered into the family room, still dressed in the suits they had worn to worship service.

"Church was good today," Mr. Arrington said. "Should have been there, ladies."

Indigo read the look Shelby gave her mom as a silent plea for support.

"You guys know why we stayed home," Shelby said with an edge to her voice. "It would have been too much, too soon."

Indigo reminded herself that, other than Shelby, no one knew the real reason for the breakup. She was sure that Shelby's mother and Brian's mother had been trading phone calls and speculating why she and Brian had ended their engagement. Was it Brian's fault or Indigo's? Had one of them found someone else?

Mrs. Arrington was fond of her, but Indigo knew she loved Brian like the son she'd never had. She was fiercely loyal to him, and to his mother.

Indigo wondered this afternoon whether that would change if she knew Brian's secret. She was sad that his unwillingness to be real meant they both had to live under a shadow of suspicion. She decided in this moment, however, that she could handle it. Regardless of whether the Arringtons or the Harpers accepted her, she would hold her head high.

The phone rang and Mr. Arrington stretched to grab a cordless receiver from one of the end tables. He gazed at caller ID and his pensive stare told Indigo it was Hunt.

"Are you going to answer, Daddy?" Shelby asked. "Hunt promised to call around this time."

He sighed and pressed Talk on the third ring.

"Arrington residence," he said dryly. "Oh, hello, Hunt. I'm doing well. You been to church today? Uh huh. We'll have to talk more about these kinds of things the next time you come to visit. Or better yet, maybe the next time you call. Here's my daughter."

He extended the phone toward Indigo and she passed it to Shelby. Mr. Arrington stuffed his hands in his pockets and left the room. Mrs. Arrington waved lightly and followed him.

"Tell Hunt I said hello," she mouthed to Shelby before she was out of sight.

Now Indigo understood. Shelby didn't want a wedding because she didn't want her own folks acting like fools. She had said her mom liked Hunt and was happy about their engagement, but clearly Mr. Arrington wanted to haze his future son-in-law.

"Yeah, babe," Shelby said into the phone. "I miss you too."

She glanced at Indigo and again seemed filled with sympathy.

"Let me call you back a little later, okay? Indie's still here and I want to make the most of our time together. Don't worry about Daddy. We'll pair him and your mom at the wedding reception so they can commiserate."

Shelby chuckled and hung up. She turned toward Indigo and sighed. "You see why I'm thinking about skipping the wedding? We can get married at Grace Temple, with Pastor Richardson and just two witnesses."

Indigo nodded. "I see why you're stressed. I'm surprised that your daddy is tripping like this."

"That's because he likes to control everything. He already had me married off, to his law partner's son. But I haven't seen Garrett Lee in three years—plus, we've never dated. I told him he had to give that pipe dream up; I wasn't into arranged marriages."

They covered their mouths to stifle their laughs.

"What about your mom?" Indigo asked.

"She really likes Hunt, and she says she can tell that he genuinely loves me," Shelby said. "That's all that matters to her. She wants me to be loved, treated with respect, and taken care of properly."

Indigo chuckled again. "That sounds like the description of a Southern belle beauty queen, not some little woman who just went through the Navy's most rigorous training program, with dreams of flying helicopters and space shuttles."

Shelby pushed the chair away from the computer and walked over to the palladium window. Her eyes traveled to her neighbor's backyard, and Indigo saw her watching a group of kids frolic on a swing set.

"Nothing about my life is that uncomplicated, or typical, anymore," Shelby said.

Indigo joined her at the window to watch the happy children. "I concur, Officer Arrington. But maybe this is how God intended it. If everything were cookie-cutter perfect, I guess we wouldn't rely on him to lead us, right? The main thing is to walk in truth and in love, with everybody—yourself, Hunt, your parents, and his. Don't let someone else's hang-ups keep you from following your heart. You make the memories you want for you and Hunt, as long as they honor God."

Shelby turned toward Indigo and gazed at her a few minutes without speaking. "You're a good friend, Indie. I did what I did—or didn't do—because I love you and I wanted the best for you. I'm sorry if I let you down, and I'm grateful that you love me enough to forgive me and to be here in Austin with me, as hard as this must be for you."

Indigo smiled halfheartedly. "It is hard, but what would be harder would be to lose my sister-friend over something that neither of us can change. Just be real with me from now on, Shel. And find the courage to be real with yourself."

Shelby looked at her young neighbors again and saw two little girls, about three, pause to hug each other. She smiled and a tear slid down her cheek. "Dreams don't necessarily die, do they? They just come in packages that God knows are a better fit for us than we could have designed."

She motioned for Indigo to join her again at the computer. "Come on. Let's decide on these dresses so we can outline a plan for the rest of the wedding."

When Shelby was seated again, she pulled an envelope from a drawer in the computer armoire and placed it on Indigo's lap. Indigo frowned when she opened it.

Shelby raised her hand to halt Indigo's protest. "You might want to give me that wedding dress, but I asked my mother to write a check to your parents, since they were picking up the tab. I'll be honored to wear the dress that you picked out and have it altered to fit me. You just help me plan my special day and be there to share it with me and Hunt. That will be gift enough."

52

Indigo loved back-to-school shopping, even if she were a grown woman well beyond the crayon-and-glue-stick stage.

In her case, she was shopping for bed linens, towels, and curtains for her New York apartment. Yasmin had recently returned from modeling camp, feeling like a fashion and design connoisseur, and had come along to offer advice. Somehow, though, she had quickly escaped to the shoe department, to hunt for one more pair of sandals to be ready for ninth grade.

Indigo spotted the two cute kids as she strolled through the section for bedroom comforters and accessories. They were about five or six and had to be fraternal twins, because although one was a boy and the other a girl, they were each other's spitting image. They tumbled into a floor-model beanbag and tickled each other incessantly, growing louder by the second.

Indigo was startled when Max Shepherd came into view. He rounded the corner and playfully scooped the two children up by their collars. She watched from a few feet away, amused by his attempt to be stern.

"Didn't I tell you two to stay where I could see you? I guess there will be no movie and popcorn today."

"We're sorry, we're sorry!" the kids pleaded with puppy dog eyes.

Indigo giggled. Had they been in her care, she would have melted.

Max turned in her direction and did a double take.

"Hey, you," he said. "How long have you been standing there?"

Indigo approached him and accepted his hug.

"Long enough to see you manhandling these two sweet children," she teased.

Max threw back his head and laughed. Indigo noticed every inflection.

"Believe me, Fric and Frac here deserve it. These are my little cousins Katerri and Joseph."

Indigo extended her hand to each of them, and they shook it.

"You're pretty," Katerri said. "Are you Cousin Max's girlfriend?"

Indigo blushed. Before she could respond, Max replied.

"Not yet, little nosey rosey. Not yet." He smiled.

Indigo raised an eyebrow. Max turned to the kids and stooped to make eye contact.

"You have my permission to play on the beanbag for two more minutes, got it? Just two. Then we have to go." He stood and faced Indigo. "So how you been?"

Indigo shrugged. "I can't complain. You?"

He hesitated and Indigo could tell that he knew.

"News travels fast in Jubilant. I'm sorry about your broken engagement," Max said.

Indigo folded her arms. "Based on what you just told your cousins, you don't seem too sorry."

Max looked down and then straight into her eyes. "Truthfully, I guess I'm not. I'm more sorry for Brian than anything. You're something special. I've realized that in the short time I've known you."

253

Indigo wanted to roll her eyes at his come-on line, but didn't, out of respect for the fact that they were photography colleagues. Maybe he really meant it, but right now she was jaded on anything that resembled smooth talk.

"I'm not looking to date anyone right now, Max," she said. "I'm leaving for New York soon and I just want some time to myself."

His curly hair bobbed as he nodded.

"Understood. I'll be around whenever you're in town," he said. "And I'll be in New York, speaking at SVA in about a month, about the transition from student to owning my own photography business. If you're up to it, maybe I can take you out for coffee or something then."

This guy was persistent. He was handsome too, Indigo admitted. But if Brian had taught her nothing else, she had learned that checking out the inside was more important than focusing on the packaging.

"We'll see," she told Max. "Look me up when you get to town, okay?"

She walked away to find Yasmin, but not before noting that funny feeling in her heart that seemed to surface whenever she was in his presence.

Something about him was magnetic, but she had to be careful. There was too much at stake to get caught up in the wrong game.

To top it all off, he seemed to be a mind reader.

"Just so you know," Max called after her, "I don't pick up girls at the mall all the time. You happen to make me do strange things, Indigo Burns."

She waved to him without turning around and kept walking, but inside, she was smiling. Max might not be "the one," but he was a signpost that someday soon she was going to learn to love again.

53

*N*izhoni became an official part of the Burns family when she showed up at the family cookout and ate a plate of chitlins with Indigo's dad.

Indigo loved her father, but she wasn't going to eat pig intestines for anyone.

"You have wrapped yourself around my daddy's heart, girl," Indigo told her friend. "Welcome."

Nizhoni laughed. "Believe me, I've eaten odder things on an Indian reservation. Other than the smell, this isn't bad. My dad won't even eat them. I'll have to let him know that I'm one up on him."

Indigo walked over to Aunt Melba, who stood on the backyard patio beaming like a proud mother.

"Did you see that girl over there eating chitlins? Do you see her hair flowing down her back?"

Indigo had noticed. There was no braid.

"Working in your salon is doing her some good, huh?"

Aunt Melba smiled. "Being around good people anywhere can do that to you, Indigo. You remember that when you get to New York. Don't cast your lot with people who have nothing to show for themselves or no drive to work hard for something. They'll only hold you back or hold you down. And I'm not just talking about material things. I'm talking dreams, ambitions, and opportunities. You cast your lot with other winners, like yourself, and you humbly serve the others in the hopes that some of them will get there."

Indigo tucked the advice in her mental memory bank. "How did you become so wise?"

"Just listening to my mama and daddy, at first, and then adding in the ultimate source—the Word of God, baby," Aunt Melba said. "It will never lead you wrong."

Indigo scanned the crowd and monitored the side gate as guests continued to arrive. He had promised he would come, but the cookout had been in full swing for two hours.

"Who are you looking for?" Aunt Melba asked. "Brian?"

Indigo shrugged. "Maybe."

"Did you invite him?"

"Yes," Indigo said. "He said he'd think about it."

Talking about him must have conjured him up, because minutes later, he came strolling into the backyard, accompanied by Shelby and Hunt.

The three of them looked good, especially Brian.

Indigo noticed some of the female friends of the family following him with their eyes. She watched as he surveyed the crowd, searching for her.

When his eyes landed on her, she waved, and he came over to the patio.

He hugged Indigo's mom, Aunt Melba, and then Indigo. It wasn't a lingering hug as usual, but it was sincere.

Indigo felt as if the two of them were onstage. R&B singer Anthony Hamilton's "The River" blared from the surround sound speakers as what seemed like everyone waited to see how they interacted.

Indigo motioned for him to follow her inside.

"Thanks for coming," she said once they were alone. "I know you leave for flight school next week. Your parents let you out of their sight?"

Brian chuckled. "Briefly," he said. "When I said I was coming here, they were all for it. They haven't given up hope."

Indigo smiled, surprised that the resentment that occasionally surfaced didn't flare. What she felt instead was something special for him. Pity, she supposed, for the journey she knew he faced.

"I'll always love you, Indie," he said softly. She saw in his eyes that he wanted to kiss her, so she let him. It was tender and sweet, but also bittersweet.

She started to tell him the truth—that on the night he revealed his issues, she had been planning to break their engagement anyway. But looking at him now, and seeing that he was working so hard to be at peace with himself and with the fact that he had given her up, she decided that some personal truths didn't need to be shared.

Brian would face enough regrets, rejection, and loneliness in the days ahead; she didn't have to crush him.

"I'll always love you too, Brian," she said. "You take care of yourself."

They hugged and returned to the end-of-summer cookout.

Brian wandered off to talk to her father and she resumed her position on the patio, where she had a full view of the entire backyard.

Yasmin sat under a shade tree, making sure she didn't get too much sun, in case Sasha called with a modeling job. She flipped through a portfolio of recent photos she had taken for various magazines, and her friends oohed and aahed.

Rachelle approached Indigo and extended a soda. She followed Indigo's gaze and shook her head.

"You know that Taryn wants to model now, right?"

Indigo laughed. "Never say never," she told Rachelle. "Wouldn't it be cool to have two supermodels in the family?"

"Hmm," Rachelle said and grabbed a cupcake from a tray that Aunt Melba was bringing outside for guests. "Too much pressure. I surely wouldn't be eating like this."

Gabe walked up and hugged her from behind. "I like everything I see," he said.

Indigo frowned in mock disgust. "You guys are sickening." She laughed.

Indigo was preparing to walk away when Rachelle pulled her by the arm and leaned into her ear.

"Don't worry, Indie, your blessing is coming. You wait and see," she said.

Indigo smiled. "I know. God's got it. He'll send him my way when we're ready for each other."

Indigo joined her father at the grill and watched him baste the ribs. She looked toward the fence again, wondering where her special guest was. Brian had shown up and that should be enough, but it wasn't, no matter how much she wanted it to be.

54

He arrived on Sunday morning, about eighteen hours late.

The doorbell rang as the Burnses were rushing through breakfast so they could make it to Sunday school.

"I'll get it," Indigo said, not wanting to hope, but doing so anyway.

She was rewarded.

Reuben had come home.

She wanted to ask him why he had missed the cookout and what had taken him so long to find the courage to return to Jubilant. But she didn't.

The fact that he was here was enough.

She stood in the doorway and drank in an eyeful of him: tall, ebony, and handsome. The spitting image of their deceased father, whose pictures still graced Mama and Daddy's walls.

She hadn't seen her brother since her graduation in May; he didn't know she had been engaged and was newly single. Before that, she hadn't seen him since her high school graduation.

Something about being in Jubilant wounded his soul. In all of the counseling that she, Mama, and Daddy had undergone with Dr. Danvers to help Yasmin, they had come to understand that.

Reuben was twelve when their parents were killed in the car crash. He remembered them more than Indigo or Yasmin and had experienced this major loss at a pivotal age. His life had been uprooted when everything in his world should have been steady and rock solid.

Dr. Danvers warned them that he might never come home again, especially if the memories of what he'd lost suffocated him because he hadn't dealt with them.

This time, though, Reuben had found his way.

In all practicality, she hadn't done or said anything compelling to draw him here. Her email had been brief:

```
The family cookout is in three weeks, on
Saturday as usual. Would love to have you
here with us.
```

Indigo knew God had answered her prayers.

She held open the door to let him enter and opened her arms wide. She hesitated to verbally welcome him home, lest that whole notion caused him to flee. She just wanted him to know that he was loved.

Reuben scooped Indigo into his arms and gave her one of the bear hugs that had been a trademark of their childhood bond.

"It's wonderful to see you, big brother," she said. "You've made my day."

Probably curious about who would be visiting at eight a.m., Mama and Daddy approached the front door.

Mama took just a few steps and fell to her knees when she saw her son/grandson.

"Thank you, Father!"

Daddy stood beside her, trembling.

Reuben approached him and hugged him. Their tender embrace

lasted until a cry pierced the air. Reuben seemed to remember he wasn't alone.

"I brought you a surprise," he told his parents. "Wait here."

Seconds later, Reuben ushered in a petite brown-skinned woman with locks that brushed her shoulders. She was carrying a baby dressed in blue.

"This is my wife, Peyton." Reuben beamed. "And this is our son, Charles David Burns. He's six months old."

Indigo couldn't hold back her tears when she saw that Daddy's cheeks were wet. When he had composed himself, Daddy uttered the words Indigo had been afraid to: "Welcome home, Son. Welcome to you and to your beautiful family."

55

*N*othing would be the same after today.

Indigo sat in Bush Intercontinental Airport in Houston counting down the minutes until she boarded her flight to New York, to her new life. She couldn't wait.

So much had happened this summer that she was sure she would someday look back on this summer and believe it was all a dream. But it hadn't been. She had grown up so much.

She had learned that when life knocked you down, you'd better listen to your Daddy and pick yourself up. She meant both Daddies—her grandfather who had raised her as a daughter, and her heavenly Father, who still had so much to teach her.

She sat here, convinced that when she boarded this flight, not only would she be headed toward a destiny crafted around photography and her growing achievements in the industry; she also would be expanding her world in ways that would resonate for eternity.

Rachelle had driven her, Mama, and Daddy to the airport and had shared how her childhood best friend, Jillian, had been a professional photographer who traveled the world before losing a battle with cancer.

"I eventually decided that the cancer didn't win," Rachelle told her. "Because Jillian still lives on through the great photos she took that are displayed in all parts of the world, and through the lives she touched with her friendship and love. She lives on through me, whenever I pull out my list of goals and remember how she inspired me to reclaim my life.

"That's the thing about this journey, Indigo. We have to remember that we're only here for a set period of time, and we don't get to 'do over' some things. So it's for our best to do them well the first time around. That's a lesson I've learned the hard way and continue to learn, even now.

"But you start thinking like that now, at your age, and when opportunities or obstacles present themselves, you'll figure out a way to either overcome them or plow through them."

Indigo reflected on Rachelle's advice and wished she could share it with Brian and Shelby. Both of them were on their way to their respective flight schools. She would see Shelby in six months, when she served as maid of honor in her best friend's wedding.

She wasn't sure when she would cross paths with Brian again, but while she was thinking about it, she wanted to let him know she was in his corner.

```
Hey, future Navy pilot, do your best. Give
your all, & remember, u will succeed. God-
speed!
```

Indigo sent the text and seconds later, received a reply.

```
Godspeed, Indie. Always yours, B.
```

He had attached a picture of a red rose.

Always, indeed, she thought. Nothing would ever change that.

DISCUSSION QUESTIONS

What was the overall theme of this book and how was this thread displayed in each major character's life?

What was Indigo's truth, and why was it so hard for her to accept? What could have made it easier?

Was Brian wise or foolish for trying to get help from Craig to figure out who he was?

Were Rachelle and Gabe's views about marriage accurate? Why or why not?

Was Shelby right or wrong not to share what she knew with her friend? What would you have done?

Why was Rachelle an important role model for Indigo as well as for Yasmin and her daughter, Taryn?

Do you think Brian's mother knew the particular issue he was struggling to resolve? If so, should she have confronted him?

What did Yasmin's illness reveal about the impact of family dynamics on a child's life?

Was Indigo's forgiveness of those who hurt her realistic? Was it wise?

What was your initial reaction to Brian's secret?

Do you think Brian's faith will truly help him heal or was his plan for moving forward unrealistic?

Each of the pastors in the book talked about trusting and resting in God, yet the younger characters seemed to struggle with that. Why is this such a challenge, for Christians at all levels of maturity?

In what area of your own journey has this book caused you to reflect?

What one life lesson will you take away from spending time with these fictional characters?

ACKNOWLEDGMENTS

Acknowledgments get harder and harder to write, because the list of people I'd like to thank for offering their prayers, encouragement, and support continues to grow.

First and foremost, I offer praise, glory, and gratitude to God for using me as his vessel once again.

I thank my husband, Donald, and children, Syd and Jay, for allowing me to grace their world and for understanding when I steal away to write. As always, I thank Muriel Miller Branch for offering a listening ear and a writing sanctuary so I could hammer out portions of this manuscript. I also thank my friends and first readers, Sharon Shahid, Carol Jackson, and Teresa Coleman.

Gratitude is extended to my agent, Steve Laube; my editors, Lonnie Hull Dupont and Barb Barnes; Twila Bennett, Michele Misiak, Carmen Pease, and the entire Revell Books marketing and publicity team; and Nathan Henrion and the Revell Books sales team. It's a group effort to birth a book, and your support isn't taken for granted!

A special thank-you is also extended to Charmaine Spain, Joe and Gloria Murphy and the entire Murphy clan, Deborah Lowry and family, Bobbie Walker Trussell, Barbara Grayson,

Henry Haney, Sandra Williams, Patsy Scott, Gwendolyn Richard, Barbara Rascoe, Lori Willis, Toyce Small, Yolanda Butler, Yul Cardwell, Danielle Jones, Lauren Stewart, Carol Mackey, Tyora Moody, Brendan Conroy, Marilynn Griffith, Rhonda McKnight, Tia McCollors, Kendra Norman-Bellamy, Linda Hudson-Smith, Rev. Nathaniel West, Shaun Robinson, Gwen Mansini, LaVera Williams, Helena Nyman, Gloria Thomas, Johanna Schuchert, Delores and Mac McLauchlin, the American Christian Fiction Writers—Richmond Chapter, my extended family and church family, and the Midlothian Chapter of Jack and Jill.

Many thanks to the wonderful book clubs across the country that have been so supportive and have befriended me—if I start listing names, I'll inadvertently neglect to mention one, so I'll stop at thank you! Thanks also to the bookstores that continue to sell my work and encourage readers to buy. Thanks to the radio hosts, television broadcasters, and print and online journalists who have honored me by featuring my work.

If I haven't mentioned your name, it doesn't mean I don't love you! Space doesn't permit it all.

A special thank-you is extended to you, the reader, for journeying with me into a fictional setting and into fictional lives where we all can find kernels of truth and glimpses of God to sustain us. Know that I think of you as I write, and I pray each time I sit in front of the computer that I'm given a story you can learn from or that you need. I hope I have accomplished that with this book, and that from this day forward, you'll walk in truth and in the joy that accompanies the depth and breadth of God's love.

Abundant blessings,

Stacy

Stacy Hawkins Adams is an award-winning author, journalist, and inspirational speaker. She and her family live in a suburb of Richmond, Virginia. Her other published titles include *Speak to My Heart, Nothing but the Right Thing, Watercolored Pearls*, and *The Someday List*. She welcomes readers to visit her website: www.stacyhawkinsadams.com.

NOVELS WITH *spirit*...

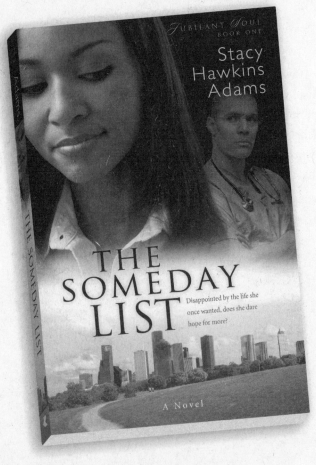

Rachelle Covington has it all. Will she give up everything to recover the past? Or will she find a reason to plan for the future?

 Revell
a division of Baker Publishing Group
www.RevellBooks.com